A Hundred Days
Till Tomorrow

A Hundred Days Till Tomorrow

A Novel

L.S. CASE

SPARKPRESS

Published by SparkPress, a BookSparks imprint,
A division of SparkPoint Studio, LLC
Phoenix, Arizona, USA, 85007
www.gosparkpress.com

Published 2023
Printed in the United States of America

Print ISBN: 978-1-68463-188-9
E-ISBN: 978-1-68463-189-6
Library of Congress Control Number: 2022919485

Interior design by Katherine Lloyd, The DESK

Dedicated to those leaving yesterday behind.

The past is a stepping-stone upon which to lunge forward. Embrace your jagged pieces, summon your inner strength, and take that leap of faith into tomorrow.

Chapter 1

S hivers penetrated Miranda's thick layers, raising prickly goose bumps and questions about "what if" and "how come." A suit of armor, complete with gauntlets and a breastplate, would have sufficed for the afternoon's meeting. Or a ball and chain and a striped prisoner jumpsuit with bold lettering–**Property of the Baxter Law Firm.**

Upholstered chairs with supportive wooden arms lined the attorney's waiting room, but Miranda occupied the saggy-cushioned couch closest to the exit. If she sat much longer or sunk any deeper, she might need a crane to hoist her slender frame from the medley of tasseled throw pillows.

March had come in like a lion, but there was no sign of a lamb. Nothing about the unseasonably cool day was ordinary except the emptiness that accompanied Miranda through time and circumstance. Clenched fists with tucked thumbs resurfaced from hiding beneath her thighs to button her blazer and upturn its collar.

Sorry, cuticles. No nibbling allowed.

While free, her nubby fingernails scratched an ever-spreading patch of neck hives before resuming their time-out.

To the left of the room, leather-bound journals with rigid spines rested on mahogany shelves. The books at the tippy top seemed unreachable, not unlike Miranda's curtailed aspirations in life.

They discriminated against those without access to a rolling ladder. Miranda was afraid of heights.

"Ms. Blair?"

A woman with a perfected librarian's bun and dangling hematite earrings summoned her from the doorway.

"Mr. Baxter will see you now." She jotted notes on a clipboard as if she were taking dictation through an earpiece on a movie set. Each of her squoval fingernails flaunted a different shade of pink polish.

Miranda drew a deep breath and exhaled through pursed lips. Rising to her feet with a clutched handbag, she mustered fragments of courage strewn across the room during her thirty-three-minute wait.

The receptionist sashayed down the hall in patent leather pumps, an inch too high and a tad shiny for a professional setting. Miranda lagged on the trail of honeysuckle perfume and stifled a sneeze. Her worn ballet flats pinched the backs of her tender heels and squashed her pinky toes.

A charcoal-gray skirt hugged the receptionist's pear-shaped figure and complemented her tailored blouse. While long-distance running fostered mindfulness, it failed to give Miranda desirable curves. And no amount of starch or elbow grease had ever made her dress shirts appear that crisp.

When they reached the doorway at the far end of the hall, the receptionist turned around. Up close, nonconforming strands escaped her slick bun. A hairstyle might offer insight about someone, but often the truth hid under the makeup. Even a foundation-covered complexion couldn't disguise a constellation of imperfections.

The woman's hollow eyes, outlined by subtle creases, mirrored a familiar sadness. Maybe her shoulders sunk from carrying too many disappointments. Had life overloaded her with burdens? Or was Miranda looking for someone—anyone—who could relate?

Inside the conference room, cumbersome drapes suffocated

rays of sunshine from peeking through the windows. And muted paisley tapestries hung from ceiling to floor, masking the four stuccoed walls.

The awkwardly plump attorney, sporting a salt-and-pepper wizard's beard, rose from his chair and extended a fleshy palm. His chubby arm jiggled with Miranda's handshake. Unlike old Saint Nicholas or Harry Potter's Dumbledore, there wasn't anything jolly about the counselor nor magical about their afternoon encounter.

"Are you alone today, Ms. Blair, or are we waiting for someone?" Mr. Baxter arched a bushy eyebrow in need of plucking.

"Just me, sir."

Perchance the misjudged receptionist would pull up a chair and come to Miranda's rescue. Maybe she, too, lacked siblings, a second parent, and the moral support of a significant other.

"Well, then," Mr. Baxter said, "let me express my condolences for your loss. It is never easy to say goodbye to a loved one." He nudged a box of tissues across the table's polished surface.

"Thank you, but I'm fine. Why am I here?" Miranda's denied cuticles longed for a nibble. Far less gratifying, she picked at them with her fingers instead. "What do you want from me?"

"Ms. Blair, this is not about what I need from you, insomuch as what you may gain. You see, many years ago, Gertrude Blair hired me to draw up her final will and testament. As her attorney and the executor of her estate, I contacted you upon her passing."

The alluded letter had been scrutinized, folded along the creases in thirds, and tucked within a zippered compartment of Miranda's handbag. Although she'd had weeks to prepare for the meeting, her grandmother's officially addressed name awakened the reality: Trudy was gone.

"According to this document, your grandmother named you the sole heir to her estate," Mr. Baxter said. His crooked smile revealed a row of typical nicotine-stained teeth.

Miranda placed a hand on her cheek, then forehead. It wouldn't take long before her underarm sweat seeped through the fabric. Her eyes darted back and forth. The room suddenly appeared smaller, as if the walls had closed in to eavesdrop. With the faux snakeskin material of bargain outlet shoes holding her feet hostage, crouching and climbing through the emergency window wasn't a viable escape.

If Miranda snuck out the door, would Mr. Baxter chase her down? And would the receptionist lift her eyes from the clipboard long enough to notice?

She tugged on her collar. Patchy hives continued to spread, creating a reddish abstract on her skin.

"I sense this is catching you off guard, Ms. Blair."

"Are you sure she chose me?"

"There is no mistake." Mr. Baxter's tone was resolute and his delivery quick. "These were Gertrude Blair's intentions, her documented final requests. A legacy left to a chosen one honors a bond. The relationship can transcend time, as it were. Think of it as extending the forecast for blue skies."

"More like patchy fog and suffocated sunshine," Miranda replied with a huff. "I never understood Trudy. How could I when she didn't give me a chance? Relationships and bonds didn't exist in my family history, so this doesn't make sense. Wasn't there anyone better suited to inherit her estate?"

"I can only decipher what's black from white." Mr. Baxter shrugged his rounded shoulders. "If you're curious about the gray areas, you'll have to venture there. We will review the contents of your grandmother's estate at our next visit. For now, there are some guidelines we must discuss. Gertrude was specific about her New England cottage on Primrose Lane in Cobblers Hill. She requested—"

"Sorry to interrupt." Miranda's slight hand raise didn't expose her underarm. "I know this sounds ungrateful, but I'm not interested in black, white, or any other color if it involves my grandmother.

I don't plan to keep what she left behind, especially her property lacking memories. I'd want to sell it as soon as possible."

"Anxious, aren't we?"

"Very," she replied, her stare unwavering. "There were many things I wished for over the years, but Gertrude Blair's estate wasn't one of them. Her assets won't buy back time, and I can't pawn them for an unconditionally loving relationship. An inherited bank account can't strengthen my family bonds, which never should have been compromised in the first place."

"Fortunately, or unfortunately, I only handle the legalities. I've had plenty of experience dealing with grieving families in the aftermath of loss, but I'm a useless therapist." The attorney's chuckle yielded an awkward giggle-snort. "I know life often doesn't make sense. Do we get what we want? Sometimes. Is it what we need? Possibly, but not always. Is it fair? Occasionally, but there are no guarantees. Are we privy to what the future holds? Sadly, or maybe luckily, never."

Miranda stifled a yawn. No one requested a monologue or a square dance routine. It shouldn't have been square anyway when he spun the conversation in circles. She wouldn't allemande left or do-si-do with the attorney. Nor would she bow to anyone, especially her estranged grandmother.

Mr. Baxter leaned in, and his protruding belly greeted the edge of the conference table like he was in his third trimester. "C'est la vie. That's life, Ms. Blair."

Not only hadn't Miranda requested a therapist, but she didn't require a translator either; two years of college French and a slew of psychology classes covered more than the basics.

"How long will this process take, and when can we proceed with the property's sale?"

"Your grandmother can address that question for you herself. While it's clear Gertrude wanted you to be her sole heir, she established a time frame for acquiring the estate—a seasonal arrangement, so to speak."

"Wait a minute." Miranda inched toward the edge of her seat and rubbed her palms against her suit pants. "Are you saying my grandmother is still calling the shots from the other side? I'm her heir but not the decision-maker here?"

The attorney repositioned his dark-rimmed glasses on his Nubian nose and peered at the engraved linen letterhead. "In time, Ms. Blair."

The grandfather clock in the room's far corner ticked steadily, preparing for its echoing of bells at the eleventh hour. There was no escaping time's passage despite attempts to detain its hands. Of course, time waited for no one; it couldn't be bought, bottled, or borrowed. When time was up, as it was for Gertrude Blair, there were no more chances.

Mr. Baxter cleared the phlegm from his throat. "Shall we proceed?"

Miranda tore off small pieces of skin from the corners of her unpolished fingernails as the attorney relayed Trudy's plans for her only grandchild. While there may have been much to gain by consenting to the old woman's arrangement, Miranda had all of herself to lose in the process.

Would she be a willing participant in her deceased grandmother's game of final requests? Or should she forfeit everything and walk away as Gertrude Blair had done all those years ago?

Chapter 2

June 21 welcomed a season long-awaited by many for its out-door leisure, generous daylight, and abundance of vitamin D. For Miranda, the first official day of summer marked her reluctant departure to New England and the countdown of a hundred days.

"I've always known I'd be horrible at goodbyes," Miranda grumbled to her mother at the curbside, their modest home providing her farewell's backdrop.

"Until now, you found reasons not to say them." Clara reached forward with the remaining suitcase but hesitated to relinquish her grip. "I'm not sure what's changed, but you can still dodge this curveball. Trudy may think she gained the upper hand by tearing us apart, but you're in the driver's seat. Don't let anyone convince you otherwise."

"Goodbye is unavoidable this time, Mom." Miranda hoisted luggage into her old Toyota's trunk and shimmied it into place. "Something is luring me to this gray area, and it's not dollar signs. Well, maybe a few. I can't explain the nudging, but I know I must go."

She shoved an overstuffed duffel bag in the vacant passenger seat and turned to Clara with her head hung low. "Now, about that suggestion you had—" Miranda's brittle voice cracked.

"What did I call it the other night? Ah, yes, a mini-vacation from communication," her mother replied with an unreciprocated giggle. "But seriously, honey, I've thought it through. We should probably refrain from contact for a while."

Clara swept back golden strands of hair from Miranda's face. "It will force us to make a move—you know, step beyond our comfort zones. Maybe I'll rediscover old friends and hobbies, and you'll make new ones. I could volunteer at the YMCA or take a few Latin dance classes." She awkwardly gyrated her hips. "Oh, the possibilities! Agree?"

Miranda flashed a customer service smile at her mother's charade. There was no denying the truth. Clara could maintain the wall constructed decades ago between mother-in-law and daughter-in-law by keeping a safe distance from Gertrude Blair's arrangement.

"The alternative would be to waste the next few months flying through our data plan and rehashing your grandmother's demands. I can hear our uninspiring phone conversations and see the string of texts about loneliness and boredom."

"And don't forget resentment."

"That too." Clara folded her arms across her chest and huffed. "I'm not sure what that evil woman was thinking with this silly arrangement, but I can tell you this—wallowing in our circumstances is *not* an option."

For two homebodies equally dependent upon one another, a wedge in communication was a long jump rather than a step. Deliberate silence made as much sense as the unorthodox plans that coaxed Miranda from the nest. She nodded while her insides churned.

The postal truck made its rounds through the neighborhood, stuffing mailboxes with anticipated letters and dreaded bills. Across the way, the eccentric cat lady placed bowls of food in her driveway for visiting strays. Neighbors expressed concern that rodents and raccoons might be among those mealtime guests. Their complaints only fueled the woman's blatant disregard for others.

A noisy sanitation truck zigzagged down the block, claiming piles of garbage and leaving behind a pungent odor that lingered like an old lady's stale floral perfume. The conscientious UPS driver made timely deliveries of various shaped and sized packages while eager homeowners peeked out their windows. It was an ordinary day in Barron Park. The grind would continue with or without Miranda Blair.

She forced the back door closed, and the entire car shook. "I may be leaving, but I won't allow anything or anyone to define me over these next few months. Especially the ghost of my grandmother." Miranda fussed for the ignition key among the jingle of others.

"That's my girl. You were never a fan of the paranormal."

"You'll see, Mom, I'll resume my position at the historical society in the fall and take more grad classes over the winter semester. It'll be business as usual."

Dark sunglasses disguised Miranda's glazed blue eyes, and the humidity tightened each curl. Threatening clouds hovered. With nothing left to pack, shift, or load, there were no reasons to delay.

"I guess this is it." Miranda nudged at a loose stone in the curb with her sneaker. She had practiced a confident posture and sure-footed strides for weeks. But this was no longer a rehearsal, and there wasn't an encore performance.

"Did you bring a water bottle for the long ride, honey?"

"Yep, two."

"What about time fillers? A season's worth of reading material? Enough art supplies?"

"Why would I need all that when you have me making friends and finding new hobbies?" Miranda smirked. "But, yes, my survival gear is packed. I even brought an Eiffel Tower wall calendar for the countdown."

"How about those inserts for your sneakers? I know they make long-distance runs more comfortable."

"Yep, got my orthotics."

"And the house key? What about the key? Can't forget the key."

"I refuse to add it to my key ring with the others, but I have it. It's burning a hole in my back pocket."

"I thought only money did that, but I guess neither of us would know. Things are going to get better." Clara lifted her daughter's chin. "The summer isn't forever. It's a single season of your life. Keep reminding yourself these circumstances are temporary—only temporary. Then we can leave this bad dream behind us."

"Only temporary," Miranda said with an exaggerated sigh.

They held each other tightly in a final mother-daughter embrace, lingering longer than the typical hug.

"Speaking of bad dreams," Miranda winced, and her white knuckles clung to Clara like a lifeline, "remember the one of people parting ways on a train station platform?"

"You mean the dream where passengers said their goodbyes? How could I forget? It haunted you every time you fell asleep. We read lighthearted books with fairy-tale endings. You drank warm milk before bed and left on the light. I even bought you a white noise machine for your birthday."

"And nothing worked. I still visited the imaginary train station, awoke in a sweat, and carried an emptiness throughout the day."

"I remember those unsettled mornings all too well," Clara said. "You would ask me the same questions over breakfast—where I thought the travelers were heading and whether they would see each other again. Unfortunately, I never had the answers, and your untouched omelet fed the garbage."

"Yet you always suggested their sad departures were for happy reasons: a new job, a golden opportunity."

"A trip of a lifetime, a fresh start," Clara added. "But you never believed me."

"I wish I could have." Miranda withdrew her arms and leaned

back. "There was no sign of joy, only tortured hearts and raw emotions. I was a helpless bystander, watching at a distance, waiting and wondering. I never did find out what led those people apart, and I still think of them sometimes. Now I understand the void they felt for having to leave."

"As do I for being left behind." Clara took baby steps away from her daughter's car. "But unlike those travelers, you know your destination. And we *will* reunite in a hundred days—that's for certain."

Miranda took her place behind the wheel. A fastened seat belt would brace her for the uphill climbs and detours ahead, but it wouldn't prevent the highway from taunting and tempting her to reconsider plans. And while she pledged to return home unscathed next fall, she risked forfeiting one familiar layer of herself with each passing mile. Change, after all, was inevitable.

As her car backed down the driveway, she gave a final wave and choked back a sob. There would be idle moments for the sting of tears when she quarantined in Gertrude Blair's time capsule.

The countdown had begun.

Temporary, only temporary.

Miranda glanced in her rearview mirror and accelerated her speed.

Chapter 3

Clouds surrendered to bright, glorious sunshine as Miranda's old Toyota rounded the final stretch of Primrose Lane. Perched on a hilltop, the disenchanted cottage came into view through the smudged windshield. Swallowing wouldn't dislodge the golf ball–sized lump in Miranda's throat, which increased by size and discomfort.

A graceful blue jay with tail feathers of the purest hue chirped a friendly greeting from the picket fence. Feisty squirrels chased one another up the stout trunk and down the draping arms of a weeping willow. At least the animals seemed content in Cobblers Hill.

Miranda permitted the engine a well-deserved rest and stepped out to greet the earthy scent of wild mushrooms, a respite from her hometown's smog. The tall, brittle grass against her calves made them itch, and her sneakers trapped gravel, crunching along the camouflaged walkway.

She would have stopped for a tick check, but the relentless afternoon sun beat down on her semi-bare shoulders. Aside from everything else she left behind, Miranda had forgotten to pack sunscreen.

The cottage resembled a dilapidated garage on stilts rather than a home built on a solid foundation. Chipped blue paint offered a glimpse of natural cedar shingles hidden beneath years of neglect.

Boards covered the two front windows like coffin lids, keeping the outside world at bay. With one shutter missing and another hanging from a corroded nail, Gertrude Blair's house was likely avoided by Halloween trick-or-treaters. Egg-throwing, shaving cream–spraying, adrenaline-seeking teenagers might have gathered there in the wee hours for a thrill. Miranda wouldn't stick around long enough to hand out candy or shoo away trespassers.

On the front step, the underlying message provided by the tattered and discolored welcome mat was "Go away!" While the door's rusted lock and bent key may have shared a long history, neither was eager to get reacquainted.

Once inside Gertrude's time capsule, Miranda maneuvered her arms like wiper blades. An army of spiders left behind silky cob-webs—wall-to-wall decorations of the creepiest kind.

"I guess this is hello again, Trudy," Miranda called out into the emptiness. "You'd probably expect me to say, 'I'm home,' but we know I'm nothing more than an extended houseguest."

The humidity amplified the mildewed basement smell, seeping through the cottage's pores like a plague. Miranda wheezed each time she drew a breath of damp air. Of her many ailments—dry eyes, anxious stomach, neck hives—asthma had never been one of them.

Floorboards creaked beneath her feet throughout the shoe-box-sized rooms. A stucco ceiling hung low in the beam of her cell phone's flashlight. Obsolete appliances, many unidentifiable, waited to reconvene with electrical outlets. Books proffering folklore and fish-ermen's tales rested on the fireplace mantel under a blanket of dust.

A patchwork quilt partially covered a metal-framed bed within the bedroom. Clips and combs for outdated hairstyles sat idly on the antique dresser. There were straw hats and gardening gloves, half-filled mason jars, broken strands of pearls, reading glasses, and beaded costume jewelry. Stuff was everywhere—Gertrude Blair's stuff.

Blood whooshed through Miranda's veins, her heart pounding obnoxiously in her ears. The remnants of her family history dwelled within this old, rotted house. But rather than dreaded photographs of the man she once called "Daddy," an array of inspirational plaques masked the dark-paneled walls. Clutching her chest, Miranda exhaled.

Trudy may have designed the plaques herself or purchased them at a craft fair for a bargain. Maybe she received them as gifts from friends to commemorate special occasions. Sadly, Miranda would never know.

The palm of her hand cradled her cell phone, and her thumb hovered over the lock screen. A single swipe and tap could bridge the gap between Cobblers Hill and home. Clara might convince her to reconsider plans; it wouldn't take much coaxing from her mother. If Miranda left now, she would arrive in Barron Park before dark with time for a rest stop along the way.

But an agreement was an agreement—even if her grandmother had a poor sense of humor to concoct such a ridiculous arrangement. The nagging question remained: "Why?" Miranda bit her thumbnail.

The rustic wood planks held the day's heat and baked Miranda in the oven of her grandmother's old bedroom. While she spent the first of many evenings by herself, wrestling with the musty fitted sheet and its overstretched elastic pockets, she wasn't alone. Shadows in the moonlight danced around the room's perimeter, and an ambitious critter logged its ten thousand steps within the walls. Miranda added mousetraps, night-lights, sunblock, and an antihistamine to her growing mental checklist.

For such a small house, the cottage bellowed a midnight symphony of clanks and whirs. She covered her head with a lumpy pillow that wreaked an eau de attic scent and counted the minutes until daybreak rather than sheep.

Sometime in the early morning hours, during the familiar good-bye sequence in her train platform dream, Miranda awoke from the discomfort of her sweat-dampened pajamas. At the first glimmer of sunlight, she leaped from the bed.

Relentless stomach growls took a back seat to her runny nose and itchy eyes. Empty boxes and aired storage bags waited on standby, but goggles and a dust mask lingered on an endless scavenger hunt list.

Had Miranda been wearing long sleeves, she would have rolled them up to her elbows. Instead, she wound her tousled hair into a tight ponytail and cracked each finger's knuckle in size order. A hundred days was a lengthy stay for any visitor, but it was hardly enough time to reflect on Gertrude Blair's items—items with an unknown history. Stuff—meaningless stuff.

The porcelain knickknacks and decorative plates were first to enter the sturdy cardboard box labeled "Donations." A stack of deteriorating magazines dropped to the bottom of a plastic garbage bag and hit the floor with a thud. Next, the rusted coffee can storing bent crochet hooks met its demise, as did unruly balls of yarn. Knitting was an old-fashioned craft in Miranda's generation anyway.

Decks of cards and artificial plants, spools of thread, and a bowl of sequined fruit awaited their fate. So did the puzzles, oil-splattered cookbooks, and overflowing bucket of buttons. Her hands flew across Gertrude's belongings like her fingers were playing ragtime on a saloon piano—a catchy tune of pack, purge, ditch, donate, and dump.

Childhood board games retreated on dusty shelves as if they had lost hope the next generation would play. Perhaps the local school could offer them another chance to instill joy.

"Wow, I never once considered—" Miranda grazed her hand across paint-clad canvases reflecting her grandmother's graceful signature in the bottom corner. "Interesting choice of colors. Warmth and detail. Had I known—" She shook her lowered head with a *tsk, tsk*. It wouldn't have made a difference.

The acrylic paintings joined the other items in the ever-growing donation pile, a windfall for the local thrift shop. Charcoal sketches and a bookcase full of classics suggested the DNA-sharing stranger mirrored Miranda's appreciation for art and literature. Trudy's modest possessions hinted at a simple life in Cobblers Hill. And the wall plaques declaring inspirational messages about the possibilities for tomorrow reflected faith. Or perhaps that's what Miranda wanted to believe about the woman who never deserved the loving title "grandma."

"It's a start," she said aloud of the boxed and bagged clutter that yielded open space. Her knees cracked as she stood and stretched. Years of running on the concrete pavement alleviated stress but instigated noisy joints. Negatives seemed to stem from positives.

A defiant crochet hook poked through one of the many over-filled garbage bags and scraped against Miranda's leg. Marks or a bruise she could handle, but blood was another story, especially without an available bandage.

Which of Trudy's disposed belongings would seek retribution next? Would the artificial plants sprout thorns and spikes and come alive with a vengeance? And might the rusted iron heat up and straighten things out? Maybe Miranda's hypocrisy, a historical society employee dismissing pieces of her grandmother's history, warranted the backlash.

With some nudging across the floorboards and one final shove, the pierced garbage bag tumbled down the backyard steps and landed with a thump. Miranda clapped the dust from her hands.

The late-morning air was undisturbed except for the metal door's bang, which set a sparrow into flight. Trudy's fractured bird-bath no longer provided a refreshing splash for feathered visitors. Dire conditions aside, at least the cottage had plumbing.

In the yard, shrubs suffocated neighboring trees, and climbing grapelike wisteria disguised an arbor. Ivy wandered across strategically placed boulders in a decorative stone wall. And the remains of a lopsided outhouse, with its crescent-mooned door, balanced on stubborn tree roots. Colleagues at the historical society in Barron Park would have been intrigued by such a relic. They may have even suggested an archaeological dig. Miranda kept her distance.

Instead, she trekked back and forth through the Kentucky bluegrass to Trudy's potting shed, her sneaker soles marking a patterned trail across the kitchen floor. The moss-covered structure wasn't one of those convenient PODS, but it would suffice as a makeshift storage unit for clutter.

"Yoo-hoo! Over here," a faint voice called from the adjacent yard.

A woman outfitted in wrinkly skin wiggled her way from behind the blueberry bushes, a wide-brimmed straw hat flopping to one side. Her cankles made a bold introduction below the hem of her housedress, but the tray resting across her sunbaked forearms captivated Miranda's attention.

"Didn't mean to startle ya, but thought ya might be hungry. Breakfast is the most important meal of the day. I reckon ya hadn't had any. Brought ya some raisin scones and tea, both freshly made. Hope ya don't mind that I added a cube of sugar. Ya ain't gotta worry about goin' light on 'em sweets with that there figure."

"How thoughtful." Miranda's smile reciprocated the old woman's warmth. "I arrived yesterday and haven't had time to get used to my surroundings, let alone eat."

"Ya have a lifetime for that, darlin'. Gettin' used to ya surroundin's, that is. Ya must be the granddaughter."

"I'm Miranda Blair."

"Been expectin' ya for quite some time but wasn't sure when. Adelaide Colby here. Friends call me Addie. Haven't seen ya since ya were itty-bitty. Anyway, tea is gettin' cold."

The mysterious woman extended the tray with outstretched arms and age-spotted hands.

Had Miranda spent more than a single summer in Cobblers Hill, she might have recalled the hospitable neighbor. Adelaide Colby was another stranger from Miranda's vague history.

"Thank you, Adelaide." She peeked under the red-checkered cloth, then closed her eyes and leaned in for a whiff. "Oh, my goodness, these smell amazing. They're still warm too! I don't remember the last time I had a homemade treat."

When Miranda looked up, the old woman was gone.

Chapter 4

Voilà!
Baking soda mixed with white vinegar and a cleaning regimen of rinse, wipe, toss, sigh, and repeat breathed new life into Trudy's relics. Despite rattles and groans, the avocado-green refrigerator kept a dozen eggs fresh and a half gallon of almond milk cold.

The pantry closet stored nonperishables, and the pine cabinets shelved mismatched glasses and hairline-cracked plates. Frayed dish towels hung from the stove door handle, and the fruit bowl sheltered a few ripe bananas and a semi-firm plum.

The cottage's sand-free windowsills welcomed elbows to lean. A panoramic view highlighted lush treetops and stone-roofed cottages, one of which belonged to the effervescent Adelaide Colby.

While some Airbnb guests might claim a place like Trudy's exuded rustic charm, most would give scathing reviews. Clean and orderly didn't mean the bungalow was, or would ever be, home.

The neighbor's breakfast tray waited idly on the counter as it had the previous day and the ones prior. A week was too long to procrastinate its return, even for an out-of-town visitor with an overflowing to-do list.

Miranda paced back and forth across the linoleum floor, following the same pattern that avoided cracks. If distance had been her ally in Barron Park, keeping others at arm's length, then an acquaintance in Cobblers Hill was a potential threat.

Joyful Adelaide hadn't come across as the obtrusive type, but that didn't mean she wouldn't meddle. Of more concern, she might have been Trudy's friend who held the key to their family's secrets.

Miranda's stomach churned, a sour taste surging from her throat into her mouth. Two decades had passed since the Blairs locked the door to what might have been. She paced into the den, across the rickety floorboards, and farther from the cloth-lined tray that reflected neighborly kindness. An unscathed Miranda would return to her disciplined routine back home in less than a hundred days. No one would be allowed to compromise these intentions, including the petite woman who pacified her appetite with raisin scones.

Hadn't Clara Blair assured Miranda she was in the driver's seat? Suppose the driver dictated a vehicle's destination and length of stay. In that case, a visit next door could be short and sweet like the southern-drawled Adelaide. It might even lift Miranda's spirits; seven days was too long to isolate among muted colors, outdated furnishings, musty smells, and ornery appliances. She grabbed the tray and headed out the back door.

In a feast for the senses, the music of swaying wind chimes welcomed Miranda into the neighboring yard. An eye-catching display of fuchsia roses entwined a white picket fence. Jewel-toned lanterns, draping from low-hanging branches, outlined a stone path.

A gentle breeze carried the comforting aroma of cinnamon and clove, honey and nutmeg, bringing to mind a crisp autumn afternoon despite the day's humidity. Come the fall, Miranda would resume her hometown's preservation projects. She could then toast the completion of Trudy's arrangement with mulled cider and a justified sigh of relief.

Adelaide leaned on her hands and knees in her garden, poking and pulling from the dirt while singing an off-key rendition of "Amazing Grace."

"Ya got out for a bit, eh?" The spunky old woman didn't turn around. "Nice to stretch 'em legs and take in the scenery. It's a glorious day to be alive, I tell ya. Put the tray on the table over yonder."

"Thank you again, Adelaide, for the treats. The scones were delicious."

"No worries, darlin'. That's what neighbors are for. You'll have plenty of time to repay the favor. Mind handin' me my snippers?"

"I'm sorry?" Miranda cocked her head. "I'm not familiar with—"

"Ah, that's my name for 'em. Most folks call 'em shears or scissors."

"Oh, you mean these guys?" Miranda handed over the tool, but the feverishly working woman failed to look up from her patch.

"Funny thin' about my garden, it knows when I'm attentive and when I've been slackin'. It ain't so happy with the latter. And that there okra is monopolizin' my time. What do ya think about okra?"

Miranda shrugged. "Never heard of it, although it sounds like a garden pest. Or some green mythical swamp creature. Oh, wait, I'm thinking of an ogre. You know, Shrek."

Adelaide let out a hearty laugh and turned around to Miranda, the joy on her face more prominent than her wrinkles. "Okra is a delicious veggie, darlin', and one high-maintenance garden snob. The patch's princess needs perfect growin' conditions—the right soil, good nourishment, hot temps, and freedom from 'em neighborin' weeds. Most northerners don't attempt to grow okra, but this southern gal here never backs down from a challenge."

Adelaide held the stem toward Miranda with her soiled gardening glove.

"Look at that there flower. Here today, gone tomorrow. And the second treasure is 'em pods. I'll harvest 'em, freeze 'em for a cool evenin', and make the most delicious gumbo. Mm, mm, mm.

Anythin' worth havin' in life is worth puttin' the time and effort into, ya hear? The proof is in the okra."

The old woman rose to her feet with shaky legs as if she had cycled a carousel too many times.

"Um." Miranda inched closer. "Here, let me help you." She extended her hand, bracing herself for the catch.

"Help me? Nonsense." Adelaide huffed and wobbled off with her head held as high as her hunched shoulders would allow.

Heat radiated from Miranda's cheeks. "Um, I meant with your garden."

"Oh, my garden. Of course, of course. I'm afraid I'm retirin' for the day, though, darlin'. Gotta tend to my oven, and it's about time for tea." She squinted at the face of her oversized watch. "Care to join me for a cup?"

Hate was too strong of a word, but Miranda genuinely disliked tea. Whereas coffee was her preferred pick-me-up beverage, she associated tea with having a nagging sore throat, missing class, and watching mindless television alongside a pile of crumpled tissues.

"Sure. I'd like that." The words escaped Miranda's lips before she could consider the repercussions.

So what if the two women shared an appreciation for structure in their day? One commonality among many disparities hardly laid the groundwork for a friendship. Besides, there must have been a reason for all the talk about okra. Maybe Adelaide was lonely too—a southerner living up north and missing her roots.

"Very well, then, we gotta table to set," the spirited senior said. "I gotta gather 'em tools and clean up. Ya can tend to my apple crumb cake. That there timer is gonna buzz. Mitts are in the drawer next to the sink. Water in the kettle is simmered but needs a good boil. Plates and cups are above. Everythin' else is on a tray," Adelaide hollered, although Miranda was only a few feet away. The pint-sized woman resumed singing the same tune but a different verse equally off-key.

The knotty pine kitchen reflected more unfamiliar walls and unspoken boundaries, especially for someone not looking to become acquainted. Miranda pulled drawers and opened cabinets as if a mouse waited to greet her on the other side. Oh, how she feared rodents!

Locate tray with tea condiments.

Check!

Oven mitts.

Check!

Cups and saucers.

Check!

Boil water.

Still waiting.

The buzz of the oven timer resembled her washing machine's completed spin cycle back home.

Shut timer off.

Check!

Remove crumb cake from the oven.

Check! Ouch, hot!

A shower was running in the adjacent room. Knobs screeched, and a bar of soap dropped. Miranda grabbed an extra place setting from the overhead cupboard just in case.

Steam rose from the piping hot cake. Ideally, it required ample time to cool, but perfect timing failed to exist in Miranda Blair's world. She glided a butter knife along the perimeter of the Bundt pan the way bakers did on cooking shows, then said a silent prayer while flipping the cake over. Even with a nudge, it resisted her taps and side-to-side jiggles.

The whistling kettle reached its boiling point, triggering an imaginary choke hold around Miranda. Her arms flailed, and the cake slipped from her cumbersome oven mitts. The bottom half plopped onto the plate while the rest of it clung defiantly to the pan. Crumbs flew into the air and scattered on the floor.

The high-pitched screech resembling a train whistle could make a hungry dog retreat from a porterhouse steak. With a shot of adrenaline surging through Miranda's veins, she wanted to ditch the cake and flee the kitchen.

It was never a suitable time for an episode of PTSD, especially when striving to leave a favorable impression. So much for Adelaide's masterpiece—so much for Miranda developing a thick skin to childhood distress.

A barefoot, half-dressed guy entered the kitchen and left a trail of wet footprints across Adelaide's floor. His muscles flexed as he towel-dried his hair with his free hand while simmering the teakettle with the other. Beads of water trickling down his bare chest and defined abs warranted an audience.

"I'm used to her teatime routine by now," he said with an incandescent smile. "Sorry if I startled you." He exited the kitchen with his khaki shorts hanging low, a loose belt undone around his waist, and the clean smell of masculinity lingering behind.

Miranda wanted to say something—say anything—but only silent words escaped when her jaw dropped. Miranda Blair didn't lose composure around men, even one like him. Her light-headedness was likely attributed to the oppressive heat and an overactive oven.

She aired out a handful of her T-shirt, the last few crumbs falling to the floor.

Adelaide's cake!

With the remaining pieces unstuck, Miranda transplanted them onto the bottom half and shimmied them into place. Then she eyed the cake from different angles before its grand introduction outside.

There was plenty of shade and a delightful breeze at the far end of the neighbor's yard. Teatime was a welcomed respite, nestled among hydrangea bushes and serenaded by a fountain's trickles. Miranda's usual afternoon break entailed a ten-minute commute from class to work while scarfing down a dry granola bar in three equal bites.

"Not used to the heat in that there kitchen, eh?" Adelaide chuckled. "Ya cheeks are nice and rosy, but ya wear the color well. Lookie at what we got here. Brava!"

Miranda placed the tray down with delicate hands and curtsied. Somehow she had traded her driver's seat for a place at the neighbor's bistro table. She was never steadfast behind the wheel anyway, having failed her road test multiple times in high school.

"So, darlin', I reckon ya have a green thumb too."

"Hardly. Our yard back home isn't large enough for a garden. Besides, it would be tough to grow anything on concrete."

"But ya here now, and ya got rich soil." Adelaide nursed her tea bag in the steaming cup of water and used her spoon to twirl it in a graceful figure-eight motion.

"True, but Trudy's property is overgrown, and the garden is a jungle. Even if it's tameable, I doubt I'm the right candidate for the job."

Miranda never intended to bring her grandmother's name into the conversation or discuss heritage rather than horticulture. She added a heaping spoonful of honey and three sugar cubes to her tea. Another cube waited on standby. "Where would I begin if I were up for the challenge? Frankly, I can't tell the flowers or fruit trees from the weeds, let alone care for them."

"There ain't no right or wrong place to begin, darlin', as long as ya start somewhere." Adelaide sliced between the Bundt cake curves and rested a piece on two of the three plates. Her straw hat occupied the empty chair.

"First, ya gotta open ya heart; then ya gotta use 'em senses. Every garden has a story to tell, so be a good listener."

Miranda accepted the smaller piece of cake and shoved a forkful in her mouth before it crumbled on the dish.

"Experience the mornin' dew when the day awakens and get to know 'em critters that visit," Adelaide said. "Ya gotta always make time for friends. Take in the afternoon breeze and 'em fragrant smells." The old woman closed her eyes and inhaled a deep, exaggerated breath. "Don't be too busy to notice 'em surroundin's."

She lifted her teacup, paused, and took a cautious sip. Miranda did the same.

"Ya gotta respect each vine, tree, and flower for its unique qualities. Abandon 'em weeds, and you'll rid the negativity that threatens ya garden's well-bein'. Weeds make their presence known. If ya ain't sure, let 'em be. Give everythin' a chance to grow, ya hear?"

Miranda nodded with a wandering eye to the back door.

"Stroll after the rain, knowin' the rich soil is providin' all 'em nutrients." Adelaide pointed a crooked finger at her. "But beware if ya keep ya head down, ya only gonna notice 'em slugs. Gotta look up to find 'em rainbows and fruit that hangs from 'em branches."

Miranda tilted her head back at Adelaide's imaginary scene across the sapphire sky.

"A new day welcomes another chance—take that chance," the old woman said. "Patience, perseverance, and passion are key ingredients; the rest is up to nature. No matter how bad 'em storms are, never give up. That there sun always shines again."

"Wow, you make it sound so profound—almost spiritual."

"That's 'cause it is. Gardenin' is a form of art, I say."

A moment of silence emphasized the significance of Adelaide's words. Wide-eyed, Miranda leaned in closer.

"Takes creativity and imagination, a captivatin' eye and self-expression," Adelaide said. "Most every lesson in life comes from that there garden. Gotta be willin' to learn from the teacher and be open to the message."

"It's intimidating, though, taking over seeds I didn't sow." Miranda placed her teacup back on the saucer. She would not become attached to anything in her grandmother's hometown—not even a garden.

"No stinkin' thinkin'. Few can take credit for bein' the initial planter," Adelaide garbled with a mouthful of cake. "That there is history now. What matters is ya garden's evolution. It's constantly changin', day by day, season to season, flower to flower. So, let go of yesterday—ya gotta appreciate today and plant 'em seeds for tomorrow."

Adelaide patted the corners of her mouth with a napkin. "Enjoy the journey, darlin', and don't go addin' any of 'em unnecessary limitations, ya hear?"

Miranda nodded, residual pain shimmering in her eyes. If only Gertrude Blair had shared treasures of personal experience unattainable from a Google search. If only there were underlying messages about nurturing healthy relationships and sprinkles of wisdom disguised in a teatime chat about plants and shrubs. If only . . .

"It would help pass the time," Miranda said after a lengthy pause assembling crumbs in the center of her plate. "And since I don't have the opportunity back home, and you say it's a form of art—one that I haven't explored—I guess I'll give gardening a chance this summer. There's nothing to lose. Right?"

"Oh, and everythin' to gain," Adelaide replied with a twinkle in her eye. "That a gal! I'm only a holler over the blueberry bushes if ya need me."

He walked out of the house, keys in hand and dark aviators resting on his visor. Miranda swallowed hard and washed down the last forkful of cake with a sip of tea.

He gave Adelaide a reverent kiss on the head and outstretched his hand to Miranda.

"I don't believe we've officially met. Jake Colby. A pleasure to meet you."

"Miranda Blair. Likewise."

"Miranda here moved next door." Adelaide's eyes sparkled.

"It's temporary. Um, I'm a visitor. A seasonal one. For the summer, is all."

"I hope you'll enjoy your visit then," Jake said. "You're going to love Cobblers Hill as much as I do. That's why I can't stay away. Right, Gram?"

"Always welcome—both y'all." Adelaide turned to Miranda. "Our yards are connected, darlin'. We'll leave the gate open for ya to come and go as ya please."

"Thank you for sharing your teatime, Addie."

A-d-e-l-a-i-d-e. Addie is reserved for friends!

The old woman beamed.

Miranda rose to her feet and gathered the cups and saucers with fidgety hands.

"Don't even think about it." Addie tapped the table. "I've got the entire afternoon, now, ya hear?"

"I guess I'll awaken the dinosaur mower and attempt to cut the grass before it gets any later or grows taller." Miranda gave an awkward chuckle she quickly regretted.

"If you don't mind me saying so," Jake chimed in, "a weed eater will trim the grass, which will make it easier to mow. I'll be happy to stop over tomorrow and give you a hand."

Addie nodded at her grandson.

"Well . . ." Miranda cleared her throat. "I'd appreciate that." She addressed her sneakers rather than the neighbors. How could she keep accepting kindness from these strangers? Under the circumstances, how could she not?

"It's a date, then," Jake said. "Not to worry, we'll have the place shaped up in a few hours. The grass should be dry by midmorning, which will make the job easier."

He placed his hand on Addie's shoulder. "I'm heading out for a few hours, Gram. I'll see you later."

Jake Colby was gone as quickly as he appeared, driving off in a roofless gunmetal-gray Jeep, raising dust and Miranda's curiosity as he accelerated down the country road.

Chapter 5

The long wooden spoon circulated the glass pitcher of lemonade enough times to create a whirlpool. Summer's quintessential beverage color coordinated with Trudy's sun-drenched kitchen.

Miranda stole sips before resting the spoon on the counter and mulling over the lemonade's sweetness. To eliminate the risk of adding poison ivy, she decided against sprigs of mint from Trudy's garden.

She appreciated Jake's willingness to help. But calling it a *date?* Miranda may not have been the only one putting too much thought into their yard endeavor. It was nothing more than lawn help and multiple check marks on her to-do list. Besides, she wasn't the dating type, much to the disappointment of guys who attempted unsuccessfully to pick through her icy layers. While she never intended to bruise egos, she avoided men and the web of emotions relationships spun.

The day might come when she would allow someone to complete her—or, more likely, Miranda wasn't meant to be half of someone's whole. She wouldn't let it happen while on borrowed time in Cobblers Hill.

A few minutes after nine, the lawn's hero walked through the open gate with safety goggles hanging from his neck. The tall handle of a gardening tool occupied one hand and an oversized gasoline container the other. With ease, Jake powered up the weedwacker and maneuvered it side to side across the grass, cutting several inches off the top with each clean sweep. The once drowsy yard came alive.

Miranda gave a friendly wave from the garden and picked weeds to heed Addie's advice—rid the negativity. Some vines surrendered with ease, while others required a tug and an unkind word. Trudy's pair of snippers worked overtime, trimming and pruning.

There was only so long Miranda could stare at the soil and analyze the plants before her eyes crossed and her shoulders begged for a stretch.

"Know when it's time to break for the day," Addie had said. She also warned Miranda about keeping her head down. "Don't be too busy to notice 'em surroundin's."

Bare skin peeked through Jake's ripped jeans, and his facial hair had grown thicker since the previous day's introduction. There was progress with the lawn too!

"Take in the afternoon breeze and 'em fragrant smells," Adelaide's words preached.

The air held sweet remnants from the freshly cut grass mixed with potent gas fumes from the mower, both undeniable summer scents.

By half past noon, the manicured lawn and semi-pruned shrubs breathed new life into the property. Jake cleaned the mower's blade and replaced the cap on the now-empty gasoline container. He removed a handkerchief from his back pocket and wiped his forehead.

"We made a big difference here, didn't we?"

"It looks amazing! It doesn't even resemble the same borderline-haunted property from earlier," Miranda said giddily, and Jake laughed. His shared credit eased her discomfort for accepting help on one of the hottest summer days. "I couldn't have done it without you."

"Don't underestimate yourself. In a few short hours, look at what you tackled in the garden."

"I've accepted that it's a work in progress. As for this rustic cottage—" Miranda tapped her chin with her forefinger. "I'm not sure of the storms it has weathered, but it looks like it's been waiting in vain. For what, I don't know."

"Maybe for the right person to come along and give it a chance to be beautiful again."

Jake trailed off toward the far end of the yard with the final bag of grass cuttings.

Although Miranda was a stranger and, more appropriately, a trespasser, she'd been chosen to breathe new life into the ruins on Primrose Lane—at least during the arrangement. Was she the right person? The neighbors seemed to think so.

"Thanks for refilling my cup of lemonade," he called out. "You never let it get half-full."

She grinned. "You must be hungry. How about a sandwich to go?"

Being a planner and an anticipator had its advantages. Earlier that morning, Miranda had stopped by the market to buy the fixings for lunch. She was guilty of being rude once, holding Addie's breakfast tray hostage; she wouldn't take neighborly kindness for granted again. At least she could pacify Jake's appetite following hours of hard work.

There hadn't been a prize for the first customer of the day. The half-asleep deli clerk fussed with disposable gloves and allowed a series of eye rolls and yawns to escape while Miranda studied the display case.

She had toggled between Italian-style roast beef and honey-smoked ham. Then salami and soppressata, bologna and mortadella. Of her many quirks, indecisiveness was the most recent. It was only sodium nitrate–cured meat, not a life-altering career move. But somehow, it mattered.

"Sure, I'll make the time for lunch," Jake said. "But if you don't mind, I'd like to check on Gram and change my clothes. I wouldn't be the best lunch date as I am."

Grass cuttings created a collage on his forearms, and a drenched T-shirt clung to his skin in all the right places. There were residual imprints around his eyes from the protective goggles. Still, Miranda only noticed the genuine goodness his smile reflected.

"Oh, of course. I seem to be wearing a layer of dirt myself over here."

There was that word again: "date." It was unrealistic that someone like *him* could take an interest in a woman like *her*. Jake would find nothing date-worthy about Miranda Blair. She needed a makeover as desperately as Trudy's cottage.

"How about packing those sandwiches to go? I'll be back in a half hour. Don't ask where I'm taking you; just trust me." Jake disappeared before she could utter a reply. "Oh, you might not want to wear sandals," he yelled from the neighboring yard.

Trust was something to build over time. And yet Jake requested it without the slightest hesitation. Miranda's inner guard that double-bolted doors and tossed keys would proceed with caution. Buttery baked goods and yard work and grandmotherly wisdom would not leave her vulnerable.

Still, Miranda relied on her instincts and first impressions—the neighbors were well-intentioned. Not only would she allow the garden gate between the cottages to remain open, but also the door of friendship.

Chapter 6

"Ladies first."

Jake held the door while Miranda climbed gracelessly into the Jeep.

Sure, she had agreed to her grandmother's arrangement and Jake's yard help. And maybe, against her better judgment, she had befriended Adelaide over tea. But how did neighborly kindness and chivalry land her beside Jake Colby?

Unlike others who enjoyed riding shotgun, Miranda preferred the driver's seat, where she couldn't be misled. As a passenger, surprises provoked anxiety, and small talk was awkward.

She clung to the Appalachian white ash basket in her lap with rigid hands and white knuckles. The wicker basket, no longer supporting a flowerless pot in Trudy's den, escaped its destiny for the afternoon to fulfill its inherent purpose.

"Have everything you need?" Jake asked.

"That depends on where we're heading."

"Sorry, no hints here. If I told you our destination, it would take away all the fun, wouldn't it?"

The Jeep began its slow descent down Primrose Lane. Dismissing the tree-shaped air freshener suspended from the rearview mirror, Miranda credited Jake for the clean, woodsy scent that filled the space between them.

"I'm sure the last few days settling in were stressful," Jake said. "For now, try not to think of anything else but getting acquainted with your new surroundings . . . temporary surroundings, that is. You're in good hands, I assure you."

He flashed a confident smile in her direction, but Miranda only sunk lower in the seat. Either her pasty complexion advertised the need for a mental health day, or it was the way she guarded the picnic basket like it contained fragile possessions she would lay down her life to protect.

She hadn't asked to be placed in another person's hands, certainly not those of easy-on-the-eyes Jake Colby. She never relinquished that much authority to anyone—at least, not before now.

As they drove through neighborhoods, none of which resembled the urban streets of Miranda's hometown, they passed gingerbread-trimmed Victorians in pastel shades of pink, blue, yellow, and green. The Queen Anne–style painted ladies were a combination of three colors found in a nursery.

Although enchanting, they lacked the simplicity of the stone-roof cottages on Primrose Lane, where tire swings suspended from stately oak trees and flowers climbed recklessly through white lattice. Even Trudy's bungalow may have exuded charm long ago when it had proper attention, a time that excluded Miranda.

"Wow! I've never seen such perfectly manicured hedges." She peered over lowered sunglasses. "I love that every home has a wrap-around porch, but their variations give the block character. Like the finials and gables on that one," she said, pointing to a Victorian on her right, "or the slated turrets over there."

"Architect?"

"Ha! More like an art lover and a historical society employee. If I had a porch like that, I'd spend hours outside in the shade and solitude, soaking up the fresh air and giving my paintbrushes a workout."

"Shade, yes, but solitude?" Jake chuckled. "Not if you were living in this town. You'd end up with visitors, a blank canvas, and a dried palette." He motioned toward four seniors playing cards and exchanging banter on a filigree veranda. "That scene justifies why town ordinances required every home in Cobblers Hill to have a porch. A half century later, people are still neighborly."

"Let me guess: they leave their porch light on for unexpected company."

"Every dusk."

Applewood Path, Cider Mill Lane, Vineyard Tangle Road, Crestridge Trail—even the engraved street signs inspired creativity for an ensuing work of art. But Miranda's countdown had begun. She wouldn't be around long enough to enjoy conversations on porches with neighbors or paint the fall foliage.

"Residents in Barron Park cocoon behind closed doors." Miranda looked away. "Our unspoken motto is 'Fences make the best neighbors.'"

"Really? And we believe if being alone is good, then being together is better. No judgment, though, only different philosophies."

Miranda loosened her grip on the picnic basket one finger at a time and swept her bangs to the side with an unmanicured hand. Jake's afternoon shave yielded a prominent jawline and flawlessly smooth, touchable face. Although it was only a casual pair of charcoal twill shorts and a crisp V-neck T-shirt, he nailed the relaxed style.

Beyond the windshield, well-maintained residences yielded to local establishments marked by gaslit lanterns. Terra-cotta flowerpots with cascading red, white, and purple-blue pansies hung from awnings. With a contagious spirit of patriotism, flags waved in the perfumed summer breeze.

"I may be partial," Jake said, "but this town has one of the best main streets. Stop by the Cobblers Hill Museum sometime for a dose of local history. The new Breathe Studio offers hot yoga classes and meditation in the courtyard, if you're into that sort of thing. And there are plenty of souvenir shops to fulfill every Christmas wish list."

Miranda would be long gone before everything became merry and jolly.

"If you're a sports fanatic like me," he continued, "there are lively places to watch the big games. And once you've worked up an appetite, grab an award-winning lobster roll from the Cutty Sark or a bowl of seafood bisque at the Waterview. There are bistro tables out back to sit with your feet in the sand."

As if on cue, Miranda's stomach gave a low growl. She cleared her throat until the rumbling subsided.

The Jeep rolled to another stop in front of the bustling town square, where Americana-themed banners draped from a cupola-roofed gazebo.

"This is where we have outdoor movie nights on the lawn. And on summer evenings, there are free community concerts here. What kind of music do you like?" Jake gave Miranda a playful once-over. "I'm gonna say country."

"Interesting. So, you think I'm a country girl?" She smoothed her frayed denim shorts, wishing she hadn't worn the checkered peasant blouse that resembled a farmer's tablecloth.

"Just a hunch. Am I right?" Jake arched a brow.

"I love all types of music. Just not explicit rap or the heaviest of heavy metal—the kind that sounds more like screaming than singing." Miranda wrinkled her nose. "Not my jam."

"That makes two of us. And for the record, I can't sing or play an instrument."

"Oh, your vocal cords can't be more challenged than mine," she insisted.

"Then it's safe to say if a good song comes on the radio, we shouldn't attempt a duet."

They looked at each other and laughed.

"What about the band Foreigner?" Jake asked. "Like them?"

"*Love* them! I have the entire *Feels Like the First Time* album on my playlist. It motivates the best runs."

"Imagine the boring workouts we'd have without music."

"Or the uninspired artwork," she added.

On any given day back home, the score from *Phantom of the Opera* or Andrea Bocelli's "Time to Say Goodbye" blasted from Miranda's playlist. Their lyrics dictated her use of color and shading, and the melody guided the overall sentiment behind each painting.

A few professors had described Miranda's art as deep and thought-provoking. Maybe they were correct in their assessment; perhaps she did have a natural talent for transferring a heightened sense of consciousness onto canvas through her brushstrokes. But she knew it had everything to do with the music.

"Later this summer, a tribute band will be performing Foreigner's greatest hits here," Jake said with teenage excitement. "We should go together. Here, take my phone and text yourself the date, August seventeenth. That way, I'll have your number as well."

Miranda cradled Jake's cell phone. A swipe would grant her access to his friend list and milestone photos. Identifying his favorite songs, frequented apps, traveled distances, logged calories, purchased items, and calendar events would be easy. With a single text, she would become part of Jake Colby's phone history.

Miranda's cell phone was supposed to be taboo for the summer, at least when communicating with Clara Blair. Her mother had claimed a healthy distance would encourage them to branch out and make new connections. Jake was now one of those connections.

"Sure, I could go for a summer concert." An intriguing Cobblers Hill version of Miranda replaced her noncommittal and quick-with-excuses self. "Sounds like good medicine."

"Great! And there's plenty of time to cancel if you change your mind."

A white steepled church stood on the hilltop, overlooking the village below as if shepherding righteousness among the townspeople. Across the street was a Tudor-style building with stained-glass windows and a Romeo-and-Juliet-style balcony.

"That's town hall where my three sisters and I attended events as kids—some fun, others not so much." Jake tugged on his lower lip as he spoke. "I remember having my seventh-grade social there. My mom made me wear a white polyester suit."

"Sounds cute."

"Humiliating is more like it. The other kids wore jeans and sneakers." Jake loosened an imaginary bow tie around his neck. "It was a balmy ninety-two degrees, and the room had no air-conditioning."

Miranda fanned herself.

"Wait, it gets better. I had this horrible bowl haircut and the first flare-up of acne. My shiny patent leather dress shoes made me slip my way across the dance floor and crash into the dessert table." Jake's belly laugh made Miranda giggle. "Picture chocolate cream donuts rolling everywhere."

"Ahh, the awkward years."

Even without the visual of a mortified tween Jake in tacky attire, Miranda's cheeks would be sore later from frequent smiles, and her sides would ache from laughter.

"They claim those times build character," he continued. "To this day, I avoid polyester and dance floors. I make sure to wear proper-fitting footwear and procrastinate getting a haircut. I'm grateful for family photo albums, though, with their reminders, you know?"

Miranda tightened her grip on the picnic basket. To have a family photo album required a family. Then there needed to be impressionable memories to fill its pages.

"See over there?" The gingerbread cottage facade of Mitchell's Luncheonette stood on the corner. "That's where I had my first summer job clearing tables at fourteen."

"Charming. It looks like something out of a storybook." She swiped the screen on her phone and took a photo.

"Yeah, on the outside. But I remember how sticky the kitchen floor was under my old Pumas and the banging of pots and pans. I saved up enough tip money to buy a BMX bike and some freedom. Good times." Jake beamed like a proud schoolboy. "And McGinley's old-fashioned ice cream parlor is where I had my first date. It has this great 1950s vibe that'll set you back in time."

Miranda rolled down her window for an uninterrupted view of the building, which resembled an aluminum rail car. Warm air mingled between them. "It's odd, like the two places have some sort of identity crisis. Shouldn't Mitchell's resemble the diner and McGinley's have the gingerbread exterior?"

Jake nodded. "It's the Cobblers Hill rendition of *West Side Story*. In the late '40s, Mitchell's Luncheonette developed a reputation for its huge portions and candy-filled counter. Stop by sometime and check out the autographed wall. You'll be amazed at how many Hollywood A-listers have visited. Anyway, McGinley's opened for business a short time later, and they competed for the same customers."

"I guess they're still duking it out?"

"Nope. Ancient history," Jake replied. "Mitchell's daughter and McGinley's son began dating and married a year later. It was a blessing to the entire town, and there's been harmony ever since."

"Surprising. I mean, I always thought love divided."

"Given a chance, I was taught it multiplied," Jake said. "After the wedding, the in-laws acknowledged they had gold mines with plenty of loyal customers. The luncheonette eliminated sweets from its menu as a peace offering, and McGinley's agreed only to serve dessert. They make a delicious rainbow cookie cake, and their strawberry rhubarb pie has taken first prize at the annual South Bay Festival for seven consecutive years. But they're best known for their homemade ice cream and toppings."

"We rarely even see an ice cream truck in Barron Park, and you have this nostalgic gem in your town. The kids must love it."

"The adults too. No one seems to mind the long wait for a table."

"I like ice cream, but I'm a simple girl," Miranda said. "No need for distractions with crushed candy and syrups and sprinkles. Hold the chocolate morsels and caramel. I prefer plain vanilla."

"If you say so." Jake raised an eyebrow at Miranda. "I bet if you gave McGinley's rocky road a chance, you'd never settle for anything plain again. We'll have to have an ice cream throwdown."

Farther along the cobblestone street, the Jeep pulled up in front of Colby's Hardware. Miranda cocked her head at the dented sign with faded lettering.

"You probably recognize the name." Jake cleared his throat. "This is our business, started by my grandfather, Pop. I know it's nothing to look at aesthetically, but it's a special place that's been in my family for decades."

Handmade fluorescent signs decorated the front bay window and advertised the weekly specials. A pale canopy hung overhead, and a rusty bell greeted each customer. The store was from another era—one that didn't belong to Jake.

"It may have weathered many storms but endured the tests of time," Miranda replied. "That's something to celebrate. It reflects character and perseverance, both admirable qualities."

"Thanks for saying so. I couldn't wait for summer to spend adventurous days here with Pop. He regarded me as a man, teaching me business principles and sharing life lessons I couldn't learn from the thickest textbook."

"He sounds a lot like Addie."

"Yeah, they were like biscuits and butter, as Gram would say."

Miranda shook her head and laughed.

"I admire that older generation, you know?" Jake said. "They didn't have much but were rich in life experience and took nothing for granted. Even with modest means, they were generous with others. And family meant everything to them."

A young woman patiently guided a fragile lady's shuffled footsteps through the front door of Colby's Hardware. Perhaps they were great-aunt and niece or grandmother and granddaughter—people taking care of people the way it should be among relatives.

"Pop taught me the meaning of integrity and grace and demonstrated the respect with which everyone deserves to be treated, from the cleaning crew and stock boys to valued customers and business associates." Jake's stare transcended through the store window. "He never missed our ball games and made time for campouts and fishing adventures. When my sisters and I needed an ear to listen or a hand to help, Pop lent us two. We could always count on him to be there for his 'grands,' as he would call us."

"Sounds like an amazing role model." Miranda fussed with the wooden handles on the picnic basket, sliding them back and forth aimlessly.

"The best. I was lucky to have had those years with my pop. That's why I feel indebted to Colby's Hardware and the memories made here. The future of this legacy is in my hands." Jake sunk lower in his seat until he was at eye level with Miranda. "Sorry if I'm boring you with too many details. I didn't mean for this conversation to become so personal."

"Not at all. It's refreshing to hear you talk about your grandfather with admiration and gratitude when others take their family ties for granted. Their ignorance comes across as entitlement. Anyway, the lessons taught by Pop shaped your character and contributed to who you are today. Those experiences will always be a part of you and the gifts you offer others."

"Thanks, Miranda. I'm glad you can relate."

"Um," she began, chewing her inner cheek, "actually, I'm an only child of a single parent with no extended family." The truth rolled off her tongue like she was immune to its bitter taste. "Memories of summertime fun with relatives didn't exist for me, and I never had a role model like your pop. It's just the way it was."

"Oh. I didn't know. I wouldn't have—"

"You have every right to celebrate your past," she replied softly. "Never apologize for that."

They exchanged glances.

Jake adjusted the rearview mirror and set the Jeep in motion. The more Miranda learned about her temporary-residence neighbor, the more she believed what he suggested earlier—she was in good hands.

Chapter 7

Miranda grabbed the Jeep's overhead handle and squeezed the passenger seat's cushioned edge. The formerly restricted picnic basket teetered on her lap. Not only had she created an imaginary brake pedal, but she jammed her foot on it, pressing it to the ground.

"Sorry about that," Jake said. "I forgot to mention the ditch. There's no way around it, but I'll give you a heads-up next time."

As much as she welcomed the afternoon's reprieve from routines and time frames, disappointments, and legalities, there was no guarantee of a next time in her countdown.

"I'm not sure you expected such a long car ride, but the good news is, we're here." Jake placed the gear in park and idled the engine.

"I wouldn't call it a long ride—it was a scenic drive with lots of landmarks and favorite places along the way. You'd make an engaging tour guide."

Rows of scarlet poppies and hearty sunflowers boasting happy faces provided splashes of color against the juniper forest's backdrop. The absence of clouds made it seem possible to extend a paintbrush to the sky and capture its cobalt color.

"Wow!" Miranda said. "This right here is pure eye candy for anyone with a canvas."

"Don't go setting up an imaginary easel yet. We still have a short hike through those woods. Think of this scene as the opening act."

"Really? It gets better?"

"Wait and see."

Armed with a bottle of insect repellent from the center console, a small cooler, and a blanket from the back seat, Jake made his way around to the passenger side.

"Here." He extended his hand. "Let me take that picnic basket from you."

"Oh, that's okay. You have enough to carry." Miranda climbed down from the Jeep with a tightened grip on the wicker lifeline.

Jake led her along a wooded path, away from poison ivy patches and threatening branches that hung at eye level. As was her tendency, she lagged a few steps behind.

Velvety moss covered the forest floor like natural carpeting for scampering squirrels. Pungent wild mushrooms clustered within the shade of prominent aspen and birch. High above, draped vines entwined with neighboring branches.

"I can't believe how much darker it is in here," Miranda said. "But not a spooky dark, more of an intriguing dark."

"The canopy of trees blocks the sun and steals the daylight. It's several degrees cooler too."

A mystery rodent scurried across Miranda's path. Her shrill collaborated with the forest echoes and rolling calls near and far. She quickened her steps while peeking over her shoulder. "I spoke too soon."

"I assure you it wasn't a Sasquatch, although that would make for an interesting afternoon, wouldn't it?" An amused Jake didn't bother to look. "It was probably a chipmunk. They dash out of nowhere and stop you in your tracks. I'm glad you wore sneakers."

It wasn't too difficult to see that Miranda was ill-adapted to the great outdoors, but when did Jake notice her footwear? And what other observations had he made?

While she was the girl next door in a literal sense, she identified with that persona—naturally pretty but understated, kindhearted yet often overlooked, available but taboo. According to the few guys she had dated, her reputation preceded her as complex and quirky. To some extent, they were valid in their assessments.

"There are many animals in these woods," Jake said, "but they won't harm you. They're more afraid of us. And you'll be happy to know we don't have poisonous snakes."

"How come?"

"Cold winters."

"Well, I can't say I'm too disappointed."

"Me either." He adjusted the backpack on his shoulder and lifted a low branch. Miranda ducked beneath it. "I prefer animals with fur."

"Or feathers. There must be a thousand varieties of birds up there." She stretched her neck back. "This place is a nature lover's paradise. You could get lost here."

"That's one way of looking at it, or you could find yourself here. This path comes alive with color in the fall. And in the winter, the pine trees make the air smell like Christmas. I've cross-country skied and snowshoed through these woods. It never disappoints."

Miranda drew a deep, nourishing breath. Foliage, snowfall, and the sun-dappled forest through the changing seasons begged for expression on canvas. Her imaginary paintbrushes yearned to dance with nature's palette of colors. But as a summer visitor eager to leave Cobblers Hill behind, she would be gone before the autumn chill arrived.

Jake turned around to face her. "Here comes the fun part—I need you to close your eyes."

"Wait, what? Jake—"

"I know, I know. But I'll guide you the rest of the way."

Jake stood by Miranda's side and held her arm with his free hand. He balanced everything else he carried in the other—everything but her picnic basket.

"Slow and steady."

"Even if you told me the hairy rodent returned with relatives, I don't think I could move much faster." She chuckled, but humor wouldn't calm her heart from pounding through her blouse.

"We aren't in a rush, and, for the record, there's no sign of the Sasquatch or any rodents. A few steps to the right." He kicked stones from her path, lifting dust into the air. "And a bit to the left. Now around this bend—"

"I can't—"

"Eh, eh, eh, I see your eyes squinting. No peeking. Keep them closed. Don't worry; I've got you."

Nobody ever got Miranda Blair before. She never leveraged that as an option. Yet there she was with shut eyes and a partially receptive mind to wherever they were heading.

"I'm not sure how much longer—"

"Okay. *Now,* you can open them."

Jake stepped to the side, and Miranda fluttered her eyes open.

There was much she could have said, but only one word escaped her lips. "Incredible!"

Chapter 8

The trees didn't hover, the birds no longer sang, and cool shade yielded to glorious sunshine. A pristine beach stretched for miles, highlighting the secluded spaces and untampered gifts nature provided. The warm, gentle breeze drifted off the water's surface and surrounded Jake and Miranda with salt-air kisses.

"I hope you like my surprise," Jake said. "The locals call it Edens Cove."

"Appropriate name. It's another Cobblers Hill masterpiece waiting to come alive on canvas." Miranda's eyes darted back and forth between the majestic dunes and rocky cliffs. "Besides the seagulls, where is everyone?"

"Crazy, isn't it? This place is free of charge—no reservation needed—and yet it's usually quiet here. If you bring a pair of binoculars, you may spot a few beachcombers in the distance or a fisherman casting a net."

Jake flung pieces of half-buried driftwood from the sand and cleared the area of intrusive rocks. Then, with Miranda's help, he spread out the generously sized blanket and secured its four corners with Colby's Hardware–labeled citronella candles.

"Even if this beach wasn't our town's best-kept secret," Jake said, "I doubt it would ever become crowded with tourists. People are too distracted by the latest technology or the newest app to notice their surroundings. It's always about wanting more and having better instead of appreciating what's around them."

"And wasting mindless hours overanalyzing social media posts."

"Exactly! I never understood why they spend so much time worrying what shade of green someone else's grass is rather than appreciating the color of their own lawn."

The breeze extinguished two of the candles. Miranda reached for the lighter and restored their flames.

"Let's see . . ." Jake dug through his cooler and tossed ice cubes into the sand while disappointed seagulls lingered for a snack. "You can join me in having a cold beer, or if you prefer, there is tangerine-flavored seltzer and pomegranate juice. I brought bottled water too, so you'd have a few options."

"Um, I've never had pomegranate juice before. I think I'll try it."

Jake untwisted the cap of the demi bottle that resembled red wine.

"You mentioned how preoccupied people are these days," Miranda said. "I try to live mindfully, but I'm as guilty as the next person for rushing through life and wearing self-imposed blinders."

"Yeah? How so?"

"Take last week's ride to Cobblers Hill, for example. I was so focused on my destination that I zoomed past those stately Victorians." She handed Jake a cracked pepper mill turkey sandwich and a small bag of kale chips in exchange for the filled flute of juice, which she wedged in the sand. "It wasn't until our drive through town earlier that I appreciated them."

"Oh, you mean my tour."

"Yes, your tour." Miranda stifled a laugh. She arranged her lunch the way she aligned her acrylics before painting. "I wish I could be one of those carefree spirits who coast through life without being weighed down by things I can't control. But unfortunately, I'm not wired that way. And since you mentioned green grass, I'll admit I expected the lawn on Primrose Lane to remain overgrown and over-looked instead of imagining its potential. You proved me wrong by changing that today. So, a toast to you and the manicured property."

Her blue eyes met Jake's gaze as she raised her drink toward him. His beer bottle greeted her flute halfway.

"Welcome to the neighborhood, Miranda."

They clinked beverages while opportunistic seagulls soared above. Waves lapped against the shoreline, providing nature's background music that serenaded them with each ripple. If only Clara Blair could see her daughter now, sipping fancy juice on a pristine beach with the guy who breathed new life into her seasonal residence. Maybe she had been right about the summer's potential.

Jake took a bite of his ciabatta. "I believe those self-imposed blinders you mentioned are removable when you're ready to see without them."

"You have to wonder, though, when your GPS stops recalculating," Miranda said, but only half-joking. "After twenty-five years, I'm set in my ways."

"It's never too late for a U-turn, but you must be willing to take it. We all change our course sometimes. I know I have." He wiped the condensation from his bottle with his hand. "Pop always said no sidewalk is without cracks and the occasional pebble. And he used to make the point every house has a broken shingle."

"Meaning we are a work in progress."

Jake nodded. "Nothing is perfect. Pop's concern was whether the homeowner took responsibility for the repair or made excuses."

The message settled in Miranda's gut, monopolizing the limited space reserved for her lunch. Not only did her childhood home have a few broken shingles like Gertrude's cottage, but the foundation had fissures too. What would Jake's grandfather say about those sidestepped cracks that manifested bad breaks and threatened the well-being of her home?

She had to switch to a safe topic. Could they fill time debating romaine, butter, radicchio, Boston, and iceberg lettuce if she commented on their balsamic vinaigrette arugula salad? Noting the freshness of their ciabatta loaves could lead to a discussion about artisan rolls and the history of Italian bread.

"Thank you for bringing the cooler of drinks," Miranda said. "You came prepared."

"And thank you for packing this delicious lunch. How did you know, aside from Gram's baking, I stick to a healthy diet?"

"A lucky guess." Miranda buried her head in the arugula, fishing for croutons with her fork. Thoughts of dripping water and Jake's defined abs were sure to make her cheeks match the pomegranate juice. Red was never her color.

Maybe women swooned over Jake, offering him their undivided attention. But Miranda wasn't like the others. Her entourage of guards was never off duty and rarely on break.

In between nibbles, she grabbed handfuls of sand and sifted warm granules through her fingers. Looking into someone's eyes was like reading their private thoughts and giving them insight into her own. Miranda was seldom without the shield of sunglasses.

"Tell me about this cove," she said. "What's over there?"

In the distance, adjoining structures with a broad base resided on a grassy island.

"That's the Cobblers Landing Lighthouse, built in 1844. Artists and writers have made it the subject of their canvases and setting in their novels."

"I can tell she's a beauty. I'm fascinated by all old buildings."

"All" did not include Trudy's rotted cottage.

"The lighthouse has two structures," Jake said. "The original resembles a medieval castle with merlons. Do you see?" He traced the battlements in the air with his finger.

"Reminds me of Hogwarts—you know, from Harry Potter."

"Kind of. The castle wasn't tall enough to be seen by ships, so they built a new lighthouse alongside it decades later. Unfortunately, the original one began to deteriorate from neglect."

"And?" Miranda leaned in closer.

"And they planned for demolition."

She gasped. "How awful! That old building has weathered the storms. Rather than be disregarded for its imperfections, the former lighthouse deserves to flaunt its scars. Like Colby's Hardware."

"Right." Jake nodded. "Vulnerable or not, our community refused to let anything happen to a piece of local history. We donated resources from our businesses and fundraised for preservation through a collaborative effort. I'm proud to say the entire Cobblers Landing Lighthouse stands respected today, listed on the National Register of Historic Places."

Jake rested back on bent elbows with his legs outstretched, unaware of his earned brownie points.

"I love a happy ending!" Miranda said giddily. "Back home, I'm an assistant to the director of my town's historical society. We preserve brick-and-mortar structures and their attached memories from long ago."

"You mentioned your job earlier. So you're a guardian of the past?"

Miranda swallowed hard and forced down another bite of her sandwich. "Okay, so here's the part where I sound like a hypocrite, and you question my integrity. I pride myself on preserving the past for old buildings and landmarks. But as for my family history and roots, I avoid looking back."

She sunk deeper into the sand.

"Fair enough. I respect that."

"Wait, you do?"

"Sure," Jake said. "Honoring a shared history is one thing. By the way, I admire you. It takes a special person to stand up and protect what others quickly dismiss. But it's a different story to delve into your past and spend time there. Unless, of course, it was flawless, which I doubt is the case for anyone. We've all had challenging times and difficult years, best left unvisited. So I don't think you're a hypocrite."

A threatening cloud passed over them and disappeared into the distance. Glorious sunshine prevailed, once again, in an azure sky.

"Anyway, the history of Cobblers Hill is important to our community," he continued. "It's one of the many reasons you'll fit right in here. Hopefully, you'll see why this New England town is a special place."

"I think I'm beginning to already." A hopeful smile emerged from deep within Miranda. She sat up taller with her gaze on the bright horizon. In time, she might fall for more than Jake's hometown.

Chapter 9

Jake stood and brushed off the sand from his legs. "Let's take a walk." He extended a hand to Miranda.

She tossed the empty lunch wrappings into the picnic basket and jumped to her feet without his assistance. The mixture of powder-soft sand and the gentle splash of water over their toes provided the ideal elements for a stroll without a destination. They meandered side by side with the wedge of two different worlds between them.

Jake knelt before an odd piece of driftwood, his hand gliding across its surface. Whereas he was in sync with nature, Miranda had limited herself to capturing it on canvas. Not only had he assured her change was possible, but it seemed to be taking hold. Never had she agreed to be a guest at a feast for the senses. Yet here she was, embraced by the sun's warm hug and crooned by the tranquil waves lapping against the shoreline.

And then there was the visual of Jake's silhouette against the ocean's backdrop. Stolen glimpses revealed his athletic build. With the right amount of muscle, Jake offered security without intimidation. The playful breeze ran through his chestnut-brown hair like a California surfer. An outing with anyone of the same caliber as Jake Colby was unlikely in Barron Park. But Miranda was in Cobblers Hill now, which seemed to make the difference.

Perhaps Jake was curious about her as well. Was it odd that Miranda was circumspect? And did he wonder what had transpired in her life to develop a resistance to her past? Or maybe he wasn't intrigued by Miranda in the first place.

"Have you found any treasures here on the shore?" Miranda asked.

"It depends on your definition of 'treasure.' With the changing tides, it's a new experience every time. I haven't come across a message in a bottle or pirate's loot, if that's what you mean. I've scored plenty of fishing lures and rusty pieces of metal, and I've acquired an extensive sea glass collection. The next time you visit Gram, check out the mason jars displayed on her mantel."

"The few beaches I have visited had rocks and broken shells," Miranda said. "Tell me about this sea glass."

"Better yet, I'll show you."

Jake reached down toward two pieces nestled in the sand and placed one in each hand.

"Look here first." He revealed brown glass in his left palm. "I'd guess this originated from someone's beer bottle. The edges are sharp, and the surface is clear. To be conditioned, it will need more time in nature."

Jake rubbed his finger over the jagged edge. Miranda flinched.

"Now, look at this one." He unveiled the second piece. "Although it had the same beginning, the edges smoothed, and the surface frosted through weathered storms. What appears hopeless may only need more time and the right circumstances to change."

Jake tossed the first piece into the water and placed the other one in her hand. "This sea glass has prepared and waited patiently for this moment to be discovered."

"So the smoother and rounder it is, the more obstacles it overcame?"

"Exactly, like your old buildings that developed character and

inherited value over time." He motioned toward the piece Miranda
was holding. "That's yours to keep."

"Thanks." She slipped it into her front pocket. "Let's see if I can
find sea glass on my own."

"Don't only look for brown," Jake called out to Miranda, who
had drifted off. "There are whites and greens too."

"Got it."

"And try not to overlook the dried seaweed piles. You'd be surprised at what you can find hiding in them."

"This is more difficult than I thought, but I like the challenge."

Aside from nature's music, several minutes of silence prevailed
as they searched the sand with lowered heads and eager eyes.

"When Kasey and I last visited here," Jake said, "we spent what
felt like hours combing this beach but came up empty-handed.
Then, before packing up for the day, we found a large piece of
cobalt sea glass next to our cooler."

"Wow, blue, huh? That must be the ultimate find."

"Any shade of blue is rare," he replied, "but I'm still waiting for
that once-in-a-lifetime piece of red. It's almost unheard of in these
waters, but I believe anything is possible."

Who was this person who strolled the beach with the emerald-eyed guy before Miranda? A friend? Family member? Or
perhaps his greyhound, although there were no identifiable signs or
animal smells during her brief time at Addie's.

"Who is Kasey?"

"My girlfriend." Jake skipped a smooth stone into the water and
kept a reserve in his other hand.

"Oh. Um. Kasey should have joined us today," Miranda said.
"Maybe she would have brought us luck finding another piece of
blue sea glass."

"Thanks, but she is spending the summer in Europe taking

culinary classes with a renowned pastry chef. It was a golden opportunity." He skipped another stone, making it hop five times on the water's surface.

Of course, Jake had a girlfriend or, more likely, an entire fan club of women. Yet a naive Miranda had fretted over his general references to a date.

The waves rushed in and retreated, her feet sinking deeper into the sand. Her footprints disappeared as if they had never existed in the first place.

Temporary, only temporary.

With her treasure hunt aborted, she attempted to skip a stone. It hit the water and fell kerplunk, sinking quickly beneath the surface.

Although Jake's girlfriend might eliminate awkwardness in a potential friendship, Kasey would be a reminder Miranda lagged behind others like a faint shadow. Had she auditioned for a lead role, Miranda assumed she wouldn't get the part anyway.

"Summer must be lonely without Kasey."

"Yes," Jake said, "but I have bucket lists to fill and hobbies to enjoy."

Miranda had only created to-do lists. Aside from preserving old buildings, painting an occasional piece of acceptable artwork, or running a familiar route, fulfillment wasn't a term recognized in her vocabulary.

"Kasey and I appreciate our time together, and we respect each other's space. It's a healthy relationship." Jake placed another flat stone between his thumb and middle finger and flicked his wrist back before its quick release. "I've always encouraged her to follow her dreams. She deserves that."

Carefree seagulls glided overhead. Their wings enabled them to soar rather than be dragged down by life's disappointments. But unlike Miranda, they chose their destination.

Didn't she deserve someone to encourage her independence as Jake did for Kasey? To instill faith where there were doubts and insecurities? To inspire tomorrow, jeopardized by yesterday?

The wind stirred up sand, and clouds permanently resided in the sky. With inclement weather threatening the forecast, it was time for Miranda to return to the cottage and subtract another day from her countdown.

Chapter 10

Jake and Miranda retraced their steps up the winding forest path until they reached the clearing.

"Edens Cove was a wonderful surprise—better than sitting on rusty lawn furniture and swatting bees in Trudy's yard." Miranda clapped her sand-filled sneakers.

"Can't argue with you there," Jake replied. "What's next on our home improvement list? Painting? Moving furniture?"

"*Our* list?" She smirked. "Since when did my to-dos become yours? I have a hunch you're plenty busy with obligations this summer without inheriting mine." She shook the remaining sand from the blanket. "Why are you so eager to help me?"

"Let's see—" Jake leaned against the Jeep's passenger door, tapping the tips of his steepled fingers together. "For starters, I was raised to be a good neighbor, and good neighbors lend a hand. Second, you and I proved that we are quite the landscaping team this morning. Shall I keep going?"

"I'm listening," Miranda said with a chuckle. She handed him the neatly folded blanket.

"Okay, then. Third, the sooner we tackle your jobs on Primrose Lane, the more time you'll have for summertime adventures. There are plenty of resources at Colby's Hardware to help you settle in comfortably with your new arrangement."

Miranda glared at Jake, the blood draining from her face, and internal alarms resounded. The Barron Park version of herself resumed a place among legalities and time frames. She tugged on the car door handle, but persistence didn't unlock it; Jake did.

He made his way around to the driver's side and took his place behind the wheel. The truck sputtered and grumbled with the engine's start, and upbeat music came from the speakers.

Jake reversed the Jeep and accelerated his speed. The afternoon's potential disappeared like the dust trail left in its path.

"Hey, I didn't mean to upset you. What just happened back there, Miranda?"

Every muscle clenched in her back and shoulders, bearing the weight of her invisible suit of armor.

"Today was fun," she said. "I admire your outlook on life and appreciate your kindness and support—really, I do. But there are parts of me you don't know."

"That's true for the both of us. Friendships develop over time."

"I wish it were simple, but it's not."

"What's not simple?"

"Everything." Miranda sharpened her tone as if Jake would better understand her sentiments that way. "Me being here. The circumstances surrounding this summer. It's not fair to drag you into my dysfunctional world."

"The last I checked, you haven't dragged me anywhere." He glanced over at her but returned his gaze to the road. "I'm not sure I understand or if you even want me to try, but I won't meddle."

Jake navigated through the radio stations. Although electric guitar strumming would have sufficed, a catchy Phil Collins song came to Miranda's rescue.

The neighbors must have had their curiosities about her arrival and the adjoining property's fate—intentions she was ashamed to admit. But, unlike others who dug into her history without an invitation, neither Jake nor Addie inquired.

Even if a bolder side of Miranda existed in Cobblers Hill, she was still a hypocrite. The historical society would have been appalled by her thoughts of demolishing the musty cottage to increase the property value.

Miranda reached her hand to the dashboard and lowered the music.

"My grandmother passed away back in February, Jake, but I've been mourning that relationship for some twenty years. It's a long story with no heroes and an unfortunate ending."

A piece of wicker protruded from the picnic basket. Regardless of Miranda's attempts to bend the stubborn piece into place, it failed to conform. "I've had my share of letdowns and frustrations, especially when it involved family."

"I got that sense from our conversation earlier."

"I missed out on those simple traditions that created lasting memories—the turkey carving at the dining room table on Thanksgiving and a competitive egg hunt with siblings at Easter. I wondered what it would be like to hear the older generation tell patriotic stories by the Fourth of July bonfire and attend a Labor Day barbecue with cousins."

"You mean you never had festive holidays growing up?"

"It depends if you consider Chinese takeout and television reruns celebratory." Miranda's eyes welled. "Relatives didn't care enough to leave behind footprints, let alone share a meal on a special occasion. Reaching milestones was as painful as having kidney stones. I should know; I had two. Kidney stones, that is. My mom and I developed a tight bond, though, through our brokenness."

Jake chewed his inner cheek, alternating between sides. He kept a heavy foot on the pedal, and his hands gripped the steering wheel in the ten and two positions.

"I counted my blessings instead of my hardships," Miranda continued. "I hoped I would find acceptance and closure in my family history one day. Were my requests unreasonable?" A single tear rolled down her cheek, followed by a steady stream of others.

Jake reached into the glove compartment and handed her a stack of Dunkin' napkins. Crumpled and coffee-stained, they were in worse shape than Miranda. She smiled at them through her tears.

"Gertrude Blair left me with vague memories and her estate, including the property here on Primrose Lane. But get this, she didn't give me the cottage to live in, rent, or sell at my discretion. She's either making me earn it or prove I'm worthy of the inheritance." Miranda dabbed her eyes with a napkin.

"She gave you the property, but not outright?"

Miranda's head bobbed. "According to Trudy's attorney, Mr. Baxter, she specified guidelines I must follow. An arrangement. I had to agree to spend an extended summer, specifically one hundred days, at her cottage. Bizarre, right?"

"Ahh, you reacted when I mentioned your arrangement," Jake said. "It was a random word with no underlying meaning but a poor choice. I'm sorry."

"It hit a trigger point. No need to apologize, though. You wouldn't have known, right?"

The Jeep accelerated down the road, racing along with her pulse. Jake raked his fingers through his hair, making it stick up on end. "Any idea why your grandmother devised this plan?"

"To test my survival skills, maybe? Or to form a final wedge between my mom and me—they were always at odds. It's like a twisted game, and I'm the token strategically being moved around the board. Even in death, could Trudy be so vindictive? Who does that? Who offers a gift but then makes you earn it?"

Jake shrugged.

"Trudy left me a separate bank account to cover the bills and expenses during these hundred days. There's even spending money for leisure. Sounds like an allowance to me. What, am I back in high school? Where was she during those awkward years we talked about earlier?"

Except for the low rumble of the Jeep, silence met Miranda's words.

"Everyone has disappointments in life," she said, "but I never overcame mine. And I resent being here, held as a prisoner against my will, like the victim I always considered myself in the Blair family. So much for my consolation prize, huh?"

"You could have declined your grandmother's plan, right?"

"Yes, of course."

"But you chose not to."

"Right." Miranda hid her forbidden cuticles under her thighs, the wicker basket teetering on her lap. "My mom and I have led simple, modest lives due to others' decisions. There weren't tough times; there were tough years. And looking ahead, it seems there'll be much of the same struggles. This arrangement presented an opportunity to own property that would provide a financial cushion. I had to surrender and accept the terms or forfeit the estate and its security. And so, I agreed to make the sacrifice for three months." She sighed. "Cobblers Hill means a great deal to you, Jake. I hope I'm not coming across as cold or ungrateful. Under different circumstances—"

"I get it." He removed his eyes from the road to glance in her direction. "I can only imagine how difficult this has been. I'm sure you did plenty of soul-searching."

"You have no idea how I struggled with this out of pride, fear, my mom's contempt for Trudy . . . a whole gamut of emotions. I'm still second-guessing my every move, but I'm here with bitterness and resentment as roommates for the summer. And, if that's not bad enough, I'm embarrassed I bothered you with this nonsense."

"Listen," Jake replied, "instead of fighting this as a personal challenge, why not be open-minded to the possibilities in Cobblers Hill? Give this town a chance. Enjoy the gift of time Trudy provided this summer, regardless of her intentions."

Shreds of consoling napkins fell in between the wicker grooves of the picnic basket. Miranda tilted the dashboard vent and redirected the cool air at her rosy cheeks.

"Gram believes God looks down the road and places people where they need to be," Jake said. "If you consider everything happens for a reason, it might be time to relinquish control and surrender to this divine plan rather than think of it as your grandmother's will."

Miranda eased into the leather seat and drew a deep breath. The pressure alleviated in her chest as she slowly exhaled. Up ahead, a glimmer of sunshine broke through the billowy clouds.

"Maybe you were meant to visit this summer for reasons you'll discover," he said. "Besides, you aren't alone. You have Gram and me and our community. And just think, in time, that previous nightmare lawn on Primrose will be greener than green—we'll see to it! That's not so bad for starters, now, is it?"

With Jake's references to "Gram" rather than "my grandmother," he seemed willing to share Addie with Miranda—as if his cherished relative belonged to them both.

"I promise you, time will fly, and we can fill it with adventures. My work schedule will be lighter until the store enters its prime September season. That allows some flexibility for summer fun. And soon enough, you will have satisfied your part of this so-called 'arrangement,' inherit Trudy's estate, and be free to return home with more security. It's only a hundred days till tomorrow."

Miranda smiled. She wasn't alone, even without her mother's calls and texts. She would embrace the theme of trust. And if the remaining days in Cobblers Hill were as enlightening as her afternoon with Jake Colby, she might not be as eager for them to end.

Chapter 11

Miranda's elbows left imprints on the windowsill. Overhead, mourning doves cooed a sorrowful tune from their resting place on a utility line. During their brief intermission, she heard Jake's truck rumble in the distance. With the Jeep's windows down, she often identified the song coming from his radio.

Addie hung wet laundry every day at 8:00 a.m. Seersucker housedresses and Jake's jeans dangled from clothespins, interrupting Miranda's view of the Colby yard.

The postal truck rounded the corner twenty-one minutes later and raised the red flag on the neighbors' clematis-covered mailbox. Then it skipped over Trudy's cottage and continued down the dirt road.

Why didn't mailboxes come with blue flags or fuschia ones since a red flag was a warning sign? While no one looked forward to getting bills, incoming mail shouldn't instigate fear. Unless, of course, the delivery contained correspondence from an attorney's office like Miranda received last winter. That letter warranted a parade of red flags and yellow caution tape wrapped around the mailbox in multiple layers.

The neighbors' lawn was plush like green wall-to-wall carpeting, while Trudy's grass had only grown taller and brittle in the summer heat. Days had passed since tackling the home improvement project and the so-called "date" with Jake.

The brown sea glass from Edens Cove rested in a porcelain dish that once held Trudy's mismatched earrings. Miranda traced its smooth form with her finger. So much for finding green and the occasional blue. The single piece was likely the extent of her sea glass collection.

Aside from a brief and coincidental encounter at the town's Red, White, and Brew coffeehouse, Miranda hadn't seen Jake. Even if she weren't notorious for declining invitations, there hadn't been mention of another adventure together in the quaint New England town. Once again, Miranda Blair was on her own.

Becoming the cottage's designated exterminator might be the scope of her summer entertainment. While the damp, musty bungalow lacked warmth on the hottest days, multi-legged crawlers found a permanent dwelling within its nooks and crannies. Purchasing bug traps and cleaning supplies would appear at the top of another to-do list.

Whereas her phone's Notes app would have sufficed, Miranda preferred using a pen and pad to create lists. Tapping and typing weren't as gratifying as gliding a pen across a page and seeing a series of bold check marks.

A desk with chipped paint and rusted handles, balancing on wobbly legs, appeared to be reprimanded to the room's corner. An overstretched rubber band on the verge of snapping secured a stack of outdated travel brochures in its top drawer. Miranda slid the matte trifolds of the Taj Mahal, Big Ben, the Temple of Artemis of Ephesus, and the Great Sphinx at Giza across the desk and into piles like she was dealing a deck of cards.

Trudy likely kept a modest home because she spent her days traveling the globe and soaking up experiences. Had Miranda's circumstances differed, she would have visited the world's wonders rather than marvel at them in history books.

Old tide charts and yellowed newspapers, expired receipts, and business cards represented a dash—the time in Cobblers Hill before

Trudy's passing and Miranda's arrival. Rather than the lack of note-paper instigating a *huff*, it was the sequence of unfamiliar memories. Everything Miranda saw, touched, and stumbled upon broadened the wedge between grandmother and granddaughter. What else in Gertrude Blair's life kept her from pursuing a relationship with her only grandchild?

After scribbling her to-do list on the back of a 1985 Sears Roebuck catalog, Miranda discarded a lifetime's worth of travel experience into the garbage pail with a clean, unforgiving sweep. The stubborn lid popped up, providing a glimpse of a Mayan temple.

Trudy's picnic basket occupied the kitchen's limited floor space in the days following Miranda's outing with Jake. She had shimmied it across the linoleum, tripped over it, and maneuvered herself around it. More than once, she stubbed a bare toe against the wicker.

The afternoon with Jake Colby had breathed new life into Trudy's arrangement. But with each passing day, it became a distant memory that labored Miranda's breath. If only she had kept the conversation light instead of word-vomiting to Jake as if he were her therapist. If only she had confronted her shortcomings rather than sidestepped them. If only—

It wouldn't have been the first time she sabotaged her happiness. Being the guest of honor at a pity party attended by "what was" and "what might have been" didn't merit a celebration. Sure, Jake lent an attentive ear, but Miranda dragged him down with "woe is me." Even for someone with Jake's physique, her emotional baggage was hefty to bear.

Miranda lifted the basket lid and peeked inside. Vibrant colors, stored as inspiration for a future painting, twirled like a kaleido-scope in her mind. There were contrasting shades of blue, rich earth tones, and hints of gold to capture the sun's rays that peeked through the forest branches. Just as a palette of acrylics would dry over time, the compelling sights of Edens Cove would fade along with reminders of abundant sunshine, pleasant surprises, and the emerald-eyed guy next door.

Jake's empty beer bottle that toasted Miranda was now sticky. Her pomegranate juice, a refreshing choice for the balmy June day, had left a crimson ring around the plastic flute. Unlike the carelessly tossed brochures, she placed the remnants from their drinks in the recycling bin below the sink. Even the ciabatta crumbs that fell from transparent lunch wrappings warranted respect. She gathered them with a wet sponge.

Without the cache of picnic memories, the empty basket revealed its paisley lining. Had Miranda noticed the series of leatherette interior straps, they may have secured the salad forks. And the overlooked zippered compartment on the underside of the basket's lid would have stored napkins. It was the perfect place to keep packets of mayo and mustard if there were a next time.

What else had Miranda overlooked when she was distracted by cold-cut selections and Jake's reference to a date? While it was unlikely she could permanently remove her self-imposed blinders, she was willing to loosen their ties. Gliding the old zipper across, she reached a hand inside the lining's pocket. Something flat and smooth with crisp edges grazed her fingertips—perhaps a takeout menu or one of Trudy's to-do lists, if she and Miranda had been anything alike.

Instead, it was a light pink envelope addressed in flowing cursive to a gentleman, Randy. The skinny "d" and long curly "y" resembled those letters on her grandmother's signed sketches. Just because Trudy wasn't a figure in Miranda's life hadn't meant she wasn't a part of someone else's history.

Of the many roles Miranda would have sought had life been different, an invader of Gertrude Blair's past wasn't one of them. She slid the sealed envelope across the kitchen countertop beyond reach and stepped away. But from every angle, it was within peripheral sight. Like the stash of travel trifolds, the garbage pail could devour

Trudy's sealed sentiments. The bold move would avoid guilt and a violation of privacy.

Miranda needed more than her grandmother's ruins, yet Jake suggested the summer might provide closure. Bitterness and resentment had made it easy to sever emotional ties with Trudy. Still, Miranda's stomach knots shouldn't have been tight like shoe leather. She had come so far, relocating and becoming vulnerable in Cobblers Hill, but the grudges were as burdensome.

She paced back and forth. If she took a different approach, getting acquainted with Gertrude Blair might expedite the healing journey. She removed and unfolded the brittle letter. Trudy's unleashed words slow danced across the page.

My Dearest Randy,

I think of you often as if you were here with me, walking beside me, hand in hand along the beach, basking in the simple joys we once shared before things became complicated. I wonder if you ever reflect on those special times. Maybe they were replaced or forgotten, or they were never cherished memories.

As I look back on my days, I long for the history we could have made. Sadly, I am left with what remains. Life had a different plan for us, and the world missed our legacy . . . yours and mine . . . ours together.

If given another chance, I would have embraced the opportunity to change what was. For this, my regrets have been heavy. Rather than easing over time, they have become more cumbersome with each passing year. I have carried mine through sweat and tears. Hopefully yours, if any, were lifted and set free.

Time waits for no one. Relationships must be handled carefully and regarded sacredly. Actions cannot be undone, just as words cannot be retracted once spoken. The bitterness left behind can sting indefinitely. For this, I am sorry. But ties do bind, and part of me will always be with you.

I leave you with this,

Gertrude

Miranda folded the love letter along its deep creases that had settled over time. Being privy to a page in her grandmother's history, she had been premature to conclude Trudy's life was perfect.

As if memories and regrets from Miranda's outing with Jake Colby weren't cumbersome enough to bear, they now entwined with the written sentiments retrieved from within the shared picnic basket.

A series of wind chimes sounding from her phone made her jump. She typed in the six-digit password and tapped on Jake's text.

Hey there, Happy 4th!
What are you doing later?
How about that ice cream challenge at McGinley's and some fireworks?
I know the perfect spot. Should I stop by around 7?

Miranda's heart sprinted as if there were a finish line in sight. The Fourth of July was an ordinary day in Barron Park. She and her mother usually spent the evening watching the fireworks show on television within the comfort of their modest den. Midway through the performance, she would be lulled to sleep by the accompanying orchestra and miss the finale.

Holidays didn't have to be ho-hum this year or ever again. Change was possible. Not only could the evening entail the smell of gunpowder and the echo of patriotic sounds from afar, but she could witness bursts of color illuminating the New England sky. She might even spot her first shooting star. But, above all, it meant a do-over with Jake Colby and the opportunity to heed Trudy's advice about second chances.

Miranda replied to Jake's text:

Sure. Sounds fun.

She hurried into the bedroom and gave each article of clothing in her limited wardrobe a once-over. The rips in her jeans—a tear from the pointy edge of a lawn chair and a gaping hole from a protruding nail under the office desk—reflected clumsiness rather than coolness. Every boxy T-shirt made her look frumpy, leaving her waistline to the imagination. And what twenty-five-year-old wore a blouse?

She slipped a sapphire-colored tank top off the hanger and held it against her milky complexion in need of self-tanner.

It would have to suffice for the occasion, along with a pair of white denim capris. Accessories were sparse in Miranda's wardrobe, as was anything flattering, trendy, red, or patriotic for America's birthday. Like a tornado's wrath, clothes were strewn across the bed and spilled onto the floor.

Trudy had been widowed early, but whether or not she remained alone in life or had a second chance at happiness was as much a mystery as the gentleman, Randy. Aside from accompanying her grandmother's travels and picnic outings—pure assumptions—what significance did he play in Trudy's life? Or could he have played in her own? What force too strong to be reckoned with—unrequited love, distance, betrayal—tore them apart? Maybe Miranda wasn't the only one who sought closure.

Addie and Jake may have been able to provide details about Gertrude Blair's past and bridge gaps in Miranda's history. But it was best to keep the relationship light with her neighbors. "Light" was more than Miranda had in previous relationships with others, and it was more than she could ask of the Colbys—for now.

Chapter 12

Jake didn't exaggerate when he said McGinley's was a gold mine. Not only was the quaint town bustling with the spirit of patriotism, but it seemed everyone in Cobblers Hill had the same idea—to celebrate with sweet indulgences.

Classic black-and-white checkerboard tile covered the floors, and high-back vinyl booths lined both sides of the nostalgic ice cream parlor. Flashing electric-blue and hot-pink fluorescent signs offered old-school roller rink vibes. The fire-engine-red Chevy, taking center stage in the crowded waiting area, distracted hungry guests. Jubilant children spun on retro barstools until they were dizzy or reprimanded by an adult, whichever happened first.

"Now I know why everyone loves this place." Miranda took in the ambiance with her aspiring artist's eye.

"Wait until you taste their ice cream." Jake swiped a menu from the hostess's station. "Here, it may be some time before we're seated. Check out the toppings, and you'll see what I was talking about."

Much like her preferred flavor, vanilla, Miranda never indulged in anything beyond the basics in life. She had convinced herself they were all she needed to be happy. Still, as the waitress walked by, supporting a tray of rich-chocolate, sweet-cinnamon, and salted caramel–infused desserts, Miranda stood on her tippy toes for a peek. She was equally intrigued by Jake Colby.

In the main dining area, couples held hands across laminate table-tops while awaiting the arrival of their summertime treats. Randy may have taken Trudy there on a special occasion or just because life was worth celebrating. Yet unlike their presumed relationship, McGinley's had weathered the storms and withstood the tests of time.

At last, a lanky girl wearing a pink ruffled poodle skirt escorted Jake and Miranda through the dining area, past noisy tables of sugar-charged children. The tantalizing aroma of toasted marshmallows lingered in the air long enough to make a calorie-conscious patron surrender to his cravings. The hostess batted her mascara-clad lashes at Jake as she directed them to a booth in the far corner.

"After you." Jake guided Miranda with an outstretched hand before taking a seat himself.

Bright, unforgiving lights hovered above. There would no longer be tinted sunglasses to hide behind, open roads ahead to focus on, or conditioned sea glass for which to comb the beach. Had Miranda considered this earlier, she might have found an excuse to decline Jake's invitation. A quiet evening in the musty cottage accompanied by her favorite playlist and Trudy's crocheted blanket somehow gained appeal. Miranda held the oversized menu upright in front of her face.

"You okay?" Jake lowered the makeshift wall between them with his hand.

She leaned in closer while scanning the room.

"Yeah, but people may question why we're here together. I'm sure they're used to seeing you with your girlfriend." Miranda's long side bang provided the benefit of a shield over her right eye. "I wouldn't want to instigate the rumor mill or anything."

Jake leaned back against the cushioned booth with his arms folded across his chest. "There's no doubt I love this town and its people, but I stopped caring about what others say or think long ago. You should too. It's a liberating way to live your life."

He offered one of his prize-winning smiles that made Miranda melt as quickly as the child's waffle cone at the neighboring table. The little boy's parents armed with a stack of napkins were seconds late. Chocolate syrup ran down his arm in a steady stream, and the rainbow-sprinkled scoop plopped on the floor. It wasn't until his stemless cherry rolled into the aisle and met the bottom of a patron's shoe that the freckled boy began to cry.

"Besides," Jake said, "people have enough to worry about in their own lives than to judge yours or mine."

"True. I like your thinking."

A middle-aged waitress resembling the stereotypical Flo snapped her gum and held an exaggerated stance by their table.

"Let's have it. What can I get you folks?"

"She's going to have the rocky road special." Jake had a competitive gleam in his eye.

"And he'll have plain vanilla ice cream," Miranda said. "Make it a triple scoop, please."

"Flo" clicked her pen emphatically. "You're not from around here, are you? Most folks don't come to McGinley's for plain anything. We've got tons of toppings. Did you see?" She pointed to the back of the menu with her long, polished fingernail. "Peanut butter clusters, cookie crumbles, candy, nuts, sprinkles, dried fruit, coconut flakes, marshmallow fluff, and that's just for starters. Take your pick."

Ignoring Jake's snickers, Miranda replied, "That's okay, just plain vanilla will do."

"You got it." "Flo" tugged the menu from Miranda's reluctant hands. "Be right back with some waters." She hurried off to deliver straws to table nine before grabbing the check at table five and wending her way through the swinging kitchen doors.

From their giggles and gawks, the ladies across the room appeared to enjoy their view of Jake's perfectly symmetrical features.

He didn't seem to notice, the weight of his stare having settled upon Miranda. Cemented at the moment, she allowed him to take her in, imperfections and all, with his hypnotic eyes. Having located the room's exits and studied the multidimensional murals, Miranda counted the seconds between each flash of neon light from the suspended "Drive-In" sign. She noted how the waitresses wore saddle shoes with iridescent laces that frequently came untied, and sibling rivalry ceased once dessert arrived.

Miranda's hands gestured as she spoke, and her head tilted back when she laughed. Others considered her smoky-blue eyes and pea-sized beauty mark attractive features, but she saw herself as plain and unassuming. Without reason to fuss, she forwent makeup and opted for a simple ponytail or messy bun.

"I haven't seen one of these in forever." She grabbed the knob of the tabletop jukebox and gave it a turn.

"Here, play a few songs for us." Jake reached into his pocket and pulled out a sealed roll of quarters. "We have enough coins for at least a half hour's worth of music."

"Do you walk around with that much change? If I hadn't known any better, I'd say you purposely came prepared."

"Guilty as charged."

"What are you in the mood to listen to?" Miranda flipped through the bands and recording artists that spanned the decades. "The Rolling Stones? A little Journey? Some greatest hits from Air Supply?"

"Surprise me."

"Okay, then."

She slid the shiny George Washingtons into the slot one by one, made several selections, and pressed the red "enter" button. Appropriately, Foreigner's "Juke Box Hero" was the first song to play. "Speaking of Journey," she said, "have you made any long-distance trips?"

"I've visited six of the seven continents, if that counts as long-distance."

Miranda leaned forward with her palms planted down on the table. "Joking, right?"

"No, it's true."

"How is it that I would have to think twice before naming each of the continents, Jake, and you have been to all but one of them? That's incredible!"

"What about you?"

"It depends if you consider the drive to work and campus long-distance." She chuckled.

Jake unwrapped the tightly wound napkin from the table setting to unveil a shiny spoon. Miranda followed his lead, but the smoothed napkin curled back defiantly into position. "I grew up more of a homebody. You probably guessed I'm still living with my mother."

"And, as you saw, I'm living with my grandmother," he replied. "Anyway, not everyone enjoys traveling. I know plenty of people who prefer their yard over a Bora Bora beach. Of the places I've visited—Ürümqi, Madagascar, Perth, Andorra—nothing compares to home."

"Yeah, you do seem well-adjusted here. It's not that I didn't have the desire to travel; I lacked the funds and opportunities."

Colleagues sought entry-level positions on the coast following graduation or pursued internships abroad. Others explored remote areas of the world without a destination. Unlike Miranda and presumably more like Jake and Kasey, they were anxious to taste what life's menu offered—carefree spirits rich in self-discovery, possessing the emotional arsenal to weather life's storms. Jake and Miranda had few commonalities, yet their differences were part of his appeal.

Had Trudy been involved in her life, Miranda may have shared that thirst for adventure. Sadly, Cobblers Hill was likely the extent of her travels.

"You're fortunate for the circumstances that allowed you to see the world. It must have been incredible."

"Assumptions can be misleading," he said. "My trips abroad were out of necessity during a vulnerable time in my life."

Anyone else might have bombarded Jake with "whys" and "how comes," but Miranda learned early how vague answers could be as frustrating as curiosity itself. A two-way inquisition might ensue if she questioned his past. She twitched, thinking about how the conversation would unfold.

The waitress returned with water glasses and extra napkins, then hurried off again.

"So you've never flown before, Miranda?"

"Nope, can't say I've held a boarding pass. I'm not sure how I would handle being up in the air. I'm afraid of heights."

She removed an edible straw from its wrapper, placed it in her glass of water, and gave it a clockwise stir, which sent the lemon wedge and ice cubes in motion. "Your travels must have served you well because you seem in harmony with life, whereas I'm unable to figure myself out. Quite frankly," she chuckled, "I might stop trying."

"If I've given you that impression, then thanks. I've been a work in progress these past few years, but aren't we all?"

From Miranda's first and second impressions, Jake Colby was a masterpiece—someone who cruised through twenty-something years effortlessly. Although he wasn't exempt from unpleasant themes running through his life, it was difficult to envision his cracks.

Oddly, though, he didn't occupy a bachelor pad with a month's supply of energy drinks and an unmade bed awaiting the next overnight guest. Southern charm, garden-picked vegetables, homemade marmalade, and afternoon tea weren't what most men would consider the high life. And as for his extensive travels, he had for-feited his bragging rights.

"I can always depend on this town to keep me grounded," Jake said. "Cobblers Hill remains a place where time stands still. In a healthy way, of course. I'm sure you can relate with . . . Where did you say you were from?"

"Barron Park."

After twirling the straw wrapper around her finger until it main-tained its corkscrew shape, Miranda arranged the sugar packets by their color—white, pink, blue, and tan. Each time she shifted ner-vous energy in her seat, the booth's vinyl cushion squeaked.

The waitress returned with shiny silver bowls boasting jumbo-sized scoops of ice cream. "You're all set, folks. Enjoy." She left the check behind on the table and disappeared into the crowd.

"Here we go!" Jake's spoon was already in motion, chipping away at the first scoop.

Typically, rocky road had a chocolate ice cream base. But there were pleasant surprises in Cobblers Hill, including McGinley's twist on the popular flavor.

"Well?" He stared at Miranda with inquisitive eyes.

"I think my taste buds just had a Halloween party. The top-pings melted in my mouth like a candy bar after a disciplined day of trick-or-treating. Yeah, it's amazing." Miranda cradled a minia-ture marshmallow and dark chocolate morsel on her spoon. "For a change, that is."

"Fair enough. And while I've always preferred ice cream with lots of toppings, or "distractions," as you called them, I'll admit McGinley's plain vanilla is delicious. There's nothing not to appre-ciate about it." Jake pointed to the bowl with his spoon as he spoke. "Except, I think a scoop of this would taste even better over Gram's homemade apple pie."

"Can't argue with that." She giggled.

The fourth track from Foreigner, "I Want to Know What Love Is," sounded through the jukebox speakers. Regretting her song selection, Miranda didn't need intuitive Jake to be aware of her shortcomings in the romance department. However, he seemed more concerned with scraping melted vanilla from the sides of his bowl with his spoon.

"If the resources were available," he said, "and you could travel anywhere in the world, where would it be?"

"Paris!" There was no hesitation in her reply, and her face lit up as bright as the jukebox.

"The City of Light, huh? It's a beauty, although I was only there for a weekend."

"Oh, yes. I'm fascinated by its history. I'd love to experience the old-world architecture and view priceless works of art." Closing her eyes, Miranda drew an exaggerated breath. "To stand face-to-face with the *Mona Lisa* and study the *Venus de Milo*. Or to stroll the Champs-Élysées and light candles at Notre-Dame Cathedral." She warmed her arms with her hands. "I get chills thinking about it. As an American in Paris, my past would no longer matter, and the future would be mine to paint with the colors I choose."

"True, but you could have a similar experience anywhere—a fresh start, a clean slate to paint—if that's what you want."

"I–I guess," she replied, her head lowered. "For now, I feel like the only art lover who works at a historical society yet hasn't stepped foot beyond the East Coast."

Jake took a long sip of water while Miranda waited for him to say something—anything. Condensation dripped down the sides of his glass, leaving behind a wet ring on the paper place mat. He slid his empty bowl to the left and leaned back with both hands outstretched on the table. The early summer sun had tanned his forearms to a golden brown.

"It's nothing to get down about. You're preparing for that

journey; perfecting the process is all. Think about how rewarding your travels will be when you eventually have them. You will get to Paris, among other places, and the wait will be worth it."

Aside from Addie, no one approached Miranda as Jake did with simple statements carrying profound messages. He placed opportunities within her reach and encouraged her to dream without expiration dates. Why couldn't she climb the Eiffel Tower someday, cruise down the Seine River, or paint, like the seasoned artists, in front of Sacré-Coeur?

"Thanks for your vote of confidence."

Jake lifted her gaze with his eyes.

"You don't need my vote, or anyone else's, for that matter."

"True, but that encouragement could have made a difference in my life. Maybe I wouldn't have settled for my plan B."

"Plan B?"

"Accepting the job at the historical society was a personal compromise. I could appreciate art and history in the past of others rather than create the future I might have wanted." Miranda addressed her blurry reflection in the almost-empty silver bowl and tucked a wisp of hair behind her ear.

"I get it. We all settle for plan B at times. No shame there. Consider it a dress rehearsal to prepare us for plan A waiting down the line."

"I sometimes think about the road not taken, Jake. I wonder about the doors that may have opened and the people I might have met had I taken an active role in art rather than a back seat."

"You mean, as an artist."

"If that's what you call someone who creates art, teaches it, inspires it, or changes lives through it. Then yes, an artist. We only had enough money to cover the basics growing up, which didn't include sketching or painting classes. So I accepted art would remain a hobby. I took a few instructional classes in college, though."

There was more to Miranda's limitations than finances. Her upbringing hadn't equipped her to embrace opportunities with confidence, while dodging life's obstacles and overcoming insecurities. Instead, she had become her own impediment.

"Don't go putting a period where there should be a comma," Jake said. "Your job at the historical society may be well suited for now, but it shouldn't define who you were meant to be. You can still pursue that plan A when the timing is right."

"About that comma you mentioned, I've also been taking random graduate classes for the past few years. Unfortunately, there's a steep price for indecisiveness known as student loans. But I love learning, and being in school makes me feel that I'm moving in a direction."

"You'd be surprised how many others haven't quite figured out life," Jake replied. "Until there's clarity, make your bucket list and prioritize emptying it. Set a goal, and go get Paris." He stuck a few bills under the check and slid it off to the side. "I assure you, Mona will be there to greet you with her half smile."

They had satisfied looks of overindulgence. Not only did the music selections run dry, but their bowls were empty. Still, Miranda couldn't recall a time more hopeful. And while she had hesitated in sharing tidbits of her life, some trivial, it was cathartic.

"Ready for some fireworks?"

"Absolutely!" She wiped a final drop of melted ice cream from the table's surface and placed the crumpled napkin beside her bowl. "Lead the way."

Chapter 13

While others secured their spot on the pier, Jake assured Miranda Emerson Rock was ideal for watching fireworks. They strolled farther from the west end's performing musicians and hustling food vendors toward more secluded spaces.

"I don't remember when I was last on a boardwalk," Miranda said. "This must be a popular place to run early in the morning before it gets hot."

"Yep," Jake replied. "Cyclists love this boardwalk too. Townsfolk claim the warmth from the day's sunshine absorbed in the wood gives Cobblers Hill its distinct beachy smell."

"How long has Addie lived here?"

"Gram is originally from Tallahassee. She moved up north after marrying Pop." Jake rubbed his jawline. "Must be fifty years or so now."

"Wow, that long, huh?"

Having lived in Barron Park all her life, Miranda had half that time invested herself. It was her forever home, providing the familiarity and sense of security she relied upon. Nothing would change that, including the inheritance of Gertrude Blair's hilltop bungalow.

"I wish I had an ounce of Addie's spunk," Miranda said. "I admire her energy and optimism."

"Even with her stubborn side, there isn't much of her not to love. I've never met anyone like her before, and I'm not saying that because I'm her grandson. The sky may be the limit for some, but that woman's faith and determination know no bounds."

"I've noticed how everything Addie says can be taken at face value, but her underlying messages make me nod," Miranda said. "They're simple yet profound and appreciated."

"You caught on quick that anyone in Gram's company becomes a student."

"I may be a good listener, but she's the perceptive one. It's as if she knows what I need to hear and guides the conversation accordingly. I absorb her wisdom and have these 'aha' moments later."

"That sums up time spent with Adelaide Colby," Jake explained.

Above the boardwalk, dimly lit lampposts hummed and dragonflies danced—summer sights and sounds as another summer day had drawn to its close. Clearance sales and end-of-season bargains would follow the celebration of America's birthday. And stores would promote everything apple cinnamon and pumpkin spice. Wasn't that what Miranda wanted, to rush the hands of time?

"Gram values an open mind and eager ear, and she sees potential where it is often overlooked," Jake said. "Have you heard her relate life to a book?"

"Not yet. But we did chat about nurturing the garden or, in other words, maintaining a healthy relationship."

"Of course you did." Jake shook his head. "I can recite those lines in my sleep. The book analogy is still my favorite, though."

"I'd love to hear it."

"There's nothing like being on the receiving end of a Gramism, as the Colbys call it, directly from its source. I'll give it a whirl without the southern accent or a pointed finger holding you accountable.

"According to Gram," Jake continued, "you can't skim through a novel, just like you shouldn't rush through life. If you recognize the value of each page, you'll learn something to apply later in the story. The more challenging chapters won't last forever. You must brave through them, though, to appreciate the rewarding ones that make you want to read more." He shifted his backpack from one shoulder to the other while keeping a steady pace toward the board-walk's end.

"Gram explains how some characters appear for a reason, others stay for a season, and a few might stick around for the rest of the story. The most important thing, she claims, is not to get stuck on any one page. Regardless of unexpected plot twists, she says to never lose faith in a happy ending. For some reason, this Gramism hits home for me."

"I can see why," Miranda said. "I've been known to inhale fiction and finish a book in a weekend. Now Addie has me thinking I'm less of a bookworm and more of a page skimmer and chapter expediter." She laughed. "I don't think I'll approach my novels the same way, thanks to your grandmother."

"You just might look at life differently too."

Miranda could benefit from more Gramisms, having never met anyone like the Colbys before. Differences in their upbringings and outlooks bordered opposite ends of the spectrum—Jake living in the moment and Miranda avoiding the past and fearing the future. But because of Trudy's will and Kasey's absence, a Colby and a Blair enjoyed the present together—even though it was temporary, only temporary.

Miranda bent down and removed a bothersome pebble from her sandal. Nonconforming blades of beach grass grew in between the boardwalk's planks and brushed up against her ankles.

"Has Addie always been such an optimist?" She stood, tossed the pebble over the ledge, and resumed her stroll.

"For as long as I can remember, yes, but for a while there, no. I'll tell you about it someday."

Someday might fall within the countdown, or it might never

come. If anyone knew the art of offering a vague reply, it was Miranda.

"What a perfect night for fireworks, huh?" Jake arched his neck back at the ceiling of shimmering stars. "Every season in Cobblers Hill offers a unique experience, but nothing compares to summer's sights, sounds, smells, and extra daylight to appreciate them. June, July, and August would be endless months if it were up to me."

Miranda cleared her throat and wrapped her arms around herself in an embrace. The boardwalk had ended, and for an awkward moment, so had their conversation. The moonlight offered glimpses of an uninterrupted stretch of beach. But as Jake and Miranda grew closer, the dunes seemed to move farther away.

"Sorry if that was insensitive," Jake said. "I know you're anxious to put this summer behind you. I get it. I do."

"Cobblers Hill is inspiring, and the people here are lovely. I see why this coastal town means so much to you."

"I sense there's a 'but' coming."

"But being here at the end rather than the beginning has instigated old wounds," she replied. "You see, I've worked hard to accept my circumstances and let go of what I can't control. I've taken enough psychology classes to write a textbook on mental health. Then I was summoned to Cobblers Hill, and the pain resurfaced. It's one thing to avoid the past; it's a different story when it's dredged up and hunts you down."

"Right. We agreed on that at Edens Cove—leaving the past in the past."

"This place could have been a part of my life while there were relatives alive and memories to make," Miranda said softly, her sentiments harmonious with nature. "But since it wasn't, I'm anxious to close the chapter and start a new one. Just don't go telling Addie I said that. She would disapprove of me rushing the pages."

Aside from the retreating waves, her words met silence. She caught a firefly in the air and let it walk across the palm of her hand. It took flight, disappearing into the darkness with its magical summer glow.

"I've hesitated to ask this," Miranda pressed on, "but, um, what do you know about my arrival here?"

Jake's slight bowlegged gait, which exuded confidence and ease, now yielded quickened footsteps toward Emerson Rock—each one equivalent to two of Miranda's smaller steps.

"Well, we are still getting acquainted, but I think you're someone open to change. You weren't who you wanted to be when you arrived, hoping for closure without revisiting the past."

Jake stole glimpses of her, but she pretended not to notice. The blur of lights that spanned the skyline sparkled like diamonds.

"I believe you have more layers than you're willing to reveal to others," he said. "Although you may limit yourself and underestimate your talents and abilities, I know you'll have a bright future. If you're willing to do your part to create it, that is."

Jake's reply seemed straightforward but sincere. He would have said something if he had been privy to the Blair family history. And had he danced around the topic, Miranda would have recognized the offbeat tempo and rhythm. Instead, he walked a direct line that permitted her leeway to dictate the conversation. A story was long overdue to be shared, and Jake had proven to be the right listener. There was only one place to start.

The absence of Victor Blair.

Chapter 14

"Um, you're right," Miranda said, lengthening her distance from the emerald-eyed neighbor. "There is more I haven't shared. I've allowed few people into my world for fear of pity or judgment. And the last thing I needed was for anyone or anything to instigate old wounds."

The abundance of twinkling stars in the evening sky watched over her as she tiptoed into the spotlight. A gentle wind, carrying the sweet scent of beach grass, nudged her from behind.

"Acquaintances back home think my father passed away when I was young." Miranda released an exaggerated sigh. "It was easier for my mom and me to keep up with that facade than accept the truth—Victor abandoned us when I was a child. He could have had another family somewhere. Or maybe he fell out of love with us. It was anyone's guess. He took a drive one day and never returned for dinner, leaving behind a widow and an orphan—or so that's how we felt."

"I can't imagine losing a parent so early in life and under those circumstances." Jake ran his fingers through his hair like a comb. "How much do you remember about your dad?"

"As much, or as little, as any kindergartner could recall. I never felt he was worthy of my memories, even if they were transparent ones," she replied softly. "His disappearance stripped my childhood of its innocence and left me feeling unwanted, like I didn't matter. I remember that much. And there were no more night-lights or security blankets. Ever since then, those doubts and inadequacies have—"

"Watch!"

Jake reached for her arm, guiding her away from a protruding plank in the sand. "You can't always spot them, but there may be rusty nails. It's no fun brushing up against one."

While Miranda may have been heading toward dangerous ground by divulging too many personal details, she had sidestepped a potential threat. For now.

"Sorry about that," he said. "Go on, please. You were saying?"

Even the lull of distant waves beckoned her to continue. "Losing my dad was one thing. The mess he left behind made matters worse. With my mom dipping into a permanent funk, it felt like I had lost both of my parents. After all these years, I still have that instinct to protect my mother. It never seemed fair to leave her behind."

"I feel the same way about Gram."

Jake's footsteps kicked up sand as he walked. The contents of his slung backpack weighed him down, and his shoulders took turns bearing the load.

"Did relatives help pick up the pieces after your father left?"

"You'd think, right?" Miranda shook her head. "My mom and Trudy battled it out and passed the blame back and forth." She demonstrated an imaginary ball toss with her hands. "Throughout their game, I was caught in the middle and leveraged as an unattainable prize."

"Ouch! That's a tough position for any kid."

"It was unbearable at times. Although I lost a father, grandmother, and extended family, others still had it worse. At least Mom and I had each other, our health, and a roof over our heads, even if it leaked during storms. That's more than some can say."

"Weren't you—you know—curious about him?"

Miranda sighed. "At times, but mostly no. I was taught not to be inquisitive. Mom and I convinced ourselves we were content with life, so we didn't dig for answers or allow others to intervene. We've maintained that approach, settling for vanilla instead of risking the rocky road." She bit her thumbnail but avoided its cuticle. "Until I agreed to my grandmother's arrangement, that is. It's out of character for me to hope for something extra from life—to accept her terms in exchange for a reward."

"It's all making sense now," Jake said. "Your modest times growing up and lack of role models."

"Fear of the unknown and frustration with my past."

"Right. You deserved more." Jake's forehead furrowed in the moonlight's glow, and he chewed his inner cheek. He seemed to plant each footstep with intent.

"It's okay. I never owned big dreams anyway. The luckier ones were born with opportunity. On the other hand, I'm still proving my worth to earn my prize."

"As with your grandmother's estate, you mean."

"Exactly."

At last, the pier's lights faded into the distance, and jutting rock formations came into view. Emerson Rock was a tucked-away inlet between the majestic dunes and rugged coastline. Nature had carved out time and made the perfect reservation for two.

"Does this spot look okay?"

"It's amazing, like having the best seats at a private planetarium." Miranda's eyes darted across the star-studded sky. "Thanks for making tonight's plan."

Miranda settled in the sand with her back pressed against a smooth boulder. She gathered her long curls, damp from the salt-air mist, and used the ponytail holder on her wrist to secure a messy bun. Wispy pieces framed her face.

Jake took a seat beside her, with Kasey's lingering presence between them. "I hope I'm not prying, but were there any opportunities to reconcile, or was that completely out of the question?"

"It's not prying. You're taking an interest. I've come to know the difference. Besides, I initiated the conversation. I wanted you to understand the circumstances that led me here, even if I'm on borrowed time. I never inquired about my father, and he didn't seek me out. At times, I've wondered if my arrival was responsible for his departure. Maybe he didn't want to be a dad or care for a family—you know, bear a financial obligation. But of all the excuses, none justify leaving us behind. That goes for my grandmother too. Her absence formed a heavier grudge."

Miranda tucked her knees into her chest and hugged them with sleeveless arms. Maybe Jake, outfitted in fleece, wouldn't notice her chattered teeth if she kept her jaw clenched.

He rummaged through his backpack and handed her a navy-blue frayed sweatshirt. Its clean scent, unmistakably Jake's, wafted in the air.

"Women never dress properly for the weather," he said, "so I brought an extra. It's a bit wrinkled, and it will swim on you, but at least you'll be warm."

The oversized alma mater sweatshirt, velvety against Miranda's semi-bare skin, enveloped her with a sense of security. Jake's fabric hug was the next best thing to being wrapped in his protective arms—a display of affection rightfully reserved for his girlfriend.

How many articles of Jake's clothing had graced Kasey's bedroom floor, the trophy prize after a romantic evening? Were there many girlfriends or just a few? And was it appropriate to ponder Jake's experiences with other women after disclosing Miranda's past?

He removed a thermos and two mugs from his camouflage backpack. "The other night, when we ran into each other at the

Red, White, and Brew, I noticed how much sugar and creamer you added to your coffee. Hope I got it right." He poured hers first. "Careful, it's hot."

"I feel like all I do is thank you," Miranda replied, her eyes smiling. "You're always a step ahead, anticipating my needs."

"Call it intuition."

"That and friendship." She warmed her hands around the mug and blew on the plume of steam. "I hope you know it doesn't go unappreciated. I'm grateful. Truly, I am. But why are you so kind to me?"

"Why shouldn't I be?" Jake cocked his head to the side. "It's how you deserve to be treated. As for your coffee, you certainly take it light and sweet. I'd drink it iced, black, decaf, or two days old—as long as it wasn't herbal tea. Now don't repeat that, or Gram will make me sleep in her she-shed."

Miranda tilted her head back and laughed.

"Anyway, you are stronger and more resilient from your upbringing. I admire your grit." He took sips of coffee while digging his feet in the sand. "Did you ever consider those childhood experiences and psychology classes might serve a purpose one day? That they prepared you for something bigger? You could be the lifeline for someone experiencing a loss or struggling to overcome adversity. People can draw strength from your yesterday, and you can provide hope for their tomorrow."

Like the joyful music and powerful lyrics of a favorite song, Miranda would replay Jake's words in her head—*resilient, strong, grit, lifeline.* She took cautious sips, savoring the coffee's bold taste. "You and Addie have taught me anything is possible. Time will tell, but you've made an interesting point. Thanks for the insight and for not judging me. You're a good egg, Jake Colby."

Warmth radiated from her cheeks despite the chill in the air. Rather than reach over and give Jake one of those nonthreatening but somewhat awkward side hugs with little contact, she let handfuls of sand sift through her fingers.

"No thanks necessary." Jake topped off their mugs with coffee and returned the near-empty thermos to his backpack. "A selfish part of me is grateful for the arrangement that brought you to town. Otherwise, we wouldn't have this summer together."

Not only had the stars aligned in the clear New England sky, but the evening's blessings had multiplied beyond those of her country's independence. Celebratory sounds boomed in the distance like an oncoming parade.

"Here we go!" Jake said.

Pyrotechnics shot into the darkness, releasing an umbrella of patriotic reds and blues that created a kaleidoscope in the sky. Flares from charter boats illuminated the harbor in a menagerie of colors.

"How about we think of nothing else and enjoy the evening? The Fourth of July only comes once a year." He glanced over at Miranda. "For us, it might be our once in a lifetime."

Chapter 15

S unlight eased Miranda into the new day. A steaming cup of coffee in an oversized mug, filled to the brim for that iconic caffeine fix, accompanied her leisurely mornings.

Back home, when time constraints dictated her day, Miranda rarely drank a few sips before her coffee became lukewarm. She would reheat her mug while preparing for work or class and discover the muddy beverage several hours later in the microwave.

Even the coffee was more uplifting in the coastal New England town. Trudy's clay mugs kept it hot while Miranda lollygagged with her thoughts. Those thoughts returned to the magic of Emerson Rock and the attentiveness of Jake Colby, who had arranged for her to have his sweatshirt and a comforting mug of perfectly prepared coffee.

The cottage was undisturbed from the previous evening and the ones prior. Aside from the small front porch, Trudy's sunroom became her favorite place to retreat. Aesthetically, it was lacking, with maroon-plaid curtains and tired furniture, but it had a scenic view of the orchard from its hilltop perspective. Glorious light infiltrated the room for several hours of the day, making it the ideal spot in which to paint or curl up with a book.

Even with Miranda's resistance, Gertrude Blair was present, her touch transcending through her belongings. Not only had her love letter roused guilt, but it awakened a once-forbidden curiosity in her granddaughter. Trudy may have sketched in the cozy sunroom, or Randy might have read literature to her from the broad selection. Perhaps her grandfather had serenaded Trudy with a fiddle or recited poetry there. And maybe Miranda's father had lounged on that same couch, contemplating life decisions during his visits.

But there was a reason why walls didn't talk, and some memories faded. Not all worlds were meant to collide.

Miranda's fingers grazed the fabric bindings that aligned recessed shelves and removed *A Wrinkle in Time* from its resting place. Madeleine L'Engle's classic could accompany her for a few evenings. So could fat-free popcorn and background instrumental music.

She flipped through the brittle pages to where another reader had wedged an old photograph of an expressionless girl between two chapters. Her corset boots and modest dress with a buttoned bodice reminded Miranda how today's fashion had evolved from matronly styles in drab earth tones. A poofy bow secured her golden curls to the side. She had Miranda's blue eyes and high cheekbones.

"Now I know who I inherited the serious and detached gene from." Miranda spoke to the black-and-white photograph in a voice barely above a whisper. "And I've noticed we share an appreciation for art and literature. Even if we're woven from the same thread, it will always be a different stitch."

Miranda smoothed the cracks and creases on the photo's worn surface. "Cobblers Hill has been a pleasant surprise, but I guess my expectations were low. At times, I don't recognize myself here. And while I learn something new each day, you've left me with many unanswered questions. Like why you brought me to your town, surrounded by everything that once defined you when you're already gone."

She tossed the book to the side, no longer caring how time became wrinkled, and propped the attentive photograph on her easel within listening distance. "And I still haven't figured out the neighbors. Am I completely naive, or are they as wonderful as they seem? Wouldn't you know? You lived next to the Colbys for—how many decades?

"I've brought your name into conversations, but unintentionally. I'm not gonna lie, I've tried to avoid it. Each time, though, the neighbors were indifferent, like you were strangers. We know how that goes, huh?"

Miranda took a sip of coffee and wiped the corners of her mouth with her thumb and forefinger. "But that suits me just fine. The fewer details I gather during these hundred days, the better off I'll be. Besides, I've been happier lately, at peace for the moment. That's not worth jeopardizing with information overload."

The loaf of warm cinnamon bread, discovered earlier on her doorstep, lured Miranda into the kitchen. While no one had claimed responsibility for breakfast or the bundle of freshly cut wildflowers wrapped in foil, there was no mistaking who was behind these acts of kindness. Miranda sliced a piece of bread with a butter knife and returned to Trudy's photograph in the sunroom. It was poor etiquette to keep an old acquaintance waiting.

"On a whim, I asked Jake what he knew about me, you know, my arrival in town. As I suspected, it wasn't much. Speaking of Jake, he's become a friend—one with no strings attached. His girlfriend clipped those."

Miranda nibbled and sipped as her eyes darted back and forth. "In another time and place, and under different circumstances, do you think a no-frills girl like me could have a chance with a man like Jake Colby?"

She gave herself a once-over.

The drawstring from her frumpy pajama pants had long disappeared in a dryer cycle, making them sag like low-rise jeans. The freebie fluorescent T-shirt from a supermarket grand opening was too large and bright without shades.

"Guys like Jake don't go for the Miranda Blairs of the world. They want a masterpiece, and I've always been a paint by number."

She licked a dab of cinnamon from her knuckle and took another sip from her mug. The bold coffee, accompanied by warm bread and an attentive photograph, dissipated the chill of loneliness.

Having stacked art books in size order from largest to smallest on the knotty pine end table, Miranda inspected her paintbrushes. Several had loose hairs or the tips no longer came to a point. Her acrylics had become clumpy and smelled sour. It was only a matter of time before her artwork fell victim to their poor quality.

"Even if Jake *were* interested in me, as ridiculous as that sounds, I've never been the girlfriend type," Miranda said to a young Trudy in the photograph. "Relationships usually end in disappointment. Aren't the Blairs proof that love divides? And yet Jake claims it multiplies. Who's right? And will I ever know, or should I spare myself the letdown?"

She crouched so the photo of Trudy was eye level with nothing between them but their past. "Had times been different, we might have had plenty of these talks like other grandmothers and granddaughters. You could have told me about Randy, my grandfather, and anyone who caught your attention. And maybe my heart wouldn't have been so broken."

There was deafening silence rather than telepathic words of encouragement from the old photograph. Only the chirping birds beyond the den window had something to say.

"Jake seems too good to be true." Miranda caressed her coffee mug. "A respectful guy who is loyal to Addie and remains faithful to his girlfriend—it doesn't get any more attractive than that! But am I missing something? How long has Kasey been hanging around? Is she as beautiful as I picture her? Better yet, is she Jake-worthy?"

Miranda fluffed a throw pillow a little too emphatically, lifting dust into the air. She leaned back against it, her propped feet revealing mismatched socks.

"He's approaching thirty. Perhaps he plans on marrying soon. Kasey Colby. Oh, that name sounds dreadful," she said with a scrunched nose. "I'm not the jealous type, and while I appreciate her presence this summer, I wonder about their connection. Jake doesn't talk about her, and she never texts or calls him when we're together. Maybe Mom and I aren't the only ones taking a mini-vacation from communication." Miranda offered a few chuckles before resuming her serious tone. "How solid can their relationship be? He must be lonely if he's looking to fill time with me."

Gertrude Blair's stare in the photograph was unwavering. Miranda took her last sip of coffee and sighed.

"I would never intervene in Jake and Kasey's relationship. I'm the last person to tamper with someone else's happiness. But I enjoy spending time with him, even if I find his determination to sell me on Cobblers Hill odd."

All along, Miranda fretted over a measly hundred days. It was a single summer—a wrinkle—not a life sentence. She smiled at Trudy's photograph. "A lot is fuzzy when it comes to Jake Colby, and yet, somehow, he's helping me see life with more clarity than ever before."

Chapter 16

The scent of fragrant lavender and freshly cut grass perfumed the air. Miranda's long, tousled hair danced recklessly with the wind as U2's "Beautiful Day" preached through her earbuds. The combination of nostalgic music and her sneakers' freedom to pound the country roads made every song seem as if the lyrics had a hidden agenda.

Rather than wallow in a bed of resentment, she had greeted the sunrise and took the neighbors' advice to remain open to life's possibilities. Everything deserved a chance, including her grandmother's arrangement. Miranda's glass didn't have to be half-empty or running dry. She could fill it to the brim like her morning coffee. It was time to remove those self-imposed blinders and enjoy the journey.

The music playlist on her phone hadn't changed, nor did the route she traveled. And while she wore the same orthotics as in previous workouts, her strides were lighter and more mindful.

Beyond an open field, a farmer wearing a brimmed hat and suspenders carried a pitchfork toward his silo. Miranda was around the bend before he could reciprocate her wave. A rustic windmill stood prominently among unoccupied acres, marking the halfway point for her run. The charming landmark's revolving steel blades, in motion yet no longer converting wind into energy, navigated out-of-towners.

Jake's affirmations propelled Miranda, as did his assurance the future was hers to paint bold masterpieces. Distancing from the close-minded person she had been in Barron Park would be a perpetual work in progress, as would having her GPS recalculate by taking a U-turn.

She stopped for a hamstring stretch at the dockyard and removed her earbuds. Crisp sails flapped against the wind, and bell buoys rattled. No longer would she ignore nature's music or only be a spectator, capturing its beauty on canvas.

The forecast called for another glorious day of sunshine and salty New England air. In the distance, the Cobblers Landing Lighthouse stood tall and proud, ready to guide boats safely into the harbor. Grizzled fishermen sorted through overflowing nets, marveling at their good fortune, while a flock of hungry seabirds soared above on a mission to find breakfast.

A weathered piece of wood interrupted Miranda's final calf stretch. Not only was it the perfect length and shape, but its surface was smooth like conditioned sea glass. She grinned at the plank, then placed it out of harm's way from moving trailer tires and resumed her run along the water's edge.

Panting for breath and covered in sweat, she pounded the country road's final stretch leading back to the Primrose Lane cottage. The revitalized Montauk daisies created a spectacle along Trudy's shared fence and offered fragrant rewards, much to Addie's delight.

Miranda stole a few refreshing sips from the hose while watering the flowers. Like Jake, his grandmother had been right about many things, including the joy inspired by a garden. It *was* an art form and a newly discovered outlet for Miranda's creativity—one that required daily attention.

Wind chimes sounded through her earbuds. She dropped the hose like it were hot to the touch and scrambled to type her phone's password. The hose flailed, spraying water everywhere, but only Jake's incoming text mattered.

Good morning, sunshine! I have a plan for today. Are you up for an adventure?

Without hesitation, she typed:

Hi there. Define the word adventure :)

Jake replied:

Let's just say this will be a wild experience, but we have a long drive ahead of us.

Miranda bit her lower lip.

I'm afraid to ask where you're taking me because I know you aren't budging on the details.

The dots revolved on her outdated iPhone until he replied:

Meet me out front in a half hour. Wear comfortable gym clothes and bring one of those ties for your hair. I'll take care of the rest. Oh, and prepare to be gone most of the day.

With sprinting thoughts, Miranda typed:

I think you're giving me too much credit.

Jake texted:

29 minutes and counting . . .

She dashed inside and kicked off her dampened sneakers. The trapped gravel in the grooves of her soles would have to wait. So would the knots in her stomach.

Following a quick shower, Miranda returned to her grandmother's bedroom, where Trudy's old photograph had lent an attentive ear to her innermost thoughts.

"Well, it looks like I have plans for today, Grandma—plans that require gym clothes."

Despite the unspoken boundaries Miranda would overstep by accepting another invitation with the handsome neighbor, "no strings attached" prevailed as her motto. But when did Gertrude Blair earn the title "grandma"?

"Hmmm, so what does one wear when accompanying a man with Jake's physique?" She rummaged through a toppling pile of clothes like a spring breaker searching for the perfect bikini.

"I wonder how many times you stood vulnerable before this mirror. Did you study your figure from different angles before an outing with my grandfather? Or, um, Randy?"

Donning a pair of snug-fitting and gravely unforgiving leggings, Miranda swayed side to side.

"Don't take this personally, Grandma, but I would've liked to inherit more voluptuous curves. And a rounder bottom too." She chuckled. "I'm sure Kasey is a stunning brunette with one of those hourglass figures you can't achieve at the gym."

Miranda stroked her dull hair, its frayed ends reminiscent of Trudy's brittle lawn.

"I could use one of those hydrating deep conditioners to add body and luster. If you were here, I'm sure you'd drag me to a salon and beg for intervention." Miranda rubbed moisturizer into her cheeks in an upward motion. Rather than bronze and glow, her pasty complexion tended to blot and burn. "A sweaty workout probably makes Kasey's skin gleam from endorphins, and her naturally extending eyelashes never require a stroke of mascara.

"I only have ten minutes left, so this will have to do. I mean, ten minutes *more* to go." Miranda gathered her wet hair and used "one of those ties," as Jake called it, to secure a tight ponytail. Others claimed her eyes often looked sad, but today they resembled sapphires. "Do you think people can change?" she asked the younger Trudy in the photo. "If so, I want to be one of those people."

She bent down and slid her feet into her soon-to-be-replaced running sneakers. The gift of spending money allocated for the arrangement would purchase new footwear, art supplies, and an updated wardrobe. She would not settle for mediocrity. It was time to kick limitations to the curb and indulge in life's extras, like the toppings served at McGinley's.

Miranda's knees cracked as she stood. She took a final glance in the mirror.

"Shoulders back and chin up. My only competition is myself. It's my time, Grandma, and I can't waste it. I'm ready to start living the life I deserve without excuses or blinders. You may have never known the old Miranda Blair, but I'm ready for us both to get acquainted with the new one!"

Chapter 17

The Jeep approached the security gate and rolled to a stop. Jake opened his window; a gust of humidity mingled with the air-conditioned space around them.

"Good morning," he said to the attendant. "We have a noon appointment for two—the last name is Colby."

Behind the checkpoint, a scrawny man wearing a fluorescent yellow vest with vertical reflectors flipped through ruffled pages on his clipboard.

"Park over there." The attendant motioned to the left with his stubbled chin. "Follow the construction cones around the bend until you get to the clearing. You can't miss it. Have fun, you two." His devilish grin made Miranda's stomach churn.

"Thank you, sir." Jake tipped his Gators cap and shifted the gear into drive.

Having planted their roots long ago, tall pine trees inhabited the grassy lot. Rusty trailers rested on uneven cinder blocks. Jake parked between two hippie buses outfitted in rust and decorated with hamsas and peace stickers. He idled the Jeep's engine, giving it a well-deserved rest following their three-hour excursion.

"One for you. Hydrate," he instructed, handing her a water bottle from the back seat cooler. "It's another scorcher out there."

Miranda untwisted the cap and took a long sip as she climbed down from the passenger seat.

"Ready?"

"I guess," she said. "Then again, I have no clue what I'm getting myself into."

"True, but you seem less jittery this time." He zipped his duffel bag, closed the hatch, and joined Miranda on the Jeep's other side. "I'd even say you were beginning to welcome the element of surprise."

"Let's not get carried away." She laughed.

Having relinquished the role of a storyteller, Miranda easily settled into Jake's passenger seat as a listener. Whereas she learned about life through books, Jake experienced it firsthand. He had regaled her with a personal narrative about his days spent wind-surfing, skiing, river rafting, and parasailing during their lengthy drive. As exhilarating as it was to hear accounts of conquered high winds and slippery slopes, Miranda prayed there wasn't an adrenaline-seeking activity in their afternoon plans.

Orange construction cones guided them on a dirt road into the woods, leaving the trailer park in the distance. Unlike Jake's boyish thirst for adventure and sure-footed strides, Miranda had a scratchy throat and hesitant footsteps.

"You have some circle of friends, Jake. I bet I can identify them by name and association now."

"I'm sure you can, after hearing me babble. No two friendships are the same, and their differences keep life interesting. And how about us?"

"Um, what about us?"

"Were you surprised to discover we have more in common than a spirit of volunteerism and good taste in music?"

He failed to acknowledge they were both forthcoming at times but vague at others.

"I was relieved to know I'm not the only one who avoids social media, fast food chains, and politics," Miranda replied with a giggle. "And to think our birthdays are only a day apart in April."

"The twenty-second and the twenty-third."

"Yep, born under the same zodiac sign," she said. "It's a good thing we aren't a Leo and Scorpio—those two are always at odds."

"I thought you steer clear of that psychic stuff."

"I do, but I follow the stars. Astrologers claim we, Taureans, have a knack for diffusing tension and regard our home as our safe place. We are artistic, reliable, and known for our loyalty. But on the flip side, we're guarded in new situations and slow to move forward."

"Sounds about right, but I'll take your word for it. Horoscopes aren't my thing," Jake said. "But I'd gladly stroll through an old bookstore together or walk a street fair or watch an eighties movie. Gotta love any John Hughes film."

They had each completed a half-marathon in their late teens. When Miranda mentioned her interest in tackling the entire twenty-six-mile race, Jake pledged to be at the finish line to capture her victorious moment. Still, he lived hours away, had a girlfriend, and remained a mystery.

The majestic evergreens closed in on Jake and Miranda, narrowing their path, and neglected porta potties balanced on overgrown tree roots.

He had offered a detour to find a clean restroom during their lengthy drive. It wasn't necessary at the time, but now the behind-the-scenes traveling circus had turned Miranda's stomach into a washing machine during an endless spin cycle.

"I'm waiting for elephants to stampede around the bend. And the little car to pull up and the silly clowns to spill out with their wild orange hair and huge feet." She mimicked their antics. "Is it me, or does the air smell like animals? What in the world is this place?" she asked lightheartedly, careful not to seem unappreciative of Jake's plans for the afternoon.

"You mean you aren't enjoying the ambiance?" He laughed. "You'll find out soon enough. In the meantime, you're going to need some of this today. I don't want you to get burned."

Miranda stared at the travel-size tube he had placed in her palm and swallowed hard. It had been a month since she arrived at the Cobblers Hill cottage on that life-changing June day. The relentless sun had beamed down on her semi-bare shoulders, leaving her pale, post-spring skin vulnerable to its rays. Unprotected and alone in her new surroundings, Miranda had lacked sunscreen and the support of someone who cared. But that rock-bottom moment in Trudy's overgrown yard was from an earlier chapter. Today, Miranda applied a generous layer of SPF 50 and basked in sunny blue skies alongside charming Jake Colby.

At last, pine needles no longer left a trail in the clearing, and an intimidating metal structure came into view.

"Here we go!" Jake rubbed his hands together briskly.

"What is that?" Miranda shuddered. She reached her hand up like a visor, squinting and gaping at the life-size pendulum.

A leathery man approached them with freckled forearms and shaggy hair.

"Howdy, folks. You must be the Colbys."

Beaming, she nodded with an outstretched hand. "I'm Miranda. Nice to meet you."

Jake followed with his introduction.

"Welcome. Call me Rex. Let's complete some paperwork and get you two fitted with safety gear."

He held out clipboards, but only Jake accepted one. Miranda stood motionless, with her hands clenched at her sides.

"It's great flying weather." Rex stared up at the cobalt sky. "I'll have you folks swinging from the trapeze in no time."

"Did he just say *trapeze?*" Panic-stricken, Miranda locked eyes with Jake.

"You mentioned you had never flown before, so it got me thinking, everyone should have the experience of flying." He arched his neck back and studied the crossbars high above. "It's not an airplane, but the circus trapeze will have to suffice for today." Jake placed his baseball hat in his duffel bag and removed his sneakers. "Just think, you can scratch that off your bucket list."

"This was never on my bucket list. I'm petrified of heights."

"You need to face your fears to overcome them." He stretched his muscular arms across his chest, then entwined his fingers behind his back. "You might end up enjoying this. Don't forget rocky road."

"That was ice cream." Miranda paced back and forth, kicking up dust in her path. "This is crazy."

"I'll go first if that'll make you more comfortable."

"Comfort doesn't exist for me. Not here, not now, not swinging like a monkey."

"If it's any consolation, I've never done this before. The closest I came to a trapeze was watching circus performers under the big tent one summer with Kasey. Even though we had terrible seats, it was still unbelievable."

Miranda's stomach churned in slow motion. How many Jake and Kasey summers—"Jasey" summers—had there been?

"Can you give us a moment, Rex?" Jake asked.

"This ain't my first rodeo." The leathery man stepped to the side. "After thirty years of teaching trapeze, I've learned to factor in time for pep talks."

Jake placed his hands on Miranda's shoulders, her heart fluttering with his unexpected touch. He lifted her chin from where it hung.

"Don't say anything. Hear me out. Aren't you tired of self-imposed limitations? Aren't you ready to prove yourself to yourself?

No more living your life afraid of those shadows. You've earned the spotlight, don't you agree?"

Jake might have overheard her earlier conversation with Trudy's photo through the thin cottage walls. More likely, he believed in Miranda. It was time she believed in herself.

"I'll go first."

Chapter 18

Breaking her spellbinding connection with Jake, Miranda removed herself from his hold. She reached for the pen dangling from the clipboard and scribbled her signature on the liability release form.

"I knew you would get fired up and rise to the occasion—no pun intended." Jake made imaginary boxing fists.

"I didn't say I would enjoy it, Colby, but I'll do it."

Miranda approached the trapeze without making eye contact with the steel bars or sea of netting.

"Safety first." Rex placed a thick belt around her that hugged below the rib cage.

"Wow, that's tight. I feel like I can't breathe." Miranda twisted left and right and back again.

"If I had a buck for every time I heard those words . . ." Rex snickered. "The good news is the feeling will subside. But it's gotta be tight." He gave the strap one final tug that made her entire body jolt. "There, that ought to do it. Now listen closely. You'll make your way up this ladder. We have chalk powder in that tin bucket over there. It'll help with sweaty palms."

"I was hoping the bucket was for queasy stomachs."

"No such luck," Rex replied, wiping his forehead with his T-shirt. "When you see the solid white rung, you've reached the halfway point. It's time to shimmy around to the opposite side of the ladder, so you're facing out, not in. There'll be safety netting beneath you for the rest of your climb. So far, so good?"

There was a reason why Miranda's bottom kitchen cabinets were cluttered, yet the top shelves that required a step stool remained empty. And while the other kids had jumped off the high diving board, creating a splash and earning cheers at the town pool, Miranda spent her adolescent years watching from the shallow end. Now Jake and Rex expected her to perform a circus act thirty feet above the ground.

"You'll need to take a large step onto the suspended platform and let go of the ladder simultaneously." Rex's calloused hands gestured as he talked, and his shaggy mustache moved with his breath. "It may feel a bit unsteady up there, but I'll be waiting to grab you and provide further instructions. Got it?"

The leathery man's words—*suspended, platform, let go, unsteady*—formed a lump in Miranda's throat that she struggled to swallow.

He climbed ahead, leaving Miranda frozen at the bottom of the narrow ladder. While her heart encouraged her to reach for the first rung, her lethargic limbs wouldn't budge. The blistering rays beamed like a spotlight, making her skin crave another lathering of Jake's sunscreen.

"Break it down one step at a time," Jake coached while being fitted with his safety belt. "Focus only on getting to the first rung. You got this!"

Resisting the urge to hurl her morning breakfast, she took her first hesitant step, then a second and a third. The wobbly sensation in her limbs was a welcome distraction from the suffocating harness. Each rung taunted her to back down from the challenge, but she kept her momentum—reaching and stepping, resting, and repeating until she was eye level with the white marker. Aside from her racing pulse, everything else moved in slow motion while she shimmied to the ladder's other side.

"You're halfway there!" Jake shouted, his voice farther in the distance. "One rung at a time."

Heeding the warnings and resisting the urge to cry, Miranda didn't look anywhere but straight ahead as she propelled herself clumsily to the top. Once she grabbed Rex's outstretched hand, she didn't let go. It wasn't until she planted both feet on the platform and double-checked that her newborn giraffe legs were still attached to her body that she exhaled.

"I did it! I actually did it!"

"Well done," Rex said in his raspy smoker's voice. "You see? That wasn't so bad, was it? Here's where the magic happens." He attached cables to Miranda's harness; the tugging of clips made her gasp.

It wasn't a heart attack, just imaginary chest pains. As a prisoner of panic, Miranda traded acrophobia for claustrophobia and a mild case of hypochondria. Perhaps Trudy had passed down those genes too.

"These safety lines will lower you into the net after releasing the bar," Rex said. "Guiseppe is keeping a tight grip on the other end."

A gaunt, wire-haired man waved from below with a black-gloved hand. Miranda jolted her head back, and the platform swayed. She clung to Rex with white knuckles, ignoring the scent of day-old sweat and stale cigarette smoke. He needed a shave as desperately as a shower.

"All righty then. I want you to lean forward on the platform's edge and reach for the bar, first with your left hand and then both, like this—" Rex demonstrated with an imaginary prop. "I'll be holding you back from your harness until you are ready to release into flight."

Miranda would have surrendered to the urge to bite her cuticles had they not been lathered in the mixture of chalky powder and salty perspiration. Her morning breakfast revisited her mouth for a second time.

"When you hear me yell, 'Hep!' leap from the platform, holding firmly onto the bar with both hands. Let it propel you forward and glide you back. The trapeze has nothing to do with upper body strength, so don't be intimidated, but challenge yourself. Try lifting your legs and tucking them around the bar."

He cleared his throat, making a garbled sound. Maybe his morning breakfast had revisited him too.

"Only half of our flyers have success with the knee hang," Rex continued, "but I'm gonna assume you'll be one of them."

Miranda knew assumptions could be misleading. Jake said so himself.

"Then, on the third swing, grab hold of the bar again, unwrap your legs and let them dangle, so your body is fully extended." Rex demonstrated with another imaginary prop, and the platform shook again. "When you hear me yell, 'Forward, backward, forward!' follow along with your legs to build momentum. Then release the bar, tuck your knees into your chest, and try to roll back as you descend. Guiseppe will lower you down gradually, as I mentioned before."

"Wait," Miranda said. "Let me get this straight. You want me to exit with some sort of backflip dismount? You know this is my first time, right?"

Unlike the other kids, she never jumped on a trampoline or did gymnastics. G-force wasn't included in her exercise routine. Now Rex wanted her to knee-hang, backflip, and trust someone named Guiseppe.

"I know there are many details, but we like to set the bar high. You'll see. It'll all come naturally. People are surprised by what they're capable of once the trapeze is in motion. So believe in yourself, and give your man something to brag about."

The unrealistic reference to Jake released more butterflies in Miranda's stomach. Even with Rex's motivational pitch, she couldn't lean forward. Free-falling off the platform wasn't an option.

Her life in Barron Park had been safe but stifling compared to Cobblers Hill, which was full of possibilities. If she hadn't accepted Trudy's arrangement, she would have missed invaluable lessons in the quaint New England town. She would have missed out on Jake Colby. Indeed, her grandmother would have taken the plunge if given a second chance at happiness with Randy.

Miranda could retrace her footsteps down the ladder or embrace the theme of trust and take the leap.

Yielding to a rush of adrenaline, she placed both hands on the bar and leaned forward at a forty-five-degree angle, with Rex holding onto her harness from behind.

She closed her eyes, summoned her faith, waited for Rex's call, and plunged into the air.

Chapter 19

With Jake's encouraging whistles, Miranda conquered the knee hang and surrendered to the life-size pendulum.

Rex called out, "Grab hold of the bar again, and release your legs."

Maneuvering in midair with the sun forcing her eyes closed, Miranda freed her lower limbs from the bar just in time. Her attempted backflip yielded a belly flop into the safety net. Although the cables were still attached to Miranda's harness, her spirit was already free. Guiseppe assisted her down from the net, and she wobbled toward the man responsible for her first flight and so much more that summer.

"You were awesome up there! It's all on video." Jake held up his cell phone. "How does it feel to nail it on your first try?"

"Incredible!" Miranda panted. She fell to her knees as if she had just landed on the moon. "Thank you . . . for making . . . me do this."

"Whoa, I didn't make you do anything, nor would I."

Miranda gave him a smirk that generated an exuberant smile.

"Okay, so I booked the reservation and brought you here. I offered a few encouraging words, but the rest was all you today."

"I can't thank you enough, then, for helping me face my fear of heights." Miranda reached for her water bottle with a trembling hand.

"Jake, you're up next," Rex called down.

"You're a tough act to follow, kiddo. Wish me luck." He gave her a nudge as he walked by.

"You don't need luck—you've got this."

Miranda stole a glimpse of him when he wasn't looking. The dry wick tank top barely covered his broad shoulders, and the basketball shorts clung to the rest of him. Kasey was the big elephant in what had become their private circus. Time and distance, Trudy's arrangement, and Miranda's aversion to relationships presented the other obstacles. But even without those variables, it didn't guarantee Jake's interest in anything more than friendship.

Miranda huffed.

How would she handle someone like Jake anyway? Being exclusively his was more intimidating than swinging from the circus trapeze. But kiddo? *Kiddo?*

So she was a few years younger than Jake with limited life experience. That didn't mean she was less of a woman than his beloved Kasey. "Kiddo" made Miranda a player on a different team out of his league.

Jake demonstrated courage and stealth in his effortless climb to the ladder's top rung. He didn't delay stepping onto the suspended platform or reaching for the bar with both hands. With goose bumps prickling her arms, Miranda discovered it was possible to sweat and have chills at the same time. Jake gave a quick wave from above, and she replied with a thumbs-up. Then, without hesitation, he plunged into the air, swooping forward and back. Miranda cheered his valiant efforts from below.

While Jake failed to knee-hang, he compensated with a perfect backflip dismount and exited the net.

"Woo-hoo! That was awesome!" he shouted. Beads of sweat glistened on his neck and forearms. "Gotta love that adrenaline rush. But how were you able to knee-hang? My legs wouldn't budge."

Miranda shrugged.

He untwisted the cap of his water, chugged half the bottle, and said, "Just don't go leaving me for the Big Top. We still have a few more weeks together."

She tilted her head back and laughed.

Rex called down from the platform. "Miranda, your turn. Take two."

Her eyes darted from Jake to the trapeze to Rex and Jake again. "He's kidding, right? He's just messing with me."

"Nope. We have encore performances."

Miranda cracked a rigid smile as she stumbled onto her feet and paused until her surroundings no longer spun. There was no time for vertigo, tired muscles, or achy hands when Jake had gone to great lengths to make the afternoon possible.

Ignoring each rung's taunts and resisting the urge to look down, Miranda reached the platform in half her initial time. It was typical of Jake Colby to see things favorably, but the arrangement was almost half over. When did months turn into weeks that would soon become days? Thoughts of returning home should have offered solace. Instead, they were more troubling than Miranda's impending plunge.

"You're going to knee-hang again, but let's try something different." Rex gave a devilish grin. "You know, shake things up a bit."

With her legs still shaking from her first flight, Miranda wasn't ready for different.

"Henry is going to be your catcher on this one." Rex pointed to a buff man with a handlebar mustache standing on the other platform.

"Listen closely for my prompt—timing is everything. When you hear me yell, 'Hep!' on the third swing, reach forward with both arms. Henry will greet you halfway. Grab hold of his wrists while unhooking your knees from the bar. He will swoop you the remainder of the way and then release you on the return for your descent into the net."

The knee-hanging catcher was now gliding effortlessly on the opposing trapeze. His zebra-striped leotard wasn't difficult to miss; his outstretched hands would be another story.

"Again, timing is everything here." Rex's beady eyes settled on Miranda. "You gotta wait for my prompt, and don't release the bar a second before or after."

Timing *was* everything. It encompassed the arrangement, dictating Miranda's plans and influencing her decisions. For Trudy and Randy, time hadn't been in their favor. For Jake and Miranda, time wasn't on their side either. For the future of the cottage, time was uncertain. But for Miranda's happiness, it was about time. *Time*. It was all a matter of time.

She wouldn't allow anything to jeopardize her earlier achievement. Seizing the moment with a deep nourishing breath, Miranda reached for the bar with her free hand and plunged gracefully through the air while awaiting Rex's prompt. Everything depended on his judgment and her trust in the art of trapeze. Life in Cobblers Hill had taught her to believe.

At last, Rex called, "Hep!"

Miranda swung forward with outstretched arms and a silent plea. *Please be there. Please be there.*

She and the catcher joined hands with impeccable timing and swooped forward. While such a circus act was known to generate audience applause, Jake's cheers from below were all she needed to hear.

"Way to go!" Jake shouted, blowing air through his pinkies. He ran to greet her with double high fives. "You were amazing up there! It was a seamless flight, like you had practiced it for years."

Panting, Miranda leaned over with her hands resting on her knees. "That . . . right . . . there . . . was . . . downright . . . petrifying."

"But you're smiling."

"I was never . . . so relieved . . . to hold hands . . . with a stranger in my life." Miranda breathed heavily through her nostrils.

Jake laughed. "Even if you didn't connect with Henry, the safety net would have caught you. You'd brush it off and try again. What matters is you never backed down from fear."

"This has been an incredible experience—a day I'll never forget." Miranda looked up at him, her eyes beaming.

"Yep, it's the day you officially grew your wings. Consider them another souvenir from your hundred days in Cobblers Hill. You now have what it takes to soar."

Chapter 20

The scent of freshly baked cinnamon pinwheels wafted through the Colby yard on the same summer breeze carrying the clank of wind chimes.

"This is such a lovely piece of property." Miranda captured each shape and tone with her aspiring artist's eye.

"Well, thank ya, darlin'. Kind of ya to say." Addie tapped her spoon against the porcelain teacup and placed it alongside her napkin. "It's a comfy place to live."

Beyond comfort, the Colby yard was charming and spacious with warm personal touches—the bronze weather vane, stretches of white picket fencing, a terra-cotta sundial, and an assortment of farmhouse milk jugs and decoupage watering cans.

Addie's garden bench invited visitors to sit and be soothed by the gurgles of a nearby fountain. Hand-painted birdhouses provided luxury accommodations for feathered friends to linger. But it wasn't the fragrant flowerpots perfuming the New England air that made the Colby yard special. Nor was it the sun-ripened fruit draping from vines and beckoning outstretched hands.

Love prevailed in the neighboring yard. It was the secret ingredient in Adelaide's homemade recipes and a key component in the lessons shared across the bistro table during afternoon tea. The old woman's contagious laughter and off-key tunes drifted over shrubs and flower beds like a steady current. Smiling visitors came and went freely through the opened garden gate.

Miranda and Jake had tamed the overgrowth on Trudy's property and revived the straw-like lawn to a rich green shade, as he had promised. And she had spent attentive hours sharpening her senses in her grandmother's garden. But there weren't relatives to bask in the sunshine and gather in gratitude. Joyful conversation did not flow, nor did laughter prevail. Without cornhole games and late-afternoon barbecues, it was only land, not a backyard, and a house, not a home.

"We can thank this here family tree for bein' our cornerstone." Addie blew on her tea and took a hesitant sip as steam swirled from its surface.

Deep-rooted in the Colby yard, the massive old oak provided a canopy of leaves draped around them in a sheltering embrace. High above, bushy-tailed squirrels scampered across its nubby branches in what appeared to be a game of rodent tag.

"My ol' man planted a seedlin' some twenty-five years ago. I recall like yesterday lookin' out that there window." Addie closed her eyes to the nostalgic image that lived in her memory as Jake had done in front of Colby's Hardware. Adelaide and her grandson were cut from the same fabric. But unlike Trudy and Miranda, their compatible threads wove a fine tapestry.

"He was wearin' ole britches and diggin' in the dirt on his hands and knees," Addie continued. "That man had a hankerin' for fixin' stuff. I opened the back door and hollered why he was wreckin' my grass. If I had my druthers, I would've left the yard alone. But he wanted it to be a gatherin' place for future generations."

Addie flashed a smile of dentures, and deep wrinkles outlined her mouth.

"This here oak was his vision for tomorrow. And I thought the man was crazy." She bobbed her head back and forth and rolled her eyes. "He was up in 'em years and would never see the fruits of his labor, as they say."

Having a knack for dragging out a story, the old woman took mindful sips of her tea and paused in between each one. Miranda's eyes didn't wander.

Though forgetful on occasion, Addie dabbled on various topics with ease, pulling from her plethora of life experiences. Her subject never included Gertrude Blair.

With the neighbors respecting Miranda's privacy, she could avoid trips back in time and unwelcomed visits to her family tree. It would have been counterproductive to delve into the past midway through the arrangement anyway.

"My ol' man said time would fly by whether he planted that seedlin' or not, so he was gonna give it a chance to grow. And so he did—and look!" Addie held her arms wide with a *ta-da*.

"Amazing! I admire his foresight," Miranda said.

"Now, mind ya, Jake was a young'un at the time, and he liked to play back here with 'em toy trucks. There was chicken wire around this twig in the ground, no bigger than a minnow in a fishin' pond. I figured it wouldn't survive with that boy's sense of adventure."

Miranda's heart fluttered at the mention of Jake's name. She sipped her tea as if it were a sacred cup of coffee.

"That there oak offers shade from the sun and shelter from the rain. It's the toughest soldier I know, havin' weathered many storms and still standin' tall. Like your buildin's, darlin'. Jake told me all about those preservation projects of yours."

"And like Colby's Hardware." Trudy's cottage was resilient too, but Miranda failed to exercise its bragging rights.

"Indeed," Addie replied. "They each have a story to tell; it's finding the right listener."

"Your family tree is a beauty." Miranda arched her neck back. "Such broad leaves and grooved bark."

"And don't forget 'em clusters of bumpy acorns. They'll hit ya right on ya noggin. Come the fall, ya gonna have to wear a hard hat under here, darlin'." Addie gave a hearty laugh that wiggled her shoulders, but Miranda slumped. She wouldn't be there in the fall.

Others would take Miranda's place at afternoon teatime with Addie, nourishing their spirit with wisdom and positivity. Maybe they would catch a falling leaf from Pop's oak or hide under it during an April shower. The tree would welcome future generations that didn't include her, and the open garden gate would greet new visitors.

Miranda placed her teacup on the saucer. "I love how Pop's gift reflects the Colby family's perseverance and commitment. Its growth and character. As for his vision and this oak, I'm a huge fan of a happy ending."

"Now hold ya horses. It ain't the endin'. Every spring is a fresh beginnin', darlin'. No two seasons are the same, nor should they be. This tree reminds me of some good ol' southern advice from Mark Twain. He said, 'Why not go out on a limb? That's where the fruit is.' Ain't that the truth?" Addie pointed to Miranda with her crooked finger. "Ya ain't never give up those dreams of yours. Everythin' deserves that chance to develop. Gotta be patient."

The unshielded truth dangled in front of Miranda. She could have made an elaborate salad with her missed fruit opportunities. And she had denied others from going out on a limb too. When they regarded her as the forbidden fruit, she rationalized the wrong men were harvesting the orchard.

"Thanks for sharing the story about your family tree." Miranda reached across the table and touched the old woman's veiny hand. "I'll do my best to branch out and gather life's fruit."

"So glad, darlin'. I wish my grandson would take some of that there advice. Life is like a book, and he's stuck on one of 'em pages." Addie blotted the corners of her mouth with a napkin and tucked it under her saucer. "He's a fine man, if I may say so, and he deserves to follow that heart of his. Maybe it's in the next chapter. Oh, I hope so, but he's gotta get there."

Miranda leaned forward on the bistro table with firmly planted elbows. If they dug any deeper, they would have left a permanent impression.

"I'm not sure I understand, Addie."

"He's a writer, ya know. And a dang good one. He puts 'em words together like grits and gravy." Addie's belly laugh made her eyes squint.

"Oh? I wasn't aware," Miranda said, curtailing her surprise.

"Such talent. I guess Jake didn't tell ya about his book either, then? Big dreams to be a published novelist."

"I don't believe he has." She forfeited her final sips of tea and leaned closer until she was only inches from the old woman's sun-tanned wrinkles. Miranda's complexion was likely pasty white.

"I'm sure he's got his reasons for keepin' quiet, darlin'. Or maybe he's waitin' for the right time to talk about it." Addie gathered the cups on a tray. "Timin' is everythin' in life, and the day will come for that there dream of his. Ya know what they say, every marble finds its hole."

The old woman stood and wobbled back to her cottage. Miranda picked up the tray with anxious hands and followed close behind.

"There's much to say but not a lot I can tell ya, I'm afraid," intuitive Addie said. "Ya should hear it from Jake, although he don't like talkin' about it, darlin'."

Addie tapped the kitchen counter twice, and Miranda rested the tray there.

"Once Jake shares with ya, I reckon ya can knock some sense into him."

"Definitely. You can count on me to give a gentle nudge of encouragement."

"He'll need less of a nudge and more of a good whack with a two-by-four. Whatever it takes so he picks up the pen again and turns that there page."

Miranda nibbled on her thumbnail. She would respect Jake's privacy and not overstep the circle of trust with the neighbors. Still, Jake Colby's added layers left her unsettled but excited and apprehensive. Only time would tell which of these sentiments was justified.

Chapter 21

"Wow, this is a scene from a romance novel. I've read enough of them to know."

Joanie, the town's new head librarian, placed the tote bag of art supplies down in the sand without taking her eyes off the view.

"Those were my thoughts too," Miranda replied. "Words don't do Edens Cove justice. It's a hidden gem you need to experience firsthand."

She had spent evenings there practicing yoga in the powder-soft sand and dancing merrily with nature, her newly formed wings giving her spirit flight. At other times, she combed the beach for sea glass with Jake or painted the majestic bluffs while he skipped stones.

"All that's missing is Mr. Right to come galloping down the shore on a white horse and whisk me off into paradise." Joanie batted her eyelashes. "It's a good thing I'm wearing mascara, although my cosmetics could use an upgrade. So many social media endorsements, so little time."

Rather than a slick librarian bun and granny glasses dangling from a beaded chain, Joanie sported a pixie haircut and a purple butterfly tattoo on her untoned forearm. She exerted the energy of an Olympic sprinter and was never at a loss for words.

"You still believe he's out there, even after your recent divorce?" Miranda arched a brow at her friend.

"Absolutely. So what if I made a mistake my first time down the aisle? It's a long life, and I don't plan on spending it alone. Not only is he waiting somewhere, but I plan on lassoing him in and guaranteeing happily ever after, no matter how corny that sounds. But first, we've got a sunset to capture."

Despite diligent packing of a portable easel, paints, a container of water, and assorted brushes, Miranda had forgotten a headband. She blew her bangs from her eyes and swept them to the side with her hand.

While life back home was uneventful with long weeks and lagging seasons, she blinked in Cobblers Hill and it was mid-August. The looming reality crept closer. Miranda's time in the quaint town was dwindling, like the fading sun that would soon disappear and bring the day to a close.

"This is a pleasant change from my evening routine." Joanie removed her sneakers and clapped sand from them. "If I'm not ordering or logging books during my workday, I'm cozying up with them after hours. It's a satisfying relationship—always available and rarely disappoints on those cold winter nights. That's more than I can say about 'what's his name.'"

"Your evenings sound a lot like mine." Miranda pulled items from her tote bag one at a time like she was engaging an audience with a magic trick.

"As much as I enjoy time spent with historical fiction and women's literature," Joanie said, "I have my limits before I start to twitch. Lucky for me, I get to witness a sunset on this breathtaking beach tonight while my artist friend preserves it on canvas."

"Not too much pressure." Miranda laughed, and joy decorated her face. "It's great to have your company and the extra set of hands. Besides, the beauty of Edens Cove should be shared."

"Do you paint here often? That's a silly question. Of course, you must. Who wouldn't with this rocky coastline and your talent?"

"Unlike back home, I find myself less distracted and more inspired," Miranda said. "I paint just about everywhere in Cobblers Hill with a landmark or seascape, a picket fence, or a winding path. Each delightful memory needs to be preserved in acrylic. And while my creativity runs wild here, my brushstrokes are more disciplined."

She aligned her Winsor & Newton brushes and unlocked her recently purchased case of acrylics. The artwork-enhancing, confidence-boosting supplies provided through Trudy's spending account were a gift. Still, her greatest blessing from the arrangement was the introduction to Jake Colby.

"Sounds like your brushes are getting a workout, and you're acclimating nicely to northern living," Joanie said. "You've got me by a few weeks in town, but I'm less homesick since I've branched out from the library's reference section. Not that I don't love the smoky smell of old paper and buzz of overhead lights."

"Any regrets?"

"With my decision to start over in Cobblers Hill? Not a one. It's exceeded my highest hopes." Joanie dug her feet in the sand like an exfoliating spa treatment. "Back in January, before I accepted the position as head librarian, I was dripping in stress—you know, with the divorce and all. I wore it like an unflattering costume a week after Halloween."

"I've donned plenty of those strung-out outfits myself." Miranda tilted her head back and laughed. "Not pretty."

"Time wears sneakers or heels—it either flies or moves painfully slow," Joanie said. "Last winter was a combination of platform stilettos and dismal nights. But once this opportunity at the library came my way, I had a new driving force in my life. I'm sure you've heard the expression, 'The why that makes you wanna cry.' Well, I discovered my 'why.' I wanted nothing more than to press fast-forward on life, shed the past, and greet the salty New England air for a fresh beginning. It's silly, but I even started a countdown."

Miranda busied her hands in her art supplies, formerly referred to as "survival gear" during pre-arrangement packing days. "A countdown, huh?"

"Yes. A countdown to the day I became who life meant for me to be. It's almost a month since I've settled in and begun doing what I love in this quaint town. Anyway, enough about that." Joanie grazed her fingertips over the acrylics. "There's more to being a van Gogh than I thought. No wonder you need an extra set of hands. Do you always bring that entire case with you? Can't you just anticipate the colors you'll need in advance? Bring a select few to lighten your load?"

"That may have worked back home," Miranda explained, "but I'm not sure here. Until recently, I used to only paint in my childhood bedroom, and the color scheme never varied from somber earth tones."

"So if it wasn't a color you'd find on the bottom of your shoe, then it didn't make its way onto your canvas," Joanie said straight-faced.

"That's one way of putting it. Those shades no longer reflect what I see or feel. At least, not here. Nowadays, I don't select the colors . . . my inspiration does. Tonight, it's feeling warm hues of crimson orange, sienna red, petunia pink, and a little marigold yellow. We'll see, though, what the setting sun decides."

"We sure will!"

"When the colors dance their recital on canvas," Miranda continued, "they create these magnificent shades. The way they blend and the chemistry between them make a painting come alive."

She knelt next to her portable French easel in the sand where Jake's picnic blanket had once rested. The secured canvas tilted at a comfortable sixty-degree angle.

"I have you to thank for the recent adjustments I've made to my easel," Miranda said. "If you hadn't reserved those art reference journals, I would have missed some vital tips. My controlled brush-strokes thank you."

"And if you hadn't stopped in at the library during that monsoon, I would have missed out on our friendship. You've helped me settle into my new life here. I'm grateful, Miranda."

Jake and Addie were right. God looks down the road and places people where they need to be.

"Is there time for a walk?" Joanie stared up at the sky with eager eyes. Her gold chandelier earrings framed her face and shimmered with every breath.

"Judging by the sun's height from the horizon, we have a few minutes."

Miranda tucked her no-longer-quarantined cell phone in her back pocket and hopped to her feet. Besides fostering daily communication with new friends, the phone provided a playlist of uplifting music and reminders of town events. Maybe her mother had developed a set of wings, too, that summer. Anything, Miranda had learned, was possible.

They strolled the vast stretch of uninterrupted beach. The tide had turned, depositing piles of seaweed on the shoreline, and the minutes dwindled in life's hourglass until the close of another glorious day.

"I'm sad you only have a few weeks left in Cobblers Hill." Joanie made an exaggerated frown. "It figures. I arrive here, and your bags are half-packed to leave."

"That depends on how you look at it. I still have a few more weeks. And I'll admit, I had a silly countdown too."

"Past tense?"

"Yes. I'm slowly letting go of the things I never controlled and allowing myself to enjoy the moments that matter most."

"What is it you're looking for?" Joanie studied the slimy green piles in which Miranda swept her foot.

"In this seaweed or Cobblers Hill?"

"Both, I guess. You never did say what brought you to this town."

"These piles may look like salad gone bad," Miranda chuckled, "but sometimes treasure hides within the tangles. If you don't seek, you'll never find. As for this summer, I'm spending long-overdue time with my grandma. I've needed to confront the past to move forward. But, unlike you, I didn't have high expectations here."

"*Oof!* Sounds heavy. You seem happy, though, so you must be having success."

"It's been an awakening for sure," Miranda replied with a confident gleam. "I used to be wound so tight that you'd need a pair of snippers to cut me loose. But I'm different now. I have this new-found contentment that replaced the restlessness from June when the calendar wasn't a friend and idle time an even greater enemy."

Joanie closed her eyes, the gentle breeze nuzzling against her Mediterranean skin. "I can relate. Somewhere along life's way, I made the mistake of looking for the rainbows and pots of gold. Unfortunately, they came with a hefty price tag—disappointment! Now all I want is to live simply. I'd rather be a happier version of myself than a miserable one of someone else. If I have to pretend or exert too much effort or it involves fake laughter, I'm not interested."

"Me neither," Miranda said. "I've unpacked the emotional baggage that accompanied me to Cobblers Hill and disposed of some pieces. It wasn't easy, but I'm traveling lighter now with less to transport home. I never want to accumulate that unhealthy clutter again."

"I guess that's why you and I hit it off so well," Joanie said. "We're just two out-of-towners in pursuit of better versions of ourselves. And that's just for starters. Wouldn't it be liberating if we were seagulls for a day?" She stared at the mass of white feathers that balanced on sticklike legs. "Ahh, to live at the beach, free from life's limitations."

"I've thought that myself, but now I see things differently. Have you ever noticed how they flee when they get scared? They don't stay put for too long—always on a mission to take what a fellow seagull caught or secure the next indulgence." Miranda picked up a stray feather and twirled it between her fingers. "Even in a flock, they stand guarded and alone. And while their caw may remind us of serene beach sounds, they are alarm calls. *Eeek!*"

"Wow, deep. Thought-provoking. I never even considered—"

"You haven't been in Cobblers Hill as long as I have," Miranda said with a chuckle. "Give it time, my friend, give it time." She pointed to three pelicans bobbing on the water's surface. "Those are the birds I've come to admire. They appear content and in no great urgency to arrive at their next destination. See how they move with the current and are unfazed by the ripples?"

"You're right. They seem to go with the flow," Joanie replied. "How is it that I've got at least ten years of life experience on you, but I'm the one who should be taking notes? Tell me, besides painting and an occasional visit to your local library during a thunderstorm, how else do you lift your spirits these days?"

"Runs! Long, invigorating runs. When I first set out here, I was lost—intimidated by every twist and turn of unfamiliar country road. But with each passing week, the surroundings became comfortable and welcoming, as if I belonged. And so, like Forrest Gump, I just kept running. But unlike before, I wasn't running away. I was running toward the new lease on life I deserved."

Miranda knelt to examine a piece of brown glass. One day, when it was ready, it might find its way into a beachcomber's treasure jar to be marveled at for years to come. She tossed the jagged piece of glass back into the dark depths of water and clapped sand from her hands.

"When I'm not logging miles in my sneakers or painting," she continued, "I'm combing the town paper for art exhibits, farmers' markets, and live entertainment. I'm always on the lookout for new seasonal recipes. Oh, and I've tried my hand at gardening this summer."

"Developing your green thumb? You've been keeping busy, it seems."

"Yes, lots of Martha Stewart stuff." Miranda laughed. "Back home, my day revolved around to-do lists. Now I form what-makes-me-happy lists."

Jake Colby maintained a steady position at the top of that list.

"What-makes-me-happy lists—" Joanie cocked her head to the side. "I think I need to create one of those that doesn't involve leather bindings and pages of periodicals."

"You should. This week, I'll attempt hot yoga at the Breathe meditation studio. It will be another ridiculous first. Of course, there's always the chance I'll have heatstroke and embarrass myself during the warrior pose, but I'm up for the challenge. What about you?"

"Oh, no!" Joanie held up her hands. "No hot yoga for me, thank you very much."

"I meant, what are some of your interests beyond reading?"

"You scared me there for a second. I thought you were insinuating I do downward dog in a sauna with a bunch of strangers. *Whew!*" Joanie pretended to wipe her forehead. "I enjoy attending lectures. Call me nerdy for spending leisure time where I work, but I'm eager to soak up knowledge that others are willing to share. I never know when I'll learn something trivial or paramount that makes everything else click."

Miranda tapped her chin. "I wonder."

"I see your wheels turning, Miranda. I smell the smoke too."

"What about writers' workshops?"

"What about them?"

"Are there any scheduled in the next few weeks? Or how about lectures on publishing or overcoming obstacles for writers—that sort of thing? I'm asking for a friend stuck on his author journey."

"I'm sure we'll find some helpful resources for your friend. And if there aren't any upcoming programs like you mentioned, then it's time the Cobblers Hill Library offered them, don't you think?"

"That would be amazing! I wish I had thought of this sooner. Maybe, just maybe, this could be the answer." Giddily, Miranda spun around and faced her friend, kicking sand into the air. "It would mean everything to see the words 'The End' grace the final page of his manuscript. He deserves that and so much more. I'm committed to making this his reality. For now, we'd better get moving before that horizon changes."

"This is so exciting!" Joanie quickened her footsteps toward the makeshift art studio in the sand. "Ideas for library programs, hope for your friend's novel, and the setting sun. To think this evening almost didn't happen had I stuck to my original plans of alphabetizing my bookshelf."

"That's true for many things this summer," Miranda replied.

"I'll keep quiet over here and watch you do your thing while wishing I had an ounce of talent. Imagine it's just you and endless possibilities. I have nothing more to say. Promise." Joanie pretended to zip her lips, and Miranda laughed.

Having spent her days hearing shushes, using whispers, and working alongside inanimate objects, Joanie was entitled to be chatty after hours. Miranda's coworkers often used soft voices during work hours to revere the past and unruffle the ghosts from yesterday. But when they moved beyond the historical society walls, they dug out their megaphones.

Miranda's canvas was blank, but anticipation filled the sky. Always bittersweet, the magical transformation of dusk would bring beauty for today and hope for tomorrow. But its colors, like her circumstances, were temporary, only temporary. Without Jake Colby, she might resort to painting the same drab brushstrokes as she once did in Barron Park.

At last, the sun began its slow descent, blending colors on the sky's palette. Every second mattered before the opportunity disappeared, sinking beyond the horizon like the dwindling hundred days. She worked quickly to capture her sentiments on canvas, each stroke dancing with intent and alternating between paints and brushes to seize the breathtaking spectacle. As the sky faded to gray, her canvas had come alive, preserving a permanent image forever absorbed into its fibers like Miranda's New England memories.

Temporary. Permanent. Temporary. Permanent. Which would it be?

In time, the attorney, Mr. Baxter, would summon Miranda to tidy up the final details of her grandmother's estate. While relinquishing ownership of the cottage might break her chains to the past, it would also close the door to Cobblers Hill.

Sadly, those might become more cumbersome regrets to bear than the former ones. And with the reappearance of loose threads, life might unravel once again.

Chapter 22

The bold-faced clock tower alerted the hour that united everyone by the grand gazebo. Couples strolled by hand in hand,
and teens pedaled up on bicycles.

"It's the talk of Cobblers Hill when the town announces the
season's concert series in our local paper," Jake said. "Free entertainment that brings the community together. Can't beat it, right?"

"There's no better way to spend a summer evening, and I'm not
saying that because I'm a music lover." Crouching down, Miranda
smoothed the blanket's wrinkles with her hands. "Outings like this
aren't part of the culture in my town. With everyone on a mission
to get stuff done, there's no such thing as seizing the day or soaking
up the moment."

She stood and tightened her ponytail. "Besides, we don't have
a town square. Rather than rolling hills and rugged shorelines, we
have busy avenues occupied by cookie-cutter stores and tall buildings surrounded by concrete," she explained. "There are bargain
outlets on each corner, with nail salons in between them. No one
ever characterized Barron Park as charming, but it's home."

"Hey, Colby. What's up, man?"

A goateed guy who looked to be in his early thirties approached
them. Several beach chairs draped from his muscular forearms like
tentacles.

"Good to see ya, bud," Jake said with a shoulder bump and backslap.

"We haven't seen you on the courts or at the pub. You've gotta be holding out on us." The unidentified friend glanced over at Miranda and then back at Jake, standing by her side. "Whatcha been up to?"

"Making the most of summer, that's all." Jake placed his left hand on Miranda's right shoulder. Had he reached around to her other side, it would have constituted a semi-embrace. "This is a friend, Miranda Blair."

Miranda noted the word "friend."

"PG and I go back many years shooting hoops," Jake said to Miranda. "You are looking at the best point guard on this side of town."

"It's a pleasure to meet you." She extended her hand.

"Same here." He shook firmly but raised an eyebrow to Jake, who seemed to reply with a telepathic nod. "Anthony is my real name. PG is usually reserved for the game, but I answer to both."

"How've you been, bud?" Jake asked.

"Not too bad, man. My family is setting up back there." PG pointed toward the far corner of the square. "The kids dig these events because they can wear their pajamas outside and stay up past bedtime. They'll fall asleep before the main act and never stir despite the loud music. Celise and I can enjoy a scot-free date night without paying a babysitter." He rubbed his boxer's nose. "Soon enough, you'll see what I mean."

"Soon enough" didn't include Miranda. She lowered her head.

"We are in for a real treat this time—the music of Foreigner! Who would have thunk, right? I would have killed for this back in high school." PG strummed the strings of an air guitar, and the beach chairs rattled.

"Yeah, I'm pretty jacked up over here." Jake raised both fists. "It looks like everyone else is too."

"I'd better get going before Celise texts me again to find out what's taking so long. Enjoy the show, Miranda. Hope to see you around, Colby." PG slapped his friend on the back and rushed off into the distance.

"Don't go giving up my spot on the courts," Jake called out. "I'll be back with more three-pointers, so be prepared."

Miranda fidgeted with irrelevant details on her cell phone. When Jake wasn't fixing something in Trudy's cottage or mowing her lawn, he initiated morning runs and beachcombing days with Miranda. In June, neither replacing Kasey as a pinch hitter nor hijacking Jake's social life had been her intention. But it was mid-August now, and Miranda was guilty of wanting more of Jake Colby in the remaining days.

"PG—Anthony—is a good guy, but he can be intense on the court." Jake stared across the stretch of lawn to where his friend was setting up chairs for two energetic children. "Get a few beers in him, though, and he becomes quite the comedian. When his wife allows him out of the house, that is."

"Thanks for inviting me tonight." Miranda clutched her cell phone and kept her head lowered.

"I'm glad you agreed to join me." He sat down beside her on the blanket. "I've been looking forward to this ever since we made the plan. Time flew, huh?"

"It sure did. You said it would."

"I thought you were being polite when you agreed to the concert." Jake chuckled. "Admit it, you had your excuses lined up and your guards ready to decline."

"That's not true." Her blank stare surrendered to a restless smile. "Okay, so maybe it's partly true. Was I that transparent?"

Jake demonstrated an inch with his thumb and forefinger, and Miranda gave him a playful shove. There was no place she'd rather be than in the moment together.

"Anyway, I should be the one to thank you for bringing dinner," he said.

"And you claimed dessert."

"Correction. Gram did. I don't think we had any say in the matter."

"You're right." Miranda giggled like a schoolgirl. "We didn't."

She fussed with the picnic basket's stubborn latch until it budged. Under the weight of Jake's steadfast gaze, Miranda wondered if her jeans were too snug or if the off-the-shoulder top was inappropriate for a cool evening. Several weeks into the arrangement, she was still unsure whether to feel insecure or flattered by the attention.

"I can't wait to see what's on the menu." Jake rubbed the palms of his hands together. "What does the basket have in store for us this time? It's always full of surprises."

If only Jake knew the extent of those surprises—a love letter tucked within the picnic basket fostered an unlikely connection between grandmother and granddaughter. But some things were better left unsaid.

"I figured we would do Italian tonight. We have fresh mozzarella, fire-roasted peppers, thin-sliced prosciutto." Miranda unveiled one container at a time, unleashing aromas as Jake leaned in for a whiff. "Cerignola olives, herb-stuffed mushrooms, grilled eggplant, sun-dried tomatoes. Oh, and," she continued, holding up a loaf of bread, "antipasto fixings aren't complete without semolina."

"Wow! Who's better than us right now?"

"Nobody," she said, easing back into the evening. "It's Trudy's treat. Her generous spending account and the gift of time made this possible."

She removed appetizer forks and napkins from the zippered compartment where her grandmother's love letter once waited.

"As for wine, I wasn't sure if you prefer red or white. Some people judge a book by its cover. I select wine by the artwork on its label." Miranda held a bottle in each hand. "Your choice."

"Can't go wrong with either." He reached for the cabernet and a corkscrew. "I believe we are overdue for a post-trapeze toast."

Jake held the neck of the wine bottle in his hand and removed the cork with finesse.

Miranda winced at thoughts of how many bottles he and Kasey shared for a special occasion, and how many had accompanied romantic evenings or encouraged them. Maybe Grandma Trudy and Randy had celebrated milestones in the town square when they weren't visiting Tuscan vineyards, sampling wine and farm-fresh cheese.

Jake filled both glasses and handed Miranda one.

"A toast to you." He tilted his glass toward her. "For taking that leap of faith."

Miranda was sure her complexion matched the shade of cabernet. Accomplishing something toast-worthy and capturing Jake Colby's attention were two of the many reasons to celebrate. They dined alfresco on salty antipasto while excitement brewed for the concert and wine glasses emptied.

"Tell me about your girlfriend. You never mention Kasey, and I'm sure you miss her this summer." The words escaped Miranda's lips defiantly, holding her prisoner to them. She brought her thumb to her mouth but lowered it before she could nibble a cuticle.

Jake swirled the wine around in his glass. "Okay, um, what would you like to know?"

Everything! How you met. What your intentions are.

"Whatever you'd like to share," she replied.

Jake delayed his response, whether lost in thought, caught off guard, or speechless. He filled his plate with slices of cured meat and sun-dried tomatoes, then tore off a chunk of bread. When a marinated mushroom slipped from his fork, he resorted to using his fingers.

"We met way back and had this immediate connection." Jake's eyes surveyed the square but returned to meet Miranda's gaze. His face beamed as bright as the stage spotlight, the aura blinding Miranda. "It's hard to explain, but suddenly, my life had clarity again. She renewed my purpose. When someone else's happiness means everything, you know you have created something special."

If there were a snooze button, Miranda would have smacked it like a blaring alarm clock on a rainy Monday morning. She berated herself for thinking her platonic summertime adventures with Jake could compare to what he experienced with Kasey.

While genuinely happy for Jake, Miranda grieved for herself, having never been on the receiving end of such sentiments nor the source of someone else's joy.

"What about you?" Jake reached for the bottle of chardonnay and removed its cork.

"What about me?"

"You never mentioned if you have someone special back home."

The wine seemed to release Jake's inhibitions too. It wasn't a question of whether Miranda had someone noteworthy in her life but rather why she didn't.

"No. I'm single." She squirmed on the blanket like there was a swarm of picnic-invading ants. "I never looked for him. I assumed he didn't exist, so I called off the search before it began."

Heat radiated from her cheeks. Although her feet were likely to swell from sodium overload, she shoved whole olives in her cheeks and stared at her empty glass.

"When you believe no one special is out there for you, it could become a self-fulfilling prophecy," Jake said. "I'm sure you've met some great guys who could've made you happy if given a chance. You deserve one who will sweep you off your feet and stop at nothing to make you smile. But without encouragement, you know, sending the right signals, you could miss out."

"Yeah, but my relationships always fail, so why bother getting my hopes up?"

She took the last sip of wine that lingered at the bottom of her glass, and Jake refilled it with chardonnay. The stage crew worked diligently in the distance, testing the grand gazebo's sound system. But they didn't connect the cables quickly enough to rescue Miranda from the truth—she sought excuses instead of opportunities like her mother.

"Besides," she continued, "there's an absence of role models in the Blair family—no one celebrated milestone anniversaries and declared themselves soul mates. That's why I've spent my life doubting whether everlasting love existed. I prefer to be by myself for the wrong reason than allow someone into my life for the right reason and be disappointed, if that makes any sense."

Jake refilled his plate, creating an abstract with balsamic-drizzled mozzarella and grilled eggplant. "You have to be vulnerable at times and believe something crazy good is in store. Don't you owe it to your future self to be open to the possibilities?"

He made valid points. And while Miranda never thought that far ahead in life, her worse regrets might be yet to come.

"As long as you keep looking for the clouds, Miranda, you'll never see what's waiting behind them."

"Thank you for the poetic words. Spoken like a true novelist." She cupped her mouth with her hand, but the words escaped anyway. "A little birdie mentioned your lifelong dream of becoming a published author. I wasn't aware that was on your bucket list we always talk about."

She bit her lower lip and refused to let go, but the chardonnay was broaching the topic she felt, deep down, was best to avoid.

Jake's expression told Miranda her deep-down self might be right.

Chapter 23

"I should have known Gram would leak those details sooner or later." The color drained from Jake's face, and he tugged at his lower lip. "Yes, having a published novel has been my dream, or it was a dream long ago."

"I inhale fiction as a hobby," Miranda said. "I'd love to read your novel. My friend Joanie would too."

"There isn't much to be excited about, only a rough draft without a proper ending. When the words stopped flowing and the paragraphs weren't forming, I walked away."

He slid his plate to the side and began stacking the containers, his back to Miranda. "I'll return to it someday."

"How long has it been?"

"I never jotted down dates. A few years, maybe longer," Jake replied.

"I'd love to help you overcome writer's block. I heard meditation and acupuncture can free creativity. Maybe spend some time in one of those float tanks or salt caves."

"Thanks, but it's something I've needed to figure out on my own." He took more frequent sips of wine. "As you know with your art, some pieces are more difficult to express. If you aren't in the right frame of mind, it's better to revisit them another time. Otherwise, you're disappointed by the outcome."

"You have a point there. Anyone else can admire my work, but all I see are the imperfections."

Families sprawled on lawn chairs, and couples cuddled on outspread blankets. There wasn't an unoccupied park bench or a stretch of available grass. Luckily, Jake and Miranda's spot nestled under the enormous pine, the town's main attraction for their annual Christmas tree lighting festival, offered some privacy.

"I know I'm breaking all my own rules about asking questions," Miranda said, "but what happened? Why the loss of inspiration?"

"Our plans don't always work out as we hoped. You know that yourself. I'd be the evening's buzzkill, though, if I bored you with the details."

"Not at all. You've been so kind and listened to my drama; I'm all ears when you're ready to share your story."

Two yappy dachshunds with brown hot dog–shaped bodies sprinted in different directions, and a disgruntled child dragged a tattered blanket like Linus from *Peanuts*. The parents appeared equally disenchanted as they headed toward Jake and Miranda but veered away.

"You once told me that I was in harmony with life." Jake breathed an exaggerated sigh. "That wasn't always so. I struggled to find myself during my first few semesters of college. I might have dropped out of school had it not been for this one professor. He helped me recognize my potential as a writer and encouraged me to put my creative thoughts on paper. Changing majors was a turning point for me. I wrote a few short stories, and by the time I was a senior, I had begun writing my first novel. I may be addicted to adrenaline, but expressing my creativity on paper was more exciting than a rock-climbing trip or river-rafting adventure. I'd choose my laptop over my skis any day."

Teenagers threw a Frisbee across the lawn while onlookers watched its effortless glide. A robust concession worker with a booming voice yelled, "Popcorn! Peanuts!" throughout the square. But with Addie's pecan pie on reserve for later, there was no need for refreshments and no time for distractions. Miranda's steady gaze held Jake accountable for his words.

"Having my manuscript, a stellar GPA, and the homecoming queen as my girlfriend, I felt the world was within reach." Jake grasped the air like he was capturing a firefly, but his retracted hand was empty. "I was going places, Miranda. I had big career dreams of that once-in-a-lifetime opportunity as a writer. My résumé attracted interest from some of the most sought-after firms in New York City. The anticipation, though, was short-lived."

Laughter and loud voices carried throughout the square as pacified townspeople returned from patronizing the food vendor trucks. Some feasted on lobster rolls and fiddleheads, while others spooned corn chowder from disposable bowls. Although youngsters favored the whoopie pies, there was enough fresh New England fare to appease every appetite.

"Pop collapsed one day at Colby's Hardware." Jake winced. "It was a sudden heart attack with no time for goodbyes. We should have been preparing for Easter, but instead we planned a funeral. I went from feeling like titanium to pliable plastic overnight."

"I'm sorry for your loss, Jake. You learned how fragile life is and how vulnerable you are."

"Exactly. I was wallowing and waiting for the next disappointment to strike. I returned to campus as a different man—stripped of my security."

Miranda watched his chest rise and fall through his snug shirt as he drew a deep breath and exhaled slowly. With an occasional blink, his eyes reflected an unfamiliar shade of green.

"Then came the wake-up calls. Partying friends dismissed me. And my girlfriend didn't understand that a grandparent wasn't an old forgetful person who took up space at family gatherings." Jake inserted the cork into the half-full bottle with force and tapped it with his palm. He flicked the other cork from the empty cabernet into the picnic basket. "That was a quick ending, too, when she replaced me with some reckless frat boy."

Miranda could embrace him with open arms or comfort him with sentiments. There were countless words to choose from but no guarantee of the right ones.

"I'm sorry for those tough times. I would have lost my inspiration too. And I understand how it still stings as if it happened yesterday. Some memories are harder to forget."

Nearby, picnickers lit citronella candles as nightfall settled in and fireflies danced around them. The grand gazebo was slowly coming to life, racing Jake and Miranda's conversation against time.

"Not long after, I discovered I had inherited Pop's business. I'll never forget the words read from his will, how he entrusted me with a piece of our family's history and knew I would continue to make him proud." He met Miranda's gaze. "I was only twenty-one."

"I recall you telling me a little about this during our first drive through town. Inheriting the family business was a tremendous gift," she said, dismissing her hypocrisy.

"And a difficult sacrifice as well. Do you remember at McGinley's when you shared your job acceptance at the historical society rather than pursue a career as an artist?"

"Yeah, I surprised myself with that revelation."

"Colby's Hardware became *my* plan B," Jake said. "I had no more thoughts of climbing the corporate ladder and putting my creative energy into writing. My wild ride, *poof*," he added, snapping his fingers in the air, "gone. Instead, I became an inexperienced business owner in a small town."

"I may be missing something here, but why couldn't you do both, run the business during the day and write at night?" The residual effect of the wine still toyed with Miranda's inhibitions. "You are so capable. Why limit yourself?"

"With me, it's all or nothing, Miranda. It didn't matter whether I finished my novel or began writing a sequel. Instead, I dedicated myself to Pop's legacy at Colby's Hardware and honored his final requests."

"I applaud your integrity," she replied sheepishly. Jake had forfeited his happiness to uphold a commitment while she fretted over a measly hundred-day arrangement. "Plenty of others would have ignored those requests to chase their dreams. It's a reflection of your character."

"Thanks, but what choice did I have?"

"There are always choices, but there aren't easy decisions."

"When I weigh what I would've had to turn my back on, it wasn't up for debate. I sometimes mourn the exciting life I could have had and the novelist I might have become. And looking ahead, there's no one else to take responsibility for the family business."

Jake leaned back with outstretched legs. "Given the chance for a do-over, I would have made the same decision. Everything that's happened in my life has led me to this moment—to here and now."

"Thanks for sharing a bit of history with me. I have the utmost respect for you."

He offered a pained smile. "I'm afraid that's only the beginning of my story, Miranda."

The stage lights flashed. Activity around them and between them came to an abrupt halt. Fans began to whistle and cheer.

"Hot Blooded" followed a song of another extreme, "Cold as Ice." The powerful melodies engaged the crowd to sing along with the chorus as familiar lyrics poured from their mouths. Despite the heaviness that mingled in Jake and Miranda's evening, threatening to weigh them down, the timeless music offered a reprieve.

After the fifth song and two glasses of wine, Miranda was grateful for the lull in electric guitar strumming. The crowd responded to the softer ballad "Waiting for a Girl Like You" with cheers and whistles, followed by silence and sways.

Mesmerized by the sea of flickering lights, she failed to notice Jake was standing, reaching out to her with his left hand.

"Dance with me, Miranda."

"What, here? Now? In front of all these people?"

Jake bent down close to her. "No one is paying any attention to us."

"It's not that I don't want to—" She glanced over at her empty wine glass.

"You knee-hung from a trapeze. You can dance with a friend in the town square." He rose to his feet again but kept his hand extended.

Miranda's voice of reason advised her to decline, but her heart had granted permission. There was no time to waste. Their stolen moments would soon become distant memories like her arrangement in Cobblers Hill or Trudy and Randy's relationship.

With inhibitions left alongside her grandmother's picnic basket, Miranda took Jake's hand and stood. They held each other rigidly, with a safe distance acceptable to friends. The initial awkwardness yielded to a slow-swaying rhythm that led her to a place beyond arrangements and legacies. Inching in closer, she rested her head on his shoulder and breathed in his clean scent. Her slender frame melted into his protective embrace.

In another place and time without Kasey, would crossing the line jeopardize their friendship? Or clear the boundaries for something more meaningful to develop? Shadows and moonlight, distant streetlamps and shining stars, nostalgic music and a natural cadence made anything seem possible.

Slow-dancing fans followed their lead. Despite her quirks and shortcomings, she was finally content being Miranda Blair, held by a man of integrity on a moonlit summer's night.

"Will you do something for me?"

He inched back to look at her. "Of course."

"You need to finish writing your novel. Don't deprive yourself of a dream. I know Pop would want that for you as well."

He whispered back, and she could feel the warmth of his breath. "I will, Miranda, in time. I'm a patient man when it comes to something I want. I promise you it will be worth the wait."

Miranda believed him. After all, Jake hadn't broken a promise to her yet.

Chapter 24

It had been forty-four hours, just shy of two days, since Miranda had last seen Jake. Every minute that passed was one too many.

The smell of sautéed onions guided her toward the Colby home. She balanced a blueberry crumb pie in her left hand, freshly made with ingredients from the farmers' market, and carried a meticulously wrapped gift under her other arm. As Addie had assured, the garden gate between the yards was left ajar, and the theme of open doors prevailed.

"No need to knock, let yourself in, darlin'!" Addie hollered in her southern twang.

All five feet of Adelaide Colby hovered over the stove, stirring and seasoning the gumbo in her country kitchen. She claimed the sizable cast-iron pot, their family treasure passed down through generations, provided the magic ingredient in every recipe. But Miranda knew it was the love.

"So glad ya could join us. Wouldn't be the same without ya."

"Thanks for the invite, Addie."

When the cherished old woman wasn't looking, Miranda scanned the adjoining rooms from a distance. Although there was no sign of Jake, he was nearby. An undeniable magnetism drew him to her each time as if it were their first introduction.

"I can't wait to try this okra you've been telling me about."

Miranda peered over the old woman's shoulder to steal a peek at the goodness.

"Hold that enthusiasm until after ya taste it, ya hear? But I say it's a treat to 'em taste buds and comfort for the soul. I got some good bread for *soppin'* too. What's that ya got there?" Addie eyed the wrapped package that Miranda offered with outstretched hands.

"It's a little something I made for you. A token of my appreciation."

"Ya shouldn't have, but I reckon I'll open it now." Addie tore off paper strips like an impatient child on Christmas morning.

"What am I missing in here?"

Once again, Jake had impeccable timing, like the June afternoon when he strolled into Addie's kitchen half-dressed to rescue the whistling teakettle. Though fully clothed now and no longer a stranger, he was every bit as intriguing.

Miranda still caught her breath at the initial sight of him. His skin had tanned to golden bronze, and his jawline appeared more sculpted without facial hair. His eyes reflected a different hue each time, varying from a blue green to a rich emerald, often resembling the beauty of sea glass or the deep pine on the trail leading to Edens Cove.

"Miranda here made me a gift," Addie said with eagerness. "Ain't that the sweetest?"

"I'd say so." Jake placed his keys on the hook while keeping his penetrating gaze on Miranda.

"There was a card too, but I must have left it home."

The four-letter word "home" rolled off Miranda's tongue. Previously, she had referred to it as her grandmother's cottage, and soon it would become Miranda's property. Then what?

Wrapping paper covered the kitchen counter and spilled onto the floor. A piece clung to Addie's floral dress.

"Well, I'll be!" The old woman held up the inspirational garden sign and nodded along as she read the symbolic words. "Ain't that somethin'? Ya wouldn't have known, darlin', but this was my

A Hundred Days Till Tomorrow

mama's favorite poem. It's been meanin'ful to me ever since I was a young'un. And now I've got this here sign to put in my garden."

She handed the gift off to her grandson and leaned in for a hug. Until tonight, Jake had been the last person to embrace Miranda. Those cherished moments within his protective arms in the town square had created her favorite summer memory. The display of gratitude by the old woman was a close second.

"You made this, Miranda?" Jake asked.

"I did. When I first arrived here, I had plenty of time to stare at the cottage walls and read the inspirational plaques that hung on them. They gave me the idea to create one for Addie."

"But the wood—" Jake smoothed his hand over the surface. "It's not the pressure-treated kind you'd buy in a store."

"Nope. I found it during one of my early jogs down by the marina. I stopped to stretch, and this amazing piece was practically under my feet. It was too good to pass up, so I placed it aside and went back later. With a little creativity, I figured I could transform it into art. And when I researched poems, this particular one seemed to reflect Addie's love for her garden."

"Oh, yes, indeed," the old woman said.

"I visited Colby's Hardware for materials and a staple gun." Miranda pointed to the back of the sign. "Your assistant helped me secure the wire for hanging."

"I love it, and I thank ya so much for thinkin' of me, darlin'."

A dazed Addie had overlooked the boiling gumbo.

"Gram, why don't you get some fresh air?" Jake guided his grandmother toward the back door. "We'll take it from here."

"I reckon that's a good idea. 'Em legs of mine are givin' me some trouble today." She wobbled outside and hollered, "Eleven minutes to go on the gumbo. That there bread needs attention. Don't forget the salt and peppa. Sweet tea's in the fridge. Add a few of 'em cubes. Gotta be cold, ya hear?"

A freshly shaven Jake leaned against the kitchen counter next to Miranda. His white cotton shirt was loose-fitting, with the top two buttons undone for easy access. He began rolling up his sleeves with slow, precise movements. The oversized spoon slipped from Miranda's hand, but she caught it in time before splattering Addie's stovetop.

"That was thoughtful of you. Gram doesn't lose composure often, and when she does, well . . ." He gave Miranda's shoulder a light squeeze that initiated a butterfly waltz in her stomach. "She loved her gift."

"It's the least I could do. Addie has made me feel like I belong here, even though my situation is temporary. I'm grateful for her friendship."

The word "temporary" seemed to dwell on the tip of Miranda's tongue like a canker sore. Either she was fishing for Jake's reaction or reminding herself good times weren't a forever thing.

At the precise moment Miranda grabbed a few ice cubes for the tea, Jake reached overhead for the bread basket, brushing up against her within the cramped kitchen. A cube dropped on the floor. She bent down, but another one slipped through her fingers, and then two more. Jake laughed, and Miranda giggled her way back to the freezer.

The smell of freshly baked bread mingled with the other enticing aromas in the rustic kitchen. Jake secured the risen loaf on a cutting board and sliced perfectly uniform pieces while Miranda stirred the sweet tea, the cubes rattling against the glass.

When would a gold band occupy Jake's finger? Had he considered a romantic proposal for Kasey or left a deposit on a diamond? Maybe he had plans to pop the question when she returned from her European vacation. That would be the ultimate homecoming for the chef-in-training.

If only Miranda knew his intentions and could read his mind and interpret his stares.

"I've never been quick to form relationships, but Addie has meant a great deal to me," Miranda said. "Somehow, she helped fill the void left by my grandmother's absence. It's as if Addie was supposed to be a part of my life, but it took a storm of circumstances to bring us together."

"If a storm were responsible, as you say, then you weathered it, and a double rainbow followed."

"You have a creative way with words, Jake. You always know what to say and how to say it."

"Well," he replied, "it's the truth. I'm not surprised you and Gram bonded. You're a different person than when you arrived here—more open and trusting."

"I'm trying, but I haven't been completely transparent with her about my past. I've avoided those conversations, and I feel guilty about it. I hope I haven't offended her in any way."

Miranda turned off the burner and removed the serving spoon, tapping it several times. Rice and celery bits fell back into the pot. Jake reached across her for the salt and pepper shakers, and she got a whiff of his clean scent.

"I appreciate how your grandmother has respected my privacy. And yet sometimes I think I'm not the only one who wants to dodge the topic of Gertrude Blair."

She shifted the pot to a cool burner and secured its lid. The kitchen had become eerily quiet aside from the refrigerator's low hum and the overhead clock's tick.

"Don't let the gumbo overcook now, ya hear?" Addie's warning resonated through the open window.

"Listen, I know you care about Gram and have the best of intentions. But try not to overthink some conversations or the absence of others," Jake said. "You've come so far from the past. All that matters now is where your life is heading, right?"

"Right."

"Come on. We'd better get this meal to the table before we're reprimanded by that feisty lady out there."

They looked at each other and laughed.

"A few pointers: the gumbo is spicy," he said. "Keep a full glass close by."

"What makes you think I can't handle spicy?" Miranda arched her brow.

"Just saying. And it's fair game to take the bread and soak up what Gram refers to as the essence. It's called 'sopping.'"

"Aha! So that's what Addie meant."

"And don't worry if you hear Gram say she loves pot liquor."

Miranda's eyes widened.

"Sounds illegal, doesn't it?" Jake laughed. "It's a southern term for the juice that remains after boiling green vegetables. They claim it's liquid gold because of all the nutrients."

"Okay, pot liquor. Got it."

"And lastly, okra isn't for everyone. I've had twenty-nine years to acquire a liking for southern cooking. I have a stash of junk food in the Jeep for later."

"So typical of you to look out for me," Miranda said playfully. She shut the light above the stove and opened the door for Jake, who held the steaming pot of gumbo with oven mitts. "Anything else you think I should know?"

Jake offered a half smile but did not reply.

Chapter 25

A grapevine-covered pergola occupied the far corner of the Colby yard. For such small cottages, the homes on Primrose Lane had oversized pieces of property with magnificent views of the rolling countryside.

"Your table setting is lovely, Addie." Miranda's fingers grazed the white-laced tablecloth. Taking a seat, she leaned in to smell the blue and white hydrangea bunches that created a fragrant centerpiece.

"A moment of silence to bless the meal, y'all, before we dig in," Addie ordered with prayer hands.

Miranda bowed her head with gratitude for healing, neighborly kindness, developed wings—and Jake Colby.

Each simple joy and recent stride somehow led back to the Colbys—and Grandma Trudy's arrangement. Miranda *was* a different person in Cobblers Hill, and as Jake had assured, the promise of tomorrow was all that mattered. Everything comes of age in its own time, whether it is a piece of glass, a cottage's transformation, Jake's novel, or her happiness. If the passage of time and patient conditioning could turn razor-sharp glass into something beautiful, there was hope for their futures too.

"Gram tells me you never tried okra before."

Jake nudged Miranda under the table as Addie dished out the gumbo.

"That's true." Miranda removed the fan-shaped cloth napkin and draped it across her lap. "If it tastes as good as it smells, I may have found a new favorite vegetable."

"Well, it ain't good cold," Addie grumbled.

Jake filled the goblets with sweet tea and placed the pitcher next to Miranda. The first spoonful disappeared into Miranda's mouth while the old woman eagerly leaned forward.

"Mmm. I love the sweetness of the onion and red peppers. And the sausage is smoky, with some kick to it."

Addie's eyes widened. "Andouille."

Miranda cradled green pieces of the neighbor's sacred vegetable on her spoon. "And this must be your okra. I can't say I've had anything like it. It's tender with a mellow taste."

"Glad ya approve, darlin', but ya know what the proverb says? Hunger makes the best sauce."

The weight of Jake's stare settled on Miranda from across the table. Perhaps he, too, was curious whether she was being honest or polite.

"Um, that's some collection of blue sea glass," Miranda said of the rare treasure encasing a flickering candle.

"Those there are souvenirs collected by my grandson and Kasey. Every time they'd leave the house, they'd come back with pocketsful." Addie let out a hearty laugh that shook her shoulders and made Jake smile.

"And yet we didn't find a single blue piece this summer." Miranda moved the gumbo around with her spoon, gliding it back and forth aimlessly across the bowl. Not only had Jake's girlfriend monopolized the sea glass in Edens Cove, but the sheer mention of her name made the old woman beam.

"Keep the faith," Jake urged. "We'll find some blue."

"And that once-in-a-lifetime piece of red," Miranda said, although she doubted such a rarity existed.

"Yes, someday."

But they were running out of time for that someday. According to the school calendar, summer vacation was winding down, and classes would resume in days. Only three and a half weeks remained in her grandmother's arrangement.

"Listen up, y'all." Addie tapped the back of her spoon in the air as she spoke with a full mouth. "The thing about sea glass is sometimes ya search forever for it, while it's right underneath ya nose. Ya gotta look closely for the treasure, 'cause if ya miss out on a good thing, someone else is gonna get it, ya hear? Ain't that the truth about a lotta stuff in life?"

She wrinkled her forehead at Jake, then at Miranda, and back at Jake.

Rather than exchange meaningful glances, Jake lit citronella candles and secured the lid on the gumbo pot. It wasn't until her first mosquito bite that Miranda understood why. She removed her sweater and draped it around Addie's sunken shoulders, although the old woman seemed too distracted by the activity in the air to notice.

The candlelight's glow and the lantern's dancing flicker only heightened the intrigue of Jake Colby. While his attractive features had captivated Miranda initially, it was how he made her feel—whole and safe and valued—that kept him at the forefront of her mind. If only she could complete him in ways Kasey hadn't.

"My librarian friend, Joanie, and I attended this inspiring lecture in Springfield," Miranda said. "Joel Avies is a best-selling author and triathlete. Have you heard of him?"

Jake shrugged. "You ladies drove to Springfield?"

"Yep, and it was worth the road trip. What a dynamic speaker! He engaged us from his powerful introduction until his closing words. His five-step system, Gutting Writer's Rut, is an interesting approach to overcoming barriers and liberating words." Miranda barely blinked. "I thought you might find his advice helpful, Jake, so I sent you my notes from the seminar. Hope you don't mind that Addie gave me your email address."

Had he noticed his abandoned laptop, previously out of commission due to a virus, was up and running, ready for his creativity to navigate the keys? Maybe he suspected it was the plotting of the girl next door and his grandmother rather than a stroke of good luck. If so, Miranda hoped it was perceived as a kind gesture rather than an invasion of privacy.

"Mr. Avies is an author advocate and writing coach too," Miranda said. "A few of his clients in the audience vouched for his mentorship. One woman claimed a few sessions together motivated her to pick up the pen and create paragraphs with power and purpose. That's a lot of *P*'s," she said, "but you get the idea about becoming unstuck."

Miranda reached into her pocket and slid a business card to the center of the table. "From the consensus of his social media followers, his books are as compelling."

She glanced down at the card and back at Jake. His eyes did not follow, nor did his hand outstretch.

"Don't mind if ya wanna go surf that there web, as ya folks call it, or check that mail. We gals got lots to chat about. Ain't that right, darlin'?" The old woman gave Miranda a double wink.

"Maybe later," Jake said, rising to his feet. He stacked the extra plates like an intruding busboy.

Until Miranda was privy to that slight imperfection in an otherwise perfect Jake Colby, being his muse would be a challenge.

"My grandson tells me you are becomin' quite the volunteer, darlin'," Addie said.

"Oh, he did, now, did he?" Miranda shot Jake a playful look. "Cobblers Hill has opened my eyes. I've missed enough opportunities to go out on a limb in my life, but I've found ways to compensate here. Especially at the youth center."

"Well, I'll be. Ain't that music to 'em old ears of mine."

"Every Sunday, a small group of us gather there to assemble peanut butter and jelly sandwiches for those who are food insecure." Miranda cradled pieces of sausage and okra on her spoon. "At times, I've visited the farmers' market and purchased Granny Smiths to accompany those lunches. It feels good to provide a little something extra, and what's more appropriate than the fruit, right?"

"Ahhh, Gram must have told you about our family tree." Jake sighed. "I should have known you got 'the lesson.'"

"We gals have dabbled on a topic or two," Addie replied with a chuckle. "Darlin', have ya given any thought to what comes next?"

Miranda covered her mouth with the back of her hand as she chewed her final spoonful of gumbo. Armed with a piece of bread, she outlined a figure eight at the bottom of her bowl.

"Look who's soppin'. Atta gal! The best part is the essence," Addie said with childlike enthusiasm. "Now, what were we sayin'? Ah, yes. Might it be time to belly up to the bar?"

Miranda glanced over at Jake with a silent plea.

He leaned in and whispered, "That's Gram's way of insinuating you make a bold move. You know, take the bull by its horns."

Miranda cleared the tickle from her throat. "Oh, I see."

Unlike Jake's consoling Dunkin' napkins she had shredded during their initial drive, the cloth one was more resilient. She fidgeted with it in her lap, wrapping it through her fingers and around her wrist like a cast. "I don't have a definitive plan for my studies, but this summer has helped me embrace my jagged pieces rather than disregard them. I've been giving some thought to a new career too. No more selling myself short, that's for sure."

Addie offered a blank stare, and neither she nor Jake uttered a word. Only the chirping crickets had something to say. Miranda may have provided the wrong reply or not enough of the right one.

The neighbors were entitled to be curious about plans for the adjoining property beyond the hundred days. While Miranda couldn't provide those answers yet, she could divert the conversation with oversized portions of her homemade blueberry crumb pie.

Before long, plates emptied, and tongues tired.

"Well, y'all, I reckon it's time for me to turn in." Addie gave an exaggerated yawn that revealed a lifetime of dental work. "I'm worn slap out! I trust ya kids can tidy up and shut 'em lanterns. Leave the kitchen be. It'll give me somethin' to do in the mornin'."

"Good night, Addie." Miranda reached over to kiss the old woman's wrinkled cheek. "Thank you for the lovely evening and for sharing your delicious okra recipe with me."

"We'll take care of things from here, Gram." Jake supported his grandmother's elbow as she rose slowly to her feet. He escorted her toward the back door, patiently guiding her labored steps.

"Stay as long as ya want, darlin'!" she hollered. "I love havin' ya here."

Although Miranda's heart sang with Adelaide Colby's meaningful words, she yearned to hear them from Jake.

Chapter 26

Miranda had an upper-body workout scrubbing the neighbors' cast-iron pot that weighed as much as a well-fed toddler.

"And?"

A bolder Miranda called out to Jake, who had returned from settling in his grandmother.

"And what?" He leaned against the kitchen doorframe with his arms folded.

"You're staring at me, Colby. I've got great peripheral vision, you know. Why the stare this time?"

"I can't explain it. You're different, Miranda."

"Uh-oh. A good different or a bad different?"

She attempted to toss a soap bubble at him with the cumbersome rubber glove, but water dripped down her arm instead.

"It's the best kind of different." Jake picked up the dish towel next to Miranda and dried each item like he was polishing an antique. "To continue our earlier conversation, there's something special about your relationship with Gram. Unlike others, you listen patiently to her long-winded sermons and show respect. I love seeing her smile and feel appreciated."

Miranda wondered if Kasey was one of those *others*.

"I'll admit, I've never owned my voice, but I am an attentive listener. And I do love Addie's stories." Miranda stacked the dry bowls in the vintage cupboard with delicate hands. Breathing too heavily might collapse the compromised wooden shelf.

"If you think it went unnoticed, I saw you give Gram your sweater tonight and the joy on her face when you raved about the gumbo. You've blessed Gram with your interest in her garden and southern heritage. And here you are, cleaning her kitchen. The way you treat others, how you make them feel, says a lot about you."

Rather than microwave a bag of popcorn and pull up a chair to relish Jake's string of compliments, Miranda folded the damp dish towel to match the corners. Pooled water dripped into the sink as she tilted the empty drainboard. She would have swept the neighbor's floor had a broom been nearby or tended to a load of laundry—anything to prolong the evening.

"I think you're giving me too much credit, but thank you," she said. "Growing up without much, I learned what mattered most in life was free. You can't put a price tag on someone's time and attention. And it doesn't cost anything to be kind. As for Addie, she deserves the best."

"Well, I admire you—all of you—the Miranda who overcame adversity in Barron Park and the one in Cobblers Hill who is willing to share her gifts with others. You know, Gram said you're bourbon in fine china."

"She did not!" Miranda stifled her laughter with a cupped hand.

"Yes, she did."

"I'm not sure what to make of that, but I think I'm flattered."

"You should be. That's Gram's way of saying you have inner strength disguised by delicate beauty." Jake reached for two glasses and a bottle of amaretto from the shelf. "Care to join me out by the swing? Rain is on the way, but we might steal some time for a night-cap and those snacks I mentioned."

Miranda couldn't force another bite, and she was less likely to sip a cordial.

"Sure, why not?"

Jake escorted her through the yard to the double Adirondack swing and grabbed one of the lanterns along the way. "After you."

"Wow, this is a work of art." Miranda grazed her hand across the logs carved into smooth lumber.

"Thanks." Jake took a seat by her side. He poured the amber-colored beverage into their cordial glasses and handed her one. "This swing was a project of mine from a few summers ago—a birthday present for Gram."

"Wait, you made this, and yet you fussed about my simple garden sign? Is there anything you don't do well, Jake Colby?"

"Too many things, but there are a few honorable mentions. You already know I don't sing, or as Gram says, I can't carry a tune in a bucket."

Miranda tilted her head back and laughed. "Your grandmother and those sayings."

"I'm horrible at wrapping presents. I don't ice-skate well either, and have zero talent in the rink. My arms flail, my knees buckle, and I make these crazy dance moves."

"I'd pay to see that!"

"What, me falling? It's a dreadful sight. And let's not forget, I can't knee-hang from a trapeze."

Addie's bedroom light went out, leaving them to the guardianship of the full moon's magnificent glow. Jake held the glass's thick stem in between his fingers and raised it to take a sip.

"Do you mind if I ask what your book is about?" Miranda's question sprang from the stillness and dangled in front of them. "You know how I feel about prying, so it's okay if you prefer not to answer."

"The novel is past tense for me, but I appreciate you taking an interest." Jake rested his head back and appeared to summon the galaxy of stars for guidance. "It was the forbidden journey of two lovers, separated by war and torn by circumstance."

Miranda closed her eyes, homing in on his voice and crickets serenading in the distance.

"Time didn't wait, and their paths led them in different directions. Their lives ran parallel in many ways, with occasional moments close enough to overlap. But one of them was always a milestone ahead or a step behind."

Intermittent silence no longer yielded awkward moments. Like the swing's cadence, their friendship had established a comfortable rhythm.

"While my lead characters had fulfilling journeys," he continued, "what might have been spanned the decades. Questions went unanswered, and unresolved feelings were repressed."

"So, a simple sidestep changed or shortchanged their futures."

"It depends on how you see it."

"I'm curious what brought them together and how time sabotaged what they shared. Tell me more," Miranda said.

Although he had written the first draft during his senior year in college, it held an uncanny resemblance to Miranda's relationship with him—parallel lives that might have intersected but didn't due to extenuating circumstances. It was likely that Trudy and Randy had drifted in the same direction as Jake's characters.

"Over fifty years, a forbidden bond endured through trials and triumphs, discoveries and disappointments, rewarding experiences and gut-wrenching regrets."

"Wow! And?"

"That's just it—I'm not sure. The story line hit a wall. Or maybe I was the one who crashed. Either way, I couldn't come up with an appropriate ending for my characters."

"There's a chance they'll rediscover each other, right?" Miranda's eyes fluttered open. "Maybe circumstances could lead them to enjoy old age together like those couples that fall in love in assisted living homes. I'm the last person to give romantic advice, but I've been told everything deserves a chance," she said, relaying his grand-parents' message. "And sometimes a second chance. I wonder if a lifetime's absence would change how they once felt or strengthen what they waited so long to share. It's frustrating and poignant, yet heartwarming and hopeful."

"By creating complex relationships and throwing in familiar obstacles, I wanted my debut novel to resonate with others—you know, nudge them to consider the similar themes in their lives. And give them something to reflect upon. I aspired to free my readers' emotions, so they weren't hiding behind their thoughts or trapped by their feelings." Jake halted the swing and faced Miranda. "Of course, Gram would want them never to lose faith."

"And like me, she would want a happy ending," Miranda pointed out.

"True."

He leaned his head back and stared up at the sky. She followed his gaze to the millions of fading stars in the late-night sky. Which-ever star captivated his attention was the luckiest of all.

"Thanks for asking about my book and fixing my laptop. Tonight, you reminded me how I enjoy being a storyteller on paper."

"Then tell stories, Jake. Write page-turning novels that tug at readers' heartstrings. Encourage and inspire through your written words, as you have done for me with spoken words this summer. It may not be the writing relationship you envisioned, but it's okay for it to be gray rather than black or white, as long as it makes you happy."

"Valid point. But if that's so, and life doesn't have to be all or nothing, as you say, then—"

Jake shifted his weight in the swing and cleared his throat as if on cue.

"Then what, Jake? It's okay, say it."

"Then why didn't you reach out to your grandmother in recent years and see if you two could have salvaged a relationship? Even if it wasn't the bond you needed as a child, you might have made peace with the past."

"I did. I mean, I tried."

Miranda took a whiff of her cordial but didn't sip. "When I was twenty or so, curiosity got to me. I was tired of accepting terms I never agreed to, so I did some investigative work and located Trudy at a nursing facility. That night, I chewed my fingernails to nubs while rehearsing my lines—what I would say and what I should avoid. The next morning, I skipped classes and took the long drive."

The evening sky no longer appeared as magical. The once theatrical stars now played hide-and-seek against a muted backdrop. The dense air constructed a barrier between Jake and Miranda.

"Really? You never mentioned this before." Jake shimmied to the edge of the swing. "I had no idea."

"Neither did my mom. It was best not to mention it back then. Even now, I'm not sure what purpose it serves."

"Was Trudy receptive to your visit?"

"She didn't chase me away in her wheelchair, if that's what you're asking," Miranda replied with a partial smile. "I kept the topics light, sharing tidbits about my life, school studies, the books I read, and the preserved buildings in town. I probably bored her with all that surface talk now that I think about it."

"I find that sweet. What about Cobblers Hill? Did she mention the arrangement?" Jake sat upright with his feet planted on the ground. "I hope you don't mind all the questions; it's just that seeing you with Gram made me realize what a dedicated granddaughter you would have been." He inched in closer. "So, you did form a relationship of sorts with Trudy?"

"Didn't get the opportunity. For the most part, she was non-communicative. Although I thought I noticed an eagerness in her eyes.

A Hundred Days Till Tomorrow

Then again, maybe her eyes always looked like that; I wouldn't have known. It was sad, though, seeing her as a prisoner to a catatonic state and sadder to think it was too late."

Jagged lightning bolts shot across the sky, and a low rumble followed. The stars had made an early departure for the evening.

"Maybe you caught her at an off time. I know from Gram that seniors are more lucid some days than others. Did you try again?"

"It was my only visit. I could have made other attempts, but I don't think life intended that relationship. It's not an excuse, Jake, but I lacked the encouragement and support."

If only he had been by Miranda's side all along, her glass might have been full, if not overflowing, rather than half-empty. Her story line with Trudy could have had a happy ending too. And Miranda might have even inquired about her father.

"It took courage to visit your grandmother after the void in your history. At least you can say you tried."

"Thanks," she said. "After that, I forced myself not to look back."

"So, when did you learn about her arrangement?"

"Not until years later, upon her passing. The attorney sent a letter in March that summoned me to his office. Soon after, I arrived in Cobblers Hill to begin my hundred days. That's when my emotions spiraled again. Not to rehash the past, but Trudy's plans felt vindictive, cold and distant like you'd expect from a stranger."

Miranda rubbed the goose bumps on her arms. "I still don't understand why Trudy chose me to inherit her estate. Maybe there weren't any other candidates. Then again, I saw fresh flowers with an attached balloon on her bedside table the day I visited. So someone else had been a part of her life. That's more than I can say for myself."

"Trudy was a private lady," Jake said with a shrug. He brushed his palms against his jeans. "Over the years, there were few signs of life next door."

"I figured as much. Although I never inquired whether you and Addie had a relationship with my grandmother, I assumed she was as much a mystery to you both as she was to me. If there were something to know, you would have shared it by now."

In the lantern's glow, Jake's hands gripped the edge of the swing. His gaze extended across the field as the shadows of trees danced recklessly in the distance.

"I think I made peace with my grandmother this summer. It may sound strange, but I feel her guidance from the other side." Miranda reached in front of her with a cupped hand and caught rain droplets sprinkled from above. "Trudy and I are different people than we were back then—a good different—and it's the memories of her here, in Cobblers Hill, I want to remember."

"Miranda, listen, there is something you should know." He leaned forward, resting his elbows on his knees. The light rain left a splattering of circles on his jeans. "I've needed to talk to you but was waiting for the right time."

Lightning streaked the evening sky, and thunder cracked vehemently overhead like broken tree branches. Then the heavens purged everything they could no longer withhold, drenching Jake and Miranda's clothing.

"I guess now isn't the right time after all." He reached for the lantern. A shield of torrential rain separated them. "Sorry tonight had to end like this."

"No apologies, it was wonderful." Miranda's reply competed with Mother Nature.

They ran for shelter—Jake to his grandmother's house and Miranda to the cottage, becoming more like home. Time would tell whether the sudden interruption was a blessing that rained down on them or a sign of turbulence ahead.

Chapter 27

Brittle grass, scorched by the relentless summer sun, crunched under Jake and Miranda's sneakers at Dewitt Park.

"So, what's new in your world?" Jake asked.

"Smooth." Miranda gave him a playful nudge.

"What?" he asked, shrugging.

"I know what you're trying to do, Colby, but there's no chance of distracting me—not here, not now."

"Focus on something else. Trust me, talking will help pass the time until we board."

Miranda continued to trust Jake; he hadn't given her a reason not to. Their crescendo of adventures encouraged her to reach higher and dig deeper. The further they headed into the hundred days, the closer she believed they were becoming.

"Well, I did have a productive morning."

"Come on." Jake gestured with a rolling hand as if directing her words. "Let's hear all about it."

"Joanie organized a community-sponsored program at the library to instruct children on how to paint a Labor Day still life. Unfortunately, the instructor had an emergency and canceled a few days before the event. Guess who volunteered to fill in?"

"No way, really? That's fantastic."

"I almost rescinded my offer." Miranda shifted her weight from one foot to the other and back again. "I've never worked with kids or taught a class before. The thought of doing both was as intimidating as that circus trapeze. But after combing the town for ideas, I came up with a child-friendly, patriotic-themed display, and there was no turning back."

"I'm listening," Jake said.

"My first find was a vibrant blue-and-white-striped kite at that gift shop, Angela's Attic. I suspended it from the ceiling with fish wire and positioned a fan so the kite looked like it was flying." Using her arm, she demonstrated the zigzag motion of its imaginary tail. "Pretty cool, if I may say so."

"Kids dig that stuff. You should have never doubted yourself."

"Then I found a child-sized beach chair with an attached umbrella on clearance and a large inflatable ball with gold stars. I picked up one of those giant bags of sand from your store and added two interesting shells and a piece of netting we found on the beach. I wedged a small American flag in the sand, and there you go—a Labor Day still life more appropriate for the Fourth of July." She laughed. "Aren't you sorry you asked?"

"Nope. I love how you've become involved in the community. Yoga classes and library visits." Jake held up one finger at a time. "Lectures and volunteer work with friends. And now you're teaching art to children. I can't wait to hear what's next on your agenda."

A uniformed man approached them, blowing an irritating whistle and directing everyone to gather in one of four color-coded areas. This time, the high-pitched sound didn't make Miranda flinch. While some passengers were too distracted by their cell phones to oblige, Jake and Miranda made their way toward the fluorescent orange flag staked in the ground.

A hefty woman with watery eyes and a pasty complexion crossed their path like she was searching for a bucket or an escape plan. The nearby group paced back and forth, tapped their feet, and cracked their knuckles.

With Jake as a distraction, even the industrial-sized fans weren't preying on Miranda's nerves as they once did. Not only had she taken his advice to talk, but she hadn't allowed a quiet moment.

"I'll admit," she said, "it was a thrill working alongside those kids and witnessing their unique interpretations of art. This sweet young artist, Tricia, spent most of the hour perfecting the American flag and obscuring items in the background. A real nationalist." Miranda chuckled. "Some kids painted cool abstract pieces, while others focused on details rather than broad shapes."

"I bet you left a lasting impression on them, bringing out their inner Picasso." Jake put his arm around Miranda, pulling her in next to him. "And to think those works of art are now hanging from crooked alphabet magnets on refrigerator doors for proud parents to admire."

"Hmmm. I never thought about that part." But she *had* considered the recent playfulness between them. She wanted to find meaning behind their blurred lines but attributed them to the comforts of friendship.

"What struck me," Miranda said, "was how therapeutic the experience seemed for many kids. They entered the community room with their heads hung low. A few clung to a parent's leg, and the older ones were distracted by their phones. A morning of painting, though, provided a constructive outlet. Patriotic music may have also played a role in their self-expression. I'd like to think a handful of those twelve children left the library inspired to create more artwork."

"You see? You're capable of much more than analyzing someone else's creation in a dark lecture hall. Or admiring a dusty relic in a drafty foyer. You are an artist, Miranda. I've noticed how your face lights up every time you talk about your artwork, and I've witnessed how it completes you. It's time to share your talent with others."

"Thanks. You always offer good advice."

"On that note," Jake said, "I'm glad you took my suggestion to dress warmly. I hear it gets chilly up there."

"What's your fascination with new heights? Never in my wildest dreams did I think I would be taking a hot-air balloon ride. It's extreme—over-the-top incredible."

"I don't believe in limiting ourselves, is all. If we're able to soar, then why shouldn't we?"

Why didn't Jake apply that ambitious spirit to his writing? And what if Miranda failed to become his muse as she did to capture his heart? Until she identified the roadblocks Jake hadn't shared, it was challenging to remove them.

She picked at a dab of dried paint on her arm. "Having ten toes on the ground here is far from limiting. There are plenty of unfamiliar dirt roads you could introduce me to, although you do have a knack for sweeping me off my feet. I hope I can handle the heights."

"You'll be too mesmerized by the view from up there to be nervous."

"It must be unbelievable, especially on a clear late afternoon."

"We'll find out soon enough." Jake chewed the inside of his cheek and stole glimpses of his watch. Across the field, the outspread balloons came to life, and passengers on the other line began to shuffle. Ladies took selfies to likely appear on social media with the anticipation of *oohs* and *aahs* from so-called friends. But posts could never do an experience with Jake Colby justice.

"You should continue to pursue more opportunities like today," Jake said. "The library may need an artist to conduct their community events on a more permanent basis."

Miranda was growing more comfortable with the title "artist," but the words "more permanent basis" made her heart flutter.

"I had no idea the basket was so big," she observed, using the balloon's travel compartment as a distraction. "It appeared smaller in *The Wizard of Oz.*"

While she had shared Dorothy's desperate plea to return to the security of her hometown, "home" had taken on a new meaning. Happiness prevailed whenever Miranda was with Jake. Now Jake Colby was her home. Aside from the obstacle presented by Kasey, time was a familiar enemy from which Miranda ran. The clock ticked emphatically, reminding her of the countdown in Cobblers Hill—a distraction more daunting than the industrial fan gearing up to inflate their balloon.

"I love your incurable innocence," Jake said. "It's called a gondola, but a basket will suffice. Our balloon is the largest and can hold many passengers, but I think there are only four on our flight. And the pilot, of course." He reviewed the paperwork, folded it in thirds, and tucked it in his back pocket. "Yep, two couples."

His easy use of the word "couples" made Miranda's insides perform a somersault.

"Which is your favorite?"

"Tough question. I love that hot-pink balloon over there." Miranda pointed to the one with a bold damask print and fleurs-de-lis. "It screams Paris! That's my top pick. Then again, the bright splattered colors on the other balloon remind me of a circus and our trapeze escapade. I can't help but smile."

"Perfect."

"But wait. I also like the profound message on that balloon over there." The tie-dyed bubble letters read "OVERJOYED" on a dark blue background. "I'll call that one the groovy blueberry."

"Ours is the peppermint balloon," Jake said.

"Oh, I'm sure it's a beauty too. I, um, didn't mean—"

Jake laughed. "Not to worry. All four balloons had availability when I made the reservation, but I chose the one I thought would be your least favorite for our flight. That way, you'd have the others as our backdrop. I knew you'd want to capture the scene and recreate it later on canvas."

"You're unbelievable, Jake Colby, down to the last detail. I hope you know how much I appreciate this evening and everything else you've done to make this summer memorable."

Jake's phone pinged, and he excused himself to engage in a series of back-and-forth texts. The profound smile that washed over his face told Miranda all she needed to know—he was communicating with his girlfriend. Whereas Miranda's relationship with Jake was based solely on friendship, Kasey was the girl who presumably became one with him.

Still, Miranda would embrace the fantasy that she and Jake were a couple, if only for the evening. Naturally, that's what the other passengers would assume. What constituted the term "couple" anyway? Sex didn't necessarily equate to emotional intimacy. Jake and Miranda's chemistry was undeniable. In many respects, she had never been closer to a man before.

She slipped away to where the first balloon was about to launch while Jake continued to binge text. The ground crew, exhibiting tireless effort, appeared to race against the clock, releasing the ropes and freeing the massive Paris balloon, to the delight of the eight waving passengers.

The balloon's gentle rise was a breathtaking sight. Still, Jake Colby monopolized Miranda's attention from across the field. As a sideline spectator, she watched him return his cell phone to his back pocket and initiate a conversation with an older couple. Whereas Miranda sought reasons to distance herself from others, Jake found the commonalities that drew people closer. Grandma Trudy may have entwined their lives for the summer, but Jake kept Miranda wanting more seasons.

Autumn was gearing up for its magical transformation in Cobblers Hill. But the upcoming months without Jake would leave

Miranda behind like a deflated balloon that lacked the elements to function. Then what? She caught her breath. There would be plenty of time to worry about tomorrow when it began. For today, Jake's happiness was all that mattered.

Weaving through the lively crowd, Miranda resumed her place in the fairy tale beside the man who'd become half to her whole. Before she could determine whether her brief disappearance had gone unnoticed, a burly man, sporting a cotton candy–like beard and an Indiana Jones hat, drew near.

"Hi, folks, I'm Bubba Louie—self-named, of course." He shouted over the fans while wiping the sweat from his forehead with a wrinkled handkerchief. "Anyone ever gone ballooning before?"

All four passengers stood motionless, except for the side-to-side swaying of their heads.

"You're in for a real treat, then. We'll take this baby to about fifteen hundred feet and drift above the treetops." Bubba used his stubby hand to mimic the balloon's gliding motion as their wide eyes followed. "Gimme a few minutes to get her fired up, and then the gents can assist their ladies in boarding."

Like a hibernating bear after a long winter's nap, the slumbering peppermint-patterned balloon rose from its side and slowly came to life. Although massive and intimidating, the standing balloon's red-and-white swirls resembled the sweetness of Christmas candy.

The other female passenger was first to climb aboard in her high-heeled shoes and sleeveless chiffon top. She warmed her slender arms with her hands as her hair and tiered skirt blew in the industrial fan's breeze.

"Check out what she has on," Jake whispered. "And it's only going to get cooler up there."

"We're having this conversation again, Jake, aren't we?" Miranda laughed. "I know what you're waiting to hear, so I'll just say it. I'm glad I listened to your advice to dress warmly tonight." She curtailed her playful giggles and secured a tightly wound ponytail. "Wherever would I be without you, Jake Colby?"

With a satisfied grin, Jake guided Miranda forward to board. "I don't know. But let's not find out."

Chapter 28

Miranda climbed into the gondola with ease, grateful to be wearing relaxed jeans and a cozy sweatshirt promoting Cobblers Hill in bold embroidered letters. Jake followed close behind. Whistles and cheers resonated from the lingering spectators. The ground crew detached ropes, releasing the rising balloon to the guardianship of nature. It drifted from the security of everything safe and familiar, slowly diminishing in size below.

Miranda clung to the edge of the gondola. The other two passengers were ghostly white.

"So that's it?" she whispered. "This massive thing is being held up in the air by a shooting flame that sounds like Darth Vader breathing?"

"And don't forget Bubba, of course." Jake chuckled.

The brawny pilot adjusted the burner levers while singing "Figaro," as if he were the operatic tenor Luciano Pavarotti.

"Why must he close his eyes with those high notes?" Miranda said.

When he wasn't exercising his vocal cords, Bubba made silly faces and cracked jokes at his own expense. He seemed to rely on entertainment and an infectious sense of humor to ease his travelers' apprehensions, but Miranda didn't relax her grip.

"You're aware he's the only one who knows how to fly this

thing, right? What if he becomes incapacitated in some way? Or if a bird punctures a hole in the lining?" She arched her head back. "There is no engine, no parachutes—no nothing."

"Then those wings you developed during our trapeze adventure will come in handy when we have to jump," Jake replied.

Miranda shot him a look.

"Okay, okay, no more teasing." He ran his fingers through his purposely messy hair. She loved when he did that, wishing, just once, for the opportunity. "Rather than think about what could go wrong, allow yourself to enjoy what seems right. There's more risk driving through town."

The other couple shared a similar lack of ballooning experience, but they didn't inspect the interior lining like Miranda. According to Jake, Inez Mary and Alberto Hugo were visiting the States from Spain. Their balloon ride commemorated fifty years of marriage. At least that was Jake's interpretation from what wasn't lost in translation.

Miranda relied upon universal smiles and nods to communicate with the older pair. Alberto held his wife's hand and kept her warm in his sheltering embrace. He swept silver strands of hair away from her cheeks and gazed into her eyes. It was no surprise their relationship had sustained five decades.

"What might have been" transported Miranda to hypothetical evenings spent slow dancing in Jake Colby's arms without the need for music. Wintry days together in cozy sweatshirts and fuzzy socks might have yielded candlelit evenings. Sunday morning breakfasts might have accompanied fall fireside weekends, while beach strolls and stargazing might have created endless summer nights.

Even the rising balloon and shrinking houses below couldn't interrupt Miranda's daydreams. Jake would have handpicked a simple bouquet of sunflowers and gifted them "just because" rather than for an occasion. Oh, how the smell of lilies in those elaborate floral arrangements reminded her of a funeral.

And he would have been ever-present, filling life's moments with reasons for her to smile. Jake Colby represented the sentiments of a Hallmark greeting card with the dreamiest cover.

Even with Miranda's limited relationship experience, she knew true love extended beyond romantic overtures and elaborate adventures. A loving, mutually respected relationship would take compromise and commitment. Given the opportunity in another lifetime, Miranda would strive to become the other half Jake Colby deserved.

"How's everyone doing?" Bubba Louie held up his stubby thumb. His fingernails needed a time-out almost as desperately as Miranda's once-chewed cuticles. "We are at our destination height, folks, so enjoy the serenity. We'll float from here."

"You hanging in there?" Jake asked Miranda.

"Surprisingly, I am. I've always loved the visual of hot-air balloons floating against a sapphire sky in those television commercials promoting life insurance. But I never had an aerial view of anything before other than what I saw on maps in a high school social studies class. Hilltops and treetops, coastlines, and vineyards—there's a different perspective every way I turn. And look at the geometric shapes—rectangular houses and circular pools."

"It doesn't even feel like we're moving, right?"

"Yeah, it's peaceful except for that occasional *whoosh* of the flame. But it's scary to think this balloon relies upon nature. Have you noticed there's virtually nothing holding us in this basket—I mean, gondola? No seat belts? I'd even settle for that suffocating trapeze harness right about now," she whispered. "If a fight broke out, or someone pushed us from behind, we could free-fall over the edge."

"Lucky for us, I don't foresee these two instigating a riot," Jake said of the other couple. Miranda covered her mouth as she giggled.

"That's a photo op right there." Bubba stepped toward them with lead feet and reached for Miranda's phone.

Jake and Miranda posed with rigid arms at their sides and programmed smiles.

"Come on, now. This ain't a class photo in prep school! You can do better, folks," Bubba huffed while tapping his pointy boot. The shaking gondola offered a not-so-subtle reminder they weren't on solid ground. "You're on a flight of a lifetime with the best pilot on this side of wherever. Let's capture the tender moment, for goodness' sake."

Jake grabbed Miranda in his arms, dipped her back, and planted an innocent kiss on her cheek, making her giggle and blush. The groovy blueberry balloon floated behind them, providing a colorful backdrop. Bubba captured the moment and then resumed his operations while singing, "That's Amore."

A dazed Miranda drew nourishing breaths while the sweet peppermint balloon drifted among the hopes and dreams others had entrusted to the heavens. Over time, she would revisit every detail of that photo, hoping a single memory could sustain a lifetime.

"Care to share those thoughts?" Jake asked.

"Is it possible to feel at peace yet petrified?"

"Petrified?" Jake's brows arched. "Of what? The landing?"

"No, as long as we're together, I feel safe. I'm afraid of what happens after the hundred days—fearful of never being this happy again." She gripped the ledge and didn't let go. "I don't remember when I was this much in harmony with life. I wish these feelings never had to end."

"They don't have to." He placed his hands on her shoulders as he had done during his trapeze pep talk. "This summer proved you are strong and capable. The decisions are yours from here. If you like Cobblers Hill, then extend your stay. Paint the changing seasons at Edens Cove and visit the farm stands. You'll find a fulfilling job in town while continuing to inspire others through your volunteer work. Join us for late-night bonfires and caroling during the holidays. Think of the fun excursions we can plan—hiking and kayaking and snowmobiling. We haven't even scratched the surface."

His words were spewing in one long, uninterrupted breath like he had waited all summer to free them. And while it was Miranda's decision whether or not to extend her stay, the circumstances and possible repercussions that followed weren't. Jake and Kasey had an arrangement of their own. It was only a matter of time until she fulfilled hers in Europe and returned to the States to retrieve the life she left behind.

Miranda turned her cheek from Jake. Everything responsible for making her time in Cobblers Hill meaningful would, inevitably, be swept aside like the withering leaves of the looming season.

"You make it sound easy, seamless," Miranda whispered, "but it's not that simple. Let's be honest here. This is all dwindling—the summer, Trudy's arrangement, our adventures."

"Listen," Jake whispered back, "you and I are overdue for a heart-to-heart chat. Maybe then you'll understand my hesitancy."

"I've been hesitant too, and I've avoided certain conversations all summer long—all my life long. I'm tired of being a hypocrite—I'm tired of running from the truth."

"I know. It's not an excuse, but our chat was interrupted by the downpour the other night. I figured we would pick up where we left off today. After seeing how anxious you were about our flight, I thought it was best to keep the conversation light."

"We can't talk here in the clouds. It's getting uncomfortable trying not to draw attention to ourselves." Miranda's eyes motioned to the other couple engaged in an animated conversation with Bubba, who was fluent in Spanish.

"How about we get a fresh start tomorrow after Gram's barbecue?" Jake suggested. "We can head down to the beach and spend some uninterrupted time together—you know, sort through things. Does that sound like a plan?"

Miranda gave a pressured nod but kept her gaze on the gondola floor.

"Okay, but for now, let me assure you that the connection I felt between us was real—*is* real," he said. "As you brought to my attention once before, no one can take our memories; we own them. Look at me, Miranda." He lifted her chin so her misty eyes could meet his. "This summer has been incredible, and it's not over yet."

"I'm beyond grateful for these hundred days of friendship with you, Jake," Miranda replied through frustrated whispers. "But what happens after my arrangement? There is no easy answer here. You have your life in Cobblers Hill, and I have mine elsewhere. Besides, I doubt Kasey would appreciate having me around. Being an appendage in your relationship is enough to send me packing."

She turned away. Only her grandmother, and perhaps Randy, or the characters in Jake's novel, were likely to empathize.

"Trust me, we'll figure this out." Jake offered a confident smile. "We will."

There would be no more rehearsals or facades. It was time to reveal the hidden truth—Miranda was in love with Jake Colby.

Chapter 29

Quaint Tudor shops lured tourists while benches welcomed those needing rest. Bicyclists, joggers, street-corner musicians, dog walkers—everyone in Cobblers Hill seemed to be enjoying a relaxed pace.

Smile after smile, townsfolk greeted Miranda as she meandered down tree-lined Main Street. Perhaps they recognized the day's significance in determining her future and the cottage's fate.

Inside Apple Dumpling Bakery, the hardworking staff was busy filling orders for their freshly made fruit pies and crusty artisan loaves. Across the way, ladies were stuffing baskets with the essentials for holiday entertaining, occasionally bidding a friendly "hello" to a familiar face.

Miranda browsed the boutiques, searching for a flattering sundress and a pair of sandals to complement her soon-to-be pedicured toes. If time permitted, she would replace her worn handbag with a trendier style and purchase sunglasses that accented her oval-shaped face.

The Petal Pushers florist arranged festive bouquets for Labor Day celebrations. Men drank espresso and read newspapers in the square where Miranda and Jake had slow danced under a ceiling of stars. A mason jar adorned with paper raffia ribbon—perfect for displaying sea glass memories—made her glance twice through the Potter's Wheel storefront window. So did her reflection.

Soon an improved and ever-so-irresistible version of Miranda Blair would make her debut at the Colbys' Labor Day barbecue, greeting family members fortunate to be part of Jake's heritage. And later that evening, she would empty the contents of her heart to Jake in a giant leap of faith.

Faint voices and laughter drifted from the Colby yard as the four o'clock hour approached. Miranda applied the finishing touches to her new look and stood before the floor mirror with Trudy's photo on the nearby dresser. Her new hairstyle boasted chunky layers that fell along her shoulders and a few blond highlights, which framed her face. The stylist recommended salon products that tamed curls and demonstrated how to use a round brush to straighten her hair from its roots.

A confident woman smiled back at Miranda. Sweeps of blush to her cheekbones brightened her porcelain skin, and a few strokes of mascara accented her prominent lashes. The clarity in her enhanced blue eyes reflected a vision for tomorrow.

While the yellow cotton sundress on the mannequin would have been a safe choice, the more expensive floral one was unparalleled. The spaghetti straps and hem above the knee revealed Miranda's toned arms and legs, which had suspended her from the trapeze and propelled her forward.

"It's probably only the residual effect of my makeover, Grandma, but I'm thinking more optimistically today. I would never intervene in Jake's happiness, but I did consider the possibility that Kasey and Jake have drifted apart. There's that slim chance his girlfriend connected with a fellow pastry chef in Europe, bonding over tarte tatin. In that case, it wouldn't be unreasonable to think Kasey might extend her stay, right? This summer has taught me that life's colors could change in a single season."

She sashayed from different angles.

"I'm a different person, and I have your arrangement to thank. I once resented these hundred days, but now I couldn't be more grateful for them."

She dabbed the corners of her eyes with a tissue. Tears were not allowed, even if they were happy ones. "I hope you're cheering me on. I could sure use the encouragement, Grandma. But somehow, I think you've been guiding my footsteps from the other side all along."

She drew a deep breath and exhaled through pursed lips while fanning her cheeks.

"It's a huge risk to reveal my heart to Jake tonight. It might complicate our friendship, and the awkwardness alone could close the door to Cobblers Hill. But if there is a chance, even the slightest sliver of hope, to have the greatest reward imaginable—a life spent beside Jake Colby—I'll take that risk. Wish me luck!"

Her once-fragmented heart was now whole, beating with the kind of passion reserved for romance novels. The moment had come to share her enhanced appearance and outlook with someone other than Trudy's old photograph and an antique floor mirror. She would heed Mark Twain's advice and go out on a limb where the fruit lay.

Miranda hoped it wasn't too late for the harvest.

Chapter 30

The bustling Colby yard encompassed everything that Miranda lacked—family. Had she anticipated such a large crowd of unfamiliar faces, she would have reconsidered Addie's Labor Day invitation.

There might have been time for a quick exit had two little girls failed to notice Miranda.

"Play with us," said the one with patches of freckles on her sun-tanned cheeks and streaming blue hair ribbons.

"We are having a tea party," explained the other girl, sporting curled pigtails and a Kermit the Frog bandage on her elbow.

The darling little ladies had taken Miranda by the hand and led her to a shady corner of the yard next to Addie's prize-winning rosebushes.

"Okay, but I like my tea with lots of honey," Miranda replied, her Jake radar on high alert.

He made his way across the yard, carrying folding chairs in his muscular arms, and kicked a rolling soccer ball into a makeshift goal comprised of garbage pails. The boys nearby cheered.

"I'm Emily," the little girl said, pointing to herself, "but every-one calls me Ems or Emmie. Like the letters *M* and *E*. This is my sister Laura Jayne, but we call her Laura." She put a finger to her cheek and tilted her head. "Mommy yells, 'Laura Jayne' when she is mad. What's your name?"

"I'm Miranda."

"What's your other name?" Emmie asked.

"Just Miranda. I never had a nickname. Kind of boring, right?" She wrinkled her nose, and the girls giggled.

"Everyone's got a short name." Laura prepared tea in pastel-colored Fisher-Price cups. "Maybe you forgot yours."

"Maybe you're right. Do you come here often?"

"Yep." Emmie used her plastic spoon to pretend-mix a little too vigorously for hot tea.

"Who are you visiting?" Even with her lack of experience with kids, Miranda knew they only divulged information when they had something to share.

"Our family." Emmie handed over a cup of tea, hot off the imaginary stove. "I like your lipstick and eye powder."

"Well, thank you!"

"We go to kindergarten," Laura said. "Our teacher is Ms. Roberta."

"I almost forgot school is back in session. Wow, such big girls you are!"

The fall semester would have been underway in Barron Park. Miranda still had three weeks in the arrangement before resuming her focus on Etruscan art and adolescent dysphoria or attending lectures on King Tut's tomb. Until then, it was taboo to think about classes, textbook price gouging, financial loans, and a meaningless routine without Jake Colby.

Miranda had been around the girls' age when she last visited Cobblers Hill. Although it had taken twenty years to receive another invitation, the summer compensated for the lifelong absence.

"And you wear nail polish too, I see. Pink is my favorite color," Miranda said.

The girls danced around giddily, twirling in their matching star-spangled dresses.

"I had my toes painted." Miranda wiggled them. "What do you ladies think? Do you like the color, or should I go with a different shade next time? A bright red? Or how about peach?"

"I see you've met my nieces."

Jake's voice resonated from behind, awakening her senses as it always had.

"Indeed. We are having a tea party. Isn't that right, girls?"

"Miranda is our new friend," Emmie said. "She's so pretty."

"And she smells like flowers," Laura added.

In a blink, the children wandered off to another part of the yard to catch butterflies.

"I agree with my nieces." Jake gave Miranda a once-over. "I'm speechless. You look—incredible!"

She blushed, unsure of which way to turn now that her little friends had fled.

"Here, come meet the family." Jake led her to two women discussing Columbus Day weekend plans involving private tennis lessons and a Groupon.

"Bree, Linz, I'd like you to meet Miranda Blair." Jake turned to Miranda. "These are my older sisters, Brielle and Lindsay."

"You always have to throw the age thing in there, don't you, bro?" Bree gave him a nudge. "We've heard so much about you, Miranda. It's nice to meet the mystery neighbor. No need for formalities; you can call us by our nicknames."

"Hope you've been enjoying your time here," Linz said.

"It's nice to meet you both. And absolutely! There's so much to love about Cobblers Hill. Your brother has been showing me around."

"I'm sure he has." Bree gave Jake a look, which made him turn away and Miranda wish she were telepathic.

"What a cute dress," Bree said.

"I love the shops on Main Street." Miranda offered a radiant smile as if she had just returned from her annual dental cleaning.

Linz whispered to Miranda, "It's nice to see our brother smile, too, these days. Thank you for that."

Miranda beamed from the greatest compliment of all—being credited with Jake's happiness.

"You already met Linz's girls, and Bree has four sons: Petey, Jim, Rob, and little Morty." Jake pointed to each of his nephews in age order. "The boys are involved in a competitive game of soccer. We've got the Colby World Cup going on over there." He raised his right arm and pumped his fist with a cheer.

"You're blessed with beautiful families," Miranda said to Jake's sisters. "I had make-believe tea with your daughters, Linz, and they are adorable. I heard about their class and teacher, Ms. Roberta."

"It's been an adjustment for them. My Emmie is loving school—especially the bus ride and snack time. Oh, and she's thrilled to have a unicorn backpack." Linz chuckled. "Laura, on the other hand, hasn't decided if she plans to return to school after the holiday weekend." She gave an eye roll. "Anyway, how long do you plan on staying in Cobblers Hill?"

"Excuse us," Jake interrupted, his timing, once again, impeccable. "Mind if I steal Miranda for a few? I think Gram is waiting for me to introduce her to everyone before their game begins." He said to Miranda, "Things can get pretty intense once the cards are dealt."

"Yeah, you'd better run then." Linz laughed.

"Go, go, go." Bree shooed them with her hand. "We've all learned the hard way not to keep Gram waiting."

As Jake whisked Miranda in the other direction, she whispered, "Thanks," out of the corner of her mouth.

"I've got you covered. We can avoid that question until later."

Butterflies took flight in Miranda's stomach with boundless

energy. Hickory smoke trailed from the grill, but her appetite waned.

"Are your parents here yet? I'm looking forward to meeting the two people responsible for raising such a fine man."

"No, unfortunately, they couldn't be here today. My oldest sister, Debbie, wasn't able to join us either."

"Oh, um, okay." Miranda kept her shoulders back to shield her disappointment.

Jake led her to where the rest of the family was relaxing within the shade of Pop's sheltering oak tree.

"Everyone," he announced, "this is my friend, Miranda Blair. Miranda, these are my aunts, uncles, and cousins."

"Hi, Miranda!" they yelled out in unison.

"Hi," she replied with a generic wave. "It's a pleasure to meet you all on this beautiful afternoon, perfect for a family barbecue." Miranda shifted her weight back and forth, alternating hips.

"This is ideal bike-riding weather." A woman seated on the Adirondack swing balanced a plate of piled nachos on her lap. She pulled at strands of cheese like she was playing the harp. "Has my nephew taken you to the Hendrickson Trail yet?"

"Come on now, Mary," the heavyset man, presumably an uncle, said. His brightly colored hibiscus shirt and turquoise shorts were appropriate for a Hawaiian luau. "You remember being their age once. I'm sure these kids found more creative ways to work up a sweat together." He winked and let out a puff of stinky cigar smoke through his laughter.

The older ladies fanned their hands in the air and wrinkled their noses. Mary shook her head with a *tsk, tsk.*

"I haven't been on a bicycle in as long as I can remember," Miranda said. "There aren't any bike trails back home, and most of the roads don't have a designated lane for cyclists. I do run a lot, though."

A young guy with long hair and even longer legs, reclining in an anti-gravity chair, pulled himself forward.

"Cousin Mike here," he said with a raised hand. "It's always nice to meet a fellow runner. I've been resting some tight hamstrings lately but itching for an early morning run. How many miles are you good for each week?"

"These days, um . . ." Miranda glanced up at Pop's sheltering oak, "about twenty-five, give or take."

"Impressive," the cousin replied with a thumbs-up. Then he replaced his AirPods and reclined again.

"There's something about being close to the water that energizes me here," Miranda remarked to whoever was still listening. "I find the salt air agreeable."

"Well, you'll love the trail—part forest, part coast. I'm Jake's aunt Wanda, by the way." She flashed a pearly white smile of oversized teeth.

With so many relatives, Miranda lost track of Mary.

"It's quite a workout," Aunt Wanda said. "The hills get me every time."

Multiple bracelets clunked against the woman's wrists, and a cheetah-brimmed chapeau flopped over one eye. She appeared to be anyone but an athlete with her delicate frame, but Miranda knew appearances could be deceiving.

Addie chimed in, "That's got more to do with ya ripe old age, Wanda, than anythin' else."

"Jake, remember to bring bug spray if you bike there," said the gentleman wearing brown Moses sandals over black, gold-toed socks. "Get the organic kind, DEET-free. Poison ivy is everywhere. Ticks too. I hear Lyme disease cases are on the rise this year. The trails aren't always marked well, and the less traveled ones are overgrown. You've gotta contend with thorns and invasive plants. And bring plenty of water—the filtered kind, not those faucet chemicals."

He earned every gray hair on his balding head, and his scratching made Miranda's skin itch.

"Gosh dang it," Addie said. "Hush ya mouth and loosen that there collar of yours, Ralph. Ya oughta live a lil'. I declare Jake and Miranda ain't got nothin' to worry about. Those trails are for explorin', I say. Ya oughta let that forest knock some sense into ya."

The others cheered Addie on until she took a bow, and Ralph sunk lower in his chair. Perhaps the Blairs had eccentric relatives who engaged in playful banter too. Miranda would never know.

"We've tackled a few items from our summer adventure file, but our to-do list grows. There never seems to be enough time for all we've planned." Jake reached into the snack bowl for a handful of chips and tossed them into his mouth. "We can head there for a ride one day this week," he said, crunching.

Emmie and Laura returned, taking Miranda by the hand and pulling her in another direction. Jake stayed behind to play a round of canasta with his uncles. Occasionally, she noticed him staring at her from a distance. Or maybe Jake caught Miranda being the admirer.

When the twins moved on to their next activity, hopscotch, Bree and Linz lured Miranda over to Addie's wishing well. She had to tread lightly. Their loyalties were likely to Kasey, or maybe no one was good enough for their only brother.

Small talk about Addie's great-grands and their after-school activities ensued. First, Linz and Bree chatted about the upcoming PTA meeting agenda, including a revised proposal for the district lunch program. Then they discussed new restrictions for the Halloween parade and a zero-tolerance policy for scary masks or inappropriate costumes on school grounds. With a planted smile and a stifled yawn, Miranda's head moved back and forth between the sisters' conversations as if she viewed a tennis match without knowing the game.

Linz plugged an epic candy sale at Costco and promoted a down-loadable coupon. Then Bree mentioned a school fundraiser for new athletic uniforms held at the Red, White, and Brew coffeehouse.

"Speaking of a coffeehouse, I remember my short-lived barista days back home and those mortifying milk-splattering moments while frothing," Miranda said with flushed cheeks. "The manager nitpicked my every move behind the counter and reprimanded me for adding too many ice cubes to a cold brew. No matter how many lemon wedges a loyal customer requested in their extra-large, grossly overpriced iced tea, they were only permitted two. Unfortunately, I had to learn that the hard way."

While there was an occasional chuckle from Jake's sisters, the chill dissipated when they learned Miranda had prepared a café au lait for their favorite singer. The shaggy-haired, nose-pierced vocalist Cy Kershaw had been on a book-signing tour that led him to the local bookstore in Barron Park. He and his army of no-nonsense bodyguards stopped for a caffeine break at the coffeehouse.

Linz and Bree giggled like lovestruck schoolgirls upon seeing the dated photo Miranda kept on her phone, posing with their tattooed crush. Eager for every detail, they asked what he ordered, how much he tipped, and whether she received free concert tickets to any of their sold-out shows. Once again, music had come to Miranda's rescue.

On a few awkward occasions that afternoon, Addie boasted to others about Miranda's volunteerism and commitment to maintaining her town's history. An inspired Cousin Faye, the preppy lady with taut skin around her eyes, pledged to support her local historical society. Two of Jake's uncles offered to write checks, although it was hardly Miranda's intention to fundraise.

Had Addie known Miranda's original plans to destroy the next-door cottage's history, there may not have been accolades. Still, Miranda was pleased to leave a favorable impression on Jake's relatives.

When everyone had their fill of hot dogs and cheese-laden burgers, Addie's award-winning tomato salad, and Cajun fries, they gathered for their annual Pictionary game. As was their tradition, the women challenged the men, and everyone joined in on the fun, from the youngest children to the senior relatives.

With booming voices and brewing competition, the Colby family did not allow Miranda's reservations. Thrown into the mix of animated characters, she stood at the makeshift easel and sketched silly graphics with a swift hand, gaining her fellow teammates' respect from the initial round. And while Jake's gaze had settled on Miranda rather than her drawings, she pretended not to notice.

Two intense hours of laughter and creativity led the ladies to victory, earning them the title of Pictionary champs. The losing side—the Colby men—agreed to start the bonfire and make s'mores while the winners gloated. The twins delighted in gooey marshmallows and melted chocolate that dripped everywhere. With sticky fingers and wide yawns, the girls turned in early for baths.

Once the little ones weren't around, Jake's nephews didn't waste time telling gruesome bonfire stories about avenging zombies from the underworld. Without having Jake beside her, pulling her in close, Miranda stole glimpses of him through the dancing flames. She had waited two decades to enjoy a Labor Day barbecue with family. And now, Miranda wanted to share more leisurely afternoons and festive occasions with Jake and his relatives, having felt like a Colby herself for the day.

While Jake's brothers-in-law loaded their trunks, the kids fell asleep in the back seats, presumably surrendering to exhaustion from hours of fresh air fun.

Headlights disappeared down Primrose Lane, and the last of the relatives hugged Miranda goodbye, expressing their hope to see her soon. Depending on her imminent conversation with Jake, she might never enjoy their company again.

Chapter 31

"Thanks for today's invite, Jake," Miranda said. "The Colby barbecue was everything I envisioned for a family gathering."

She was practically skipping down Primrose Lane toward the beach for their overdue heart-to-heart chat.

"Your relatives are wonderful, although playing games with them was intense. Wow, were they competitive!" She laughed. "And I might have to sleep with the lamp on after hearing your nephews' ghost stories. Those boys have some vivid imaginations."

Despite the glorious summer day, the crisp evening air offered a not-so-subtle reminder fall wasn't far behind. Jake kept his hands in his sweatshirt pockets and his gaze on the winding road ahead.

"It was too bad your parents and older sister weren't able to make the party. I was looking forward to meeting them. Another time, I hope."

Jake cleared his throat.

"You are blessed to have such a close-knit family." Miranda's rambling words likely sounded like gibberish. "I would've given anything over the years to be surrounded by that love and craziness. And those innocent little ones—I always wanted to be an aunt."

Aside from the competing hum of cicadas and crunching gravel under their sneakers, her words met silence. "I'm sorry to be monopolizing the conversation. I'm getting a little carried away by today's fun, but I've been looking forward to having our chat tonight."

Jake trudged along with labored footsteps. Despite knowing the way, he appeared lost. With the passage of each block, the silence became more deafening.

"Okay," Miranda said. "I'm listening when you're ready."

"For what?"

"For whatever is on your mind. Something in the air makes me feel like we're strangers again."

"Everything is fine, Miranda."

"Is it me? Did I do something?"

"Of course not. My family loved spending time with you today."

Separated by awkwardness, they reached the shore. Jake dropped the beach towel on the sand without securing the perfect spot free of bothersome shells. He plopped down on the wrinkled cloth and stared out over the water.

"Please join me." He patted the spot next to him. "Like you, I rehearsed conversations all summer, but I don't feel any more prepared to have them."

Neither Jake nor Miranda bothered to remove their sneakers or admire the moonlight. Instead, he reached for a beer from his six-pack and used his sweatshirt to untwist the cap.

"You opened up to me on many occasions and trusted me," he said. "I hope you'll never question my motives or my genuine concern for your happiness."

She waited for the "but" or "so" to follow. It didn't. Without offering Miranda a beer or making a toast, Jake took a swig from the bottle.

"I only told you part of my story that night in the town square. I felt it was best to wait until you—we—were ready. As difficult as those weeks were after losing my grandfather and inheriting the family business, they paled to what happened next."

Despite her trapeze success, Miranda hated amusement park thrill rides that twisted and plummeted into unchartered territory. Now she sat quietly beside Jake on the emotional roller coaster, hugging her knees and getting ready for takeoff.

"It was the last week of May, senior year of college," he started. "I had accepted my revised plans to run Colby's Hardware and looked forward to celebrating my college achievements over Memorial Day weekend. Graduation was supposed to be a happy milestone. Gram used to say it was like crossing the finish line after a challenging marathon."

Jake chugged his beer. Miranda's mouth was dry.

"I was one of the students being honored at a Phi Beta Kappa commencement ceremony three nights before graduation. I told my parents to skip the event. It wasn't necessary to extend their trip and take more time off work. But of course, they insisted on being there. If only they had listened."

Jake dug burrows in the sand with his sneakers. Along with the frequent rise and fall of his Adam's apple, his eyes winced as he spoke.

"The hours passed, and the ceremony was about to begin. My parents hadn't arrived. Even considering traffic, they were hours behind schedule. I bombarded them with calls and texts, but there was no reply. By the time the guest speaker led the Pledge of Allegiance, I was stone-cold, searching the audience for them and realizing something was wrong. Until this day, I can taste the poison that settled in my throat."

In a flashback, Miranda was five again, standing by her bedroom window in her pastel nightgown. As cozy homes were shutting down for the night, she waited in vain with her floppy-eared stuffed rabbit for her father's Buick to turn the corner.

The dampness of the sand penetrated the beach towel, which was considerably smaller and thinner than the plush picnic blanket that accompanied Jake and Miranda's summer outings. The wind whipped, and the waves crashed against the shoreline with a bitter vengeance. Nothing was as it had been, including the chill in the air that replaced the warmth they had basked in throughout the arrangement.

Jake was too fixed on the dark horizon to notice Miranda's trembles. This time, there would be no offering of his frayed sweatshirt or the comfort of hot coffee prepared light and sweet. His empty beer bottle hit the sand with a thump.

"The teenage driver misjudged the impact of her afternoon cocktail binge and crossed the divider into head-on traffic. The authorities claimed she exceeded the speed limit by thirty miles per hour." His lips quivered with each word. "It was all over in an instant. I lost them both."

Miranda gasped. "I don't . . . I'm . . . I'm so sorry for your loss—for how inconsiderate I've been. I didn't realize. You never told me—" Frantically, she blurted, "Your oldest sister?"

"Debbie's fine. She didn't attend the barbecue because she lives on the West Coast. You would have loved my parents. They meant everything to me."

Miranda leaned in and wrapped her arms around Jake without hesitation, her heart racing in sync with his.

"It's hard to believe my mom and dad never saw me graduate, and there won't be a mother-son dance at my wedding. They will never hold my first child." Jake inched back and locked eyes with Miranda. "And they will never meet you."

His indigestible words churned in Miranda's stomach, and tears expressed what her tongue didn't say.

"It was unfair to have taken so much from me in such a short period—Pop, my parents, my college years, my passion for writing, my career goals." Jake freed his hands to open another beer. "It brought me to my knees."

From an outsider's perspective, the Colbys were the quintessential all-American family with a flawless heritage, or perhaps that was the mirage Miranda wanted to believe. She had drawn from Jake's strength all summer long and prioritized self-healing while his wounds ran deep. Miranda lost one parent; Jake lost both. But whereas she had exposed some rusty links to her past, offering them up for scrutiny that summer, Jake had kept his concealed.

"I returned to Cobblers Hill as a broken man," he continued, his voice surrendering to emotion. "Getting through each day was painful and exhausting. I moved in with Gram, who was a fragile, emotional mess. She sat in her rocking chair all day, clinging to photo albums."

"Oh, Addie." Miranda shook her lowered head, but the harrowing images of pain and suffering, fragility, and brokenness lingered.

"There were days she didn't eat or communicate. It was gut-wrenching to witness Gram cocoon. That's how she coped."

"I wish I could have been there for you both." Miranda cupped Jake's face and stared into his cloudy eyes.

"I know." He placed his hands over hers and guided them down. "My life didn't serve much purpose other than caring for Gram and keeping Colby's Hardware alive. But even there, I struggled to fill Pop's big shoes."

"Thankfully, you had your family. Tell me you accepted their support. Tell me you allowed them to look after you during that time." Her body ached from their shared loss and emptiness.

"Like you, I learned quickly that each family member grieves differently. Some rise to the occasion, even if it's short-lived. Others withdraw, which was the case for many of the Colbys. My sisters had marriages and newborns to distract them. Gram and I were pretty much on our own."

Jake flicked the cap of his third Corona into the sand and downed the bottle.

"News travels fast in Cobblers Hill, but the monthly sales were poor, even with the town's support. You can't have a lucrative business when you forget to order inventory. The bills were incurring finance charges, and the phone calls started rolling in from debt collectors. I felt like a failure who had disappointed everyone, including myself."

Jake clenched his hands into fists. "I wanted my pre-tragedy life back with only trivial problems. I pulled into Gram's driveway one early evening after a brutal day at the store, shut the engine, and sat completely numb. I had reached my rock bottom."

"Yet you welcomed my pity party to town years later," Miranda said. "You helped me overcome my obstacles. You encouraged me to forgive my past and dream about a bright future. You were selfless, and I wasn't."

She turned away from the man she had fallen in love with and faced the flashing lights of a distant fishing boat.

"Please don't, Miranda." Jake stroked her hair, sliding damp strands from her tear-soaked cheeks. "I should have shared this with you sooner, but it's not something easy to discuss. I know you can relate."

He stared at his empty beer bottle, picking at its label with his fingernail. "It was that somber night when she first entered my life. We weren't friends back then, barely acquaintances, yet there she was, knocking on my car window and holding a dinner basket."

Kasey's willingness to care for a vulnerable Jake relieved Miranda.

"It was awkward accepting her hospitality," he explained. "I had never extended courtesies her way, yet her kindness overshadowed my indifference. She disguised hope in comfort food."

He gathered a mound of sand beside him, molding and smoothing its sides. Whatever he had buried deep within the pile stayed hidden.

"Our relationship didn't stop there," Jake said. "She checked on us daily and ran our errands. We spent the first unbearable holidays together. Somehow, she pulled us through them. She helped us learn how to breathe again."

Jake's muted gray eyes welled, although he hadn't permitted one tear to fall, perhaps relying on beer and the closeness of Miranda for consolation.

"After my sisters and I sold our childhood home and divided the estate, she encouraged me to take the necessary time I needed to get lost and find myself again. Only then, with her commitment to Gram and the help of my brothers-in-law, who temporarily ran the store, I traveled the continents. They were times spent wandering, but I needed to remove myself from here to gain a new perspective somewhere else."

"That's why you said your travels were self-seeking."

Kasey was more than Jake's girlfriend. As his saving grace, she'd reserved his heart long ago and integrated a portion of his soul for which Miranda was now grateful.

"I was in survival mode, and it was a healing journey." Jake zippered his sweatshirt and pulled Miranda closer. "She permitted me to find happiness again, and together we helped Gram. If it weren't for her, I honestly don't know where I would be right now."

She could feel his chest rise as he took an exaggerated breath like it was his last.

"Your grandmother saved my life, Miranda."

Chapter 32

M iranda stared at Jake with wild, fiery eyes.
"Did you say my grandmother? So all this time, you talked about Gertrude Blair, not Kasey?"

"Yes, Trudy was the one who saved Gram and me." Jake fidgeted on the beach towel like a sugar-charged child. He wiped his mouth with the back of his hand.

"We've spent the entire summer together, and all along you led me to believe Trudy was a stranger. Why didn't you mention this before tonight? Why didn't you tell me you had a relationship with her? Why, Jake, why?"

"I planned on sharing this with you sooner; it was difficult not to say anything. You arrived in town guarded and fragile, so Gram and I thought it was best to give you a few days to settle in."

"A few days? Try a few months." Miranda shouted her words as if Jake were far away rather than by her side. She rose to her feet, her frantic eyes surveying her surroundings.

"Hear me out," he pleaded, his head hung low. "The more I learned about your struggles and empathized with your past, the more I wanted to protect you. Later, when you made peace with your grandmother and her arrangement, I feared compromising your progress. I never meant to hurt you. Unfortunately, you and I were guilty of not asking questions or volunteering information."

"I know, Jake, but I deserved the truth before now, even if I didn't outright ask for it." Miranda spoke through gritted teeth. "You wanted me to trust you, and then you betrayed my trust by withholding information. And Adelaide did too!"

"Be upset with me, but please don't blame Gram. It would destroy her to know she hurt you." Jake tugged on his lower lip, twisting and contorting it. "Besides, I assured her I'd tell you about the past—both yours and ours and how they overlapped. I didn't want her reliving those painful memories."

"Okay, but you don't have an excuse," Miranda said.

He stood and reached for her, pulling her close to him. His breath smelled of stale beer, and his eyes were glazed.

"Tell me you wouldn't have regarded me as an enemy in your family struggle if you had known about my relationship with Trudy."

"Unbelievable!" Miranda paced back and forth with her arms crossed.

"You can't, can you? It's true. You would have resented me from the beginning. You wouldn't have given me a chance—us a chance."

"There is no us, Jake! There is only Kasey. I thought you were talking about her all along. I assumed she was the one to help you heal. And don't tell me what I would or wouldn't have done."

Jake ran his fingers through his messy hair and pointed to the towel. "Please, sit and let me finish before you jump to conclusions."

Miranda plopped down on the sand without an uttered reply. The crashing waves seemed to empathize with her fury. Or perhaps it was the shoreline, barraged and forever changed by the ruthless tide, to which she could relate.

"Gram and I assumed Trudy was a loner for most of the time she lived here. None of the Colbys had a relationship with her beyond an occasional wave. She didn't socialize with the other neighbors either. Things were quiet next door, even on holidays. If there were visitors, we never noticed them. Trudy spent most of her time alone in her garden—her sanctuary."

Miranda covered her head with her hands, the impact of his words like the crashing of tree limbs against the unforgiving forest floor.

"We assumed Trudy had some buried issues and respected her privacy. But looking back, we were partially responsible for helping her build a wall. I regret that now. It wasn't until our family's tragedy that Trudy revealed a different side. First, there was dinner and a few kind words, then a picnic basket of treats left on the porch, followed by an offering of iced tea in her yard for a change of scenery."

He grabbed handfuls of powdery sand and let them sift through his fingers. When the sand ran out, he reached for more.

"Trudy assured me we'd keep the conversation light, but I needed to talk. There I was, a grown man seeking the wisdom and companionship of an elderly woman I barely knew most of my life, even though she lived next to Gram. Does that sound familiar?"

Silence met his confession.

"Trudy became the grandmotherly figure I temporarily lost in Gram and the motherly figure taken from me too soon. I know these words are difficult to hear, but it doesn't change anything between you and me."

"How can you say that? It changes everything!" Miranda said. "You had a relationship with my grandmother when I, her only granddaughter, didn't. She chose to be there for you yet abandoned me like my father. All along, you hid this from me."

Jake reached over to Miranda. She jolted her shoulder.

"That's what I meant when I said you'd resent me and my relationship. Don't you see? Trudy was a broken lady who tried to compensate for shortcomings in her family by helping to restore happiness to ours. She never asked for anything in return. As Gram and I grew stronger, she became more fragile. I would visit a few times a week, mowing the lawn or fixing something around the cottage. But it was the unfinished business in her personal life that taunted her.

"One afternoon," Jake said, "Gram and I sat in your grandmother's yard. Stuttering her words, Trudy told us how her only son's mental illness had turned him into a changed man he, himself, feared. He left behind a wife and young daughter to shield them from his frightening fits of rage and depression.

"According to Trudy, she supported his decision to leave, knowing it would ensure her granddaughter's safety while he sought help. Her daughter-in-law, though, felt differently. She wanted him to take responsibility for his illness at home. She believed together they could bring him out of his depression. Who was right, and who was wrong? Gram and I didn't think it was our place to judge."

Jake extended his hand to Miranda—the same hand she had longed to hold all summer, feel his fingers entwined with hers, and acknowledge their bond. Instead, she rocked from side to side, dodging his curveballs.

"Trudy then informed us of—um—her son's untimely passing and how her daughter-in-law had blocked communication." Jake studied the palm of his rejected hand, tracing the life line with his thumb. "After the years you spent avoiding the unknown, it was difficult for me to become the provider of missing pieces. The last thing I wanted was to cause you any more pain. That's why I hesitated to share these details. Please talk to me."

Victor Blair had always been dead. At least that's what Miranda preferred to think than accept he was out there somewhere, denying his wife and child. It was only an assumption.

She rubbed her forehead, but the pressure kept building, and the pain grew deeper. Each sob reflected a different sadness: a denied relationship with her grandmother, her father's passing, and the evening's lost potential with Jake.

"Trudy sought information about her granddaughter and heard about her achievements and milestones through distant sources," Jake explained. "She celebrated her birthday every April twenty-second and thought about her each Christmas morning when she donated gifts to the orphanage. It destroyed her to be distant from her family. Maybe she could have tried harder to reconcile, but she didn't, and time was running out."

The biting chill and wind were ruthless like the unveiling of truth. With tingling in Miranda's fingers and toes, she was too numb to budge. She remained in her cocoon and prayed the storm would pass soon.

"Trudy told us about the plans in her will to summon her granddaughter to Cobblers Hill. And when she asked for my support, I made a promise."

"So that's what this is about? Our friendship fulfilled another one of my grandmother's arrangements?" The poisoned words spewed off Miranda's tongue. "You befriended me to keep a promise to her—not because you liked me, wanted to spend time with me, and believed in me?"

She doubled over, covering the open wounds that had begun to heal. "This setup was more twisted than I even imagined. It was a mistake to let my guard down and subject my heart to this. I should have known better."

"Not so. Listen to me," Jake pleaded. "There was no way of knowing how many years would pass before Trudy left us and her arrangement began. You could have come here with your husband and family. Or I could have had a wife and child. I never agreed to spend so much time with you or think of you every second we were apart."

If only Miranda believed Jake's words of conviction. If only she could restore the bond between them and salvage the night that was supposed to be unforgettable but for different reasons. If only a summertime's worth of trust wasn't broken in seconds.

"I'll never forget sharing bits of my history with you in front of Colby's Hardware," Jake said. "Even if my nostalgia triggered your childhood disappointments, you were caring and supportive, Miranda." He took more frequent swigs of his beer before pressing on. "The other friends I had shared that piece of myself with were anxious to return to a lighter, self-centered conversation. I knew then you were someone special—someone I wanted to have in my life.

"Later that day, we searched for sea glass after lunch. I watched as you combed the beach with such innocence and wonder. It made me want to open your eyes and heart this summer. We had chemistry, ease in our conversation, and respect for our differences. I didn't want to lose you before I had a chance to know you. I also didn't want to compromise Trudy's arrangement. My instincts told me if I acted on my desires, I might push you away. Are you with me?"

Miranda pulled her hood over her head and warmed her hands in her pockets, but there was no chance of resuscitating a stone-cold heart. Even the moon's glow couldn't shed light on what was transpiring.

"I figured if you knew I had someone special in my life, you wouldn't feel threatened by spending time with me. It would allow us to create a solid foundation of friendship we could build upon after the hundred days."

Miranda stood again, dusted the sand from her jeans, and took a few steps toward the water, keeping her back to Jake. The wind confronted her, pressing her clothing against her skin and forcing her eyes to close.

"So I told you about Kasey." Jake's voice cracked like a pubescent teenager. "Except I left out the one significant detail—um, we broke up after college."

Miranda gasped and covered her mouth.

"Kasey was the girlfriend who cheated on me when Pop passed. We haven't spoken since, and she probably is off in Europe somewhere, married to a rich guy who could afford her lavish life-style. I've coasted these past few years since my parents' death, trying to rebuild myself. When Trudy died, I feared I would return to that place of emptiness I had worked so hard to leave behind."

How could Miranda have been so naive and vulnerable and trusting? How would she ever recover from the disappointment inflicted by Jake Colby? How could a night of such promise become a letdown?

Miranda eyed Jake, venom surging from her throat, and asked the one question that summed up all the others. "How could you?"

"The closer we became, the more fearful I was of losing you when I had already lost so much in my life," Jake said, wiping the beer bottle's condensation and appearing as a fragment of the man he used to be. "I hoped you would forget about Kasey so I wouldn't have to keep the facade, and for a while there, I thought you did. Then you asked about her that night at the concert, and I was a coward. Rather than be honest, I complicated the situation even more. The immediate connection I mentioned was our relationship—our chemistry. And when I commented on how someone else's happiness meant everything to me, it was your happiness."

"I have to go, Jake," a defeated Miranda said in a wearied voice, barely above a whisper. "You satisfied your arrangement with my grandmother, and soon I'll have fulfilled mine."

Tears streamed down her cheeks, leaving behind parallel mascara lines in their path. It didn't matter anymore. Nothing did.

"I have to say, you had me fooled this summer. You weren't anything like the man I thought you were. All that remains is a shell of a person who violated my trust."

"I never claimed to be perfect," he replied sorrowfully. "I wish I could have lived up to your expectations."

"Good luck with your book. I'm sure you'll have plenty of juicy content from our summer together, making for an exceptional read. Say goodbye to Adelaide for me. It'll be too painful to see her before I leave. She became like a grandmother to me, even if it was orchestrated."

"Don't go! Hear me out."

"You've done enough talking. I wish I hadn't been listening."

Miranda walked with labored footsteps and then sprinted the remaining way, leaving Jake with his empty beer bottles, a dimming lantern, and the sting of bitter sentiments.

Chapter 33

F all was still days away, yet there had been a handing over of the season's torch that extinguished summer's potential.

In June, Miranda couldn't wait to put the resented arrangement in the past. When love walked into her life, she wished she could hold the clock's hands to extend her stay. Now she rushed against the sunrise to return home two weeks before her hundred-day deadline. Like Jake Colby, the passage of time had brought disappointment.

A consoling tissue box accompanied Miranda across the cottage's creaky floorboards. The den walls stared back at her blankly. All that remained on them were the dark outlines of Gertrude's inspirational plaques. They had likely offered Randy and the visiting next-door neighbors the same broken promises. Those plaques occupied the trash now so they wouldn't mislead others.

The moldy potting shed relinquished Gertrude Blair's stored belongings. Miranda couldn't expose her grandmother's keepsakes to winter's harsh elements. Trudy meant too much to the Colbys, having shared in their history. Rightfully, the neighbors were the more appropriate choice to inherit these possessions.

She resealed the cardboard with packing tape and slid the boxes off to the side. Perhaps Jake would stumble across them one day.

The fireplace mantel was bare aside from the dish where Miranda kept her so-called beach treasures. While she had hoped her life would mirror the smooth transformation of sea glass, her pieces were still jagged.

She emptied the dish of white and brown pieces into her palm and placed them in her pocket. Without knowing the obstacles they overcame, she couldn't judge their readiness. These pieces deserved to be back within the dark depths of the water where they belonged. Just because Miranda's journey in Cobblers Hill had ended, it didn't mean theirs couldn't continue.

In the bedroom's cedar closet, empty hangers dangled from a wooden bar where Miranda's new wardrobe had replaced Trudy's gingham housedresses. Donations of trendy jeans, flattering sundresses, and formfitting tops were now for sale at the Born Again thrift shop. They might boost another woman's self-esteem someday. Standing before the antique floor mirror with swollen red eyes and unwashed hair, Miranda took one last look at her reflection.

Throughout the hundred days, she had blossomed into someone with a bright future—someone worthy of unconditional love. But like the withering flowers in Gertrude's sanctuary, brittle from the changing season, Miranda lost perspective through Jake's betrayal.

The light buzzed over the kitchen sink, and the refrigerator hummed its familiar off-key tune. Miranda unplugged the appliances for the final time. The new owners would likely replace them with the latest technology without considering their history—the meals they had helped prepare, the electrical storms they had weathered, the years of overuse, and times of neglect.

Cabinets and pantry shelves were empty. The senior center graciously accepted the nonperishables on behalf of food-insecure townsfolk. Miranda had donated Gertrude Blair's oil-splattered cookbooks to the library and discarded the Colby family's cherished recipes. They suddenly lacked the essential ingredients she once found irresistible.

Lastly, she stood in the doorway of her makeshift art studio and sighed. Without Miranda's canvases—drenched in color and clad in sentiment—the sunroom begged for summertime's warmth and creativity. But those works of art depicting treasured moments on the coast with Jake Colby had become solemn diaries on which she no longer wished to reflect.

Miranda braided a twist tie around the last trash bag, nudged it outside, and scooped up her worn running sneakers that had pounded miles of breathtaking countryside. The lengthy task of dismantling her New England life was finally complete. Soon, chapters of the Jake Colby fairy tale would close. Miranda wrapped her arms around herself, but the embrace failed to provide comfort.

"Well, this is it, our final goodbye," she called out into the emptiness of the solemn cottage where her grandmother's memory would remain. "I've enjoyed visiting with you, Trudy. I'll miss what we all shared this summer, even if it was superficial." She dabbed her eyes with a wrinkled tissue. "I thought we were heading for happily ever after here. I guess the author intended a different ending to our story."

Choking back a sob, Miranda stepped out into the crisp morning air. Once the stubborn door closed behind her, it would remain locked. The unoiled keyhole would get rusty, as she feared her progress might too.

She placed her canvases by the curb beside the pile of belongings that were once hers and Trudy's and took the driver's seat. Beyond the windshield, the sun peeked its hello from the garden, bringing a new day of possibilities to life.

The yard next door was dormant from the previous evening. Despite the deceptive charm of a white picket fence, the grass wasn't greener at the Colbys. The Blairs weren't the only family with cracks, fissures, and shortchanged futures with loved ones.

It had been a week since Miranda heard Jake's voice or saw his radiant smile. She would no longer seek her reflection in his blazing eyes—emeralds that had faded to gray. While she had been foolish and naive, she never professed her feelings to him. Some words were better left unsaid, and some fantasies were more satisfying left to the imagination. Fairy tales triumphed in children's books rather than real life, and hope was best kept beyond reach.

The Toyota backed down the gravel driveway and made its final descent along Primrose Lane. Miranda's wings—which took a lifetime to build but a dishonest moment to break—hid under an abandoned pile that awaited Monday morning pickup. Time would determine if she could develop new ones without Jake Colby.

Chapter 34

The row of sycamore trees shed crumpled gray bark. Cars parked on both sides of the street, but there was no sign of friendly people or acts of neighborly kindness. Miranda would get reacquainted with her dependable yet colorless surroundings before rightfully declaring Barron Park home again. The possibility that such a place might no longer exist made her gasp for air.

She left her baggage in the one-car garage, alongside dusty boxes that hadn't seen daylight. By only unpacking the necessities—running sneakers, art supplies, inner strength—Miranda hoped to keep her bittersweet memories from Cobblers Hill quarantined. Erasing the ones of Jake Colby, though, would be impossible.

"I can't believe you're home!" Clara Blair greeted her daughter at the front door with open arms. "My goodness, I've been subtracting the days, the hours, the minutes, the seconds, and here you are two weeks early!"

Miranda had also been watching the clock and calendar for varied reasons. Now she mourned those structured time frames and countdowns.

"Thanks, Mom," she muttered, hugging her mother half-heartedly with stifled sobs.

"There, there." Clara stroked Miranda's shorter hair. "You can exhale. That dreadful arrangement is behind you. I'm sure it was worse than we imagined, but it's over. You never have to visit that awful place again."

"I'm sorry," Miranda said through sniffles as she wiped away tears with the backs of her hands. "I know this isn't the homecoming you expected. It's just that—"

"Shhh." Clara held her close, gently rocking back and forth. "You'll forget these past few months ever happened. There's no need to relive them, and I won't drill you with questions. You're home now. This will always be your haven, honey, free of meddling. Okay?" She cupped her daughter's tear-soaked face with her hands.

"It's not okay." Miranda pulled back. "Why must this house be a haven? Why do you feel the need to protect me? And what's wrong about asking questions and finding answers when we need them?"

She paced the worn shag rug, huffing with each heavily planted step.

"I'm tired of everyone thinking they know what's best without being honest with themselves. Stop sheltering me and making me feel it's acceptable to go through life without seeking the truth."

"What in the world?" Clara's mouth gaped open, and she shook her head. "I don't understand any of this fuss."

"That's because you don't ask, Mom. And you've programmed me to avoid questions. Instead of discussing anything relevant, we sweep those conversations under the outdated carpeting. I'm guilty of avoiding the truth too, but I've paid the price for my silence. Why must we live in fear of the unknown?"

"All right, then. You want questions? I'll ask one." Clara gave her daughter a once-over. "Where is the old Miranda?"

"She's gone," Miranda replied. Heat penetrated from her rosy cheeks, and pain surrendered to bitterness. "She's been replaced by a more enlightened version of herself who isn't settling for less than she deserves."

"It was a big mistake having you spend time around my mother-in-law's memories. As if that wretched woman didn't do enough damage in her lifetime, what has she done now?"

"First of all, it was my decision to leave," Miranda said through gritted teeth. "And my grandmother provided me with opportunity and surrounded me with friendship and offered me life-altering experiences through her arrangement. She supported my hobbies and introduced me to my dreams, even if they became nightmares. That's what the wretched woman did."

Miranda fled to her bedroom and slammed the door. Like the cluttered but barren cottage back in June, furnishings lingered from the past, but emptiness prevailed. The loose posts on her ripped canopy bed waited in vain for a handyman, as did the wobbly desk chair—a high school tech class project. Lopsided posters of dismembered bands stuck to the walls with stretches of tape. The pastel-colored ceiling fan, suitable for a nursery, circulated air in slow motion.

She would have drawn the curtains had they not already been closed, forbidding sunshine and shunning the outside world. Magazines and puzzles, time-fillers she intended to bring to Cobblers Hill, covered the dresser. Experiences in the quaint coastal town had been too plentiful to hide behind tabloid gossip or unassembled pieces anyway.

The wastebasket was half-filled with crumpled tissues that had consoled Miranda leading to her June departure. In time, it might overflow with those comforting her return home.

Off to the side, easels displayed artwork Miranda barely recognized. Not only did these canvases represent the feelings and limitations of the person she had been, but they validated the artist she had become during the days spent breathing in salty New England air.

While she struggled to connect with items that once defined her in Barron Park, things were also amiss on Primrose Lane. Caught in an emotional web, she dangled somewhere between the two existences, resenting them both.

Miranda fell into bed, surrounded by dust and guilt. Had she allowed time to settle in, she might not have provoked a fight with her mother. Jake was the one who allied with Trudy and hid their relationship. He was the source of her pain and disappointment. And Miranda was equally frustrated with herself, having avoided the truth from her mother, grandmother, and the neighbors.

She wrestled with twisted sheets and kicked covers to the ground. They had never been a comfort anyway. Although Miranda wanted to believe she had distanced from the past, reality lingered like a week-old headache—she had voluntarily stayed there, relying on unnecessary crutches.

She rolled onto her side and covered her head with a pillow. Tomorrow was a new day to accept responsibility and seek the truth rather than find fault in Clara's parenting. Miranda would make amends in the morning.

Chapter 35

The smell of burnt toast infiltrated Miranda's childhood home. Cocooned in a tightly wrapped bathrobe, Clara Blair hovered over the stove and fried omelets.

"I'm sorry, Mom." Miranda's voice cracked through the cloud of smoke. "I should have never lashed out at you yesterday. It was wrong and disrespectful."

"Apology accepted, and I hope you'll accept mine."

Clara reached for the coffeepot but avoided eye contact. "How did you sleep?"

"With my eyes closed," Miranda said with a forced chuckle. "I'm beyond exhausted, despite the hours I slept."

"All that soul-searching must have taken its toll, honey. A good breakfast will help."

Miranda took her usual seat at the table set for two. The expired milk carton provided a welcome distraction from the horizontal lines burrowed in her mother's forehead and the shimmer of silver roots.

She took a deep, diaphragmatic breath, the kind she had practiced at the Breathe yoga studio. "Why didn't we ever talk about my father?"

Suddenly, sounds within the kitchen became a symphony—the dripping faucet, buzzing of an overzealous fly, and ticking clock. Accepting Miranda's invitation, the past would be joining them for breakfast. Her mother polished a spoon and aligned the napkins' corners, folding them into symmetrical triangles.

"Well," Clara started, clearing her throat, "at first, I kept his memory alive, hoping he would return. When it became apparent he wasn't coming back, I had no choice but to bury his memories." She buttered her toast, evenly spreading globs of saturated fat across its surface like she was laying cement. "The survival skills I adopted for us worked, or at least that's what I thought. Eventually, you stopped asking, I stopped talking, and we became a family of two."

With shaky hands, her mother reached for the sugar bowl next. She broke up clumps using the back of a teaspoon and stirred the white granules the way she mixed cake batter.

"We both lost, Miranda, except I had the added responsibility of shielding another life. Your protection was my priority. It wasn't my intention to cause you any more heartache than you endured as a child." She sipped her coffee before adding more creamer and a heaping spoonful of sugar. And then another.

The bold-roasted cup of joe beckoned Miranda to take a sip too. Instead, she leaned forward on her elbows, narrowing the space between her and Clara for another long-overdue and intrinsically difficult conversation about her best interests. "I understand, Mom."

"Do you?" Clara arched her brows. "Do you really?"

"I'm trying. But I'm a grown woman now, even though I live at home and sleep in my childhood bedroom. We still never talk about Dad. Don't you realize I have questions and curiosities about the man responsible for bringing me into this world?"

Miranda slid her untouched breakfast plate aside and stared into her mother's sorrowful eyes. "Many women my age are married with children. How can I share my life with someone else when I don't know who I am?" Her fingers traced the coffee mug's rim. Steam no longer rose from its surface. "Hasn't it ever occurred to you that I need to piece together my identity?"

Clara dabbed the corners of her eyes with a napkin. "I honestly wasn't aware you felt this way. I figured the day might come when you'd want more information, but you seemed content all these years like it was a non-issue."

"That's because whenever I introduced the topic of family, whether it involved Dad or Grandma Trudy or others, it formed a wedge between us that lingered for days. I already lost one parent. I couldn't bear to lose you too. I had no choice but to live with unknowns and accept the incomplete picture."

"It was better we looked ahead in life, not back," Clara said in between sniffles. "I thought we had agreed not to make our disappointments an issue, but I guess I misinterpreted. I won't deny I never willingly talked about the man who walked away. I felt he didn't deserve to be a part of our world that he chose to leave behind. So I withheld irrelevant details to spare us the heartache."

"But that's just it. It was an issue—a pressing one—and it caused all sorts of doubts and insecurities. With all due respect, Mom, I think you mistook living in denial for finding closure. Those years of making assumptions left me feeling rejected when that wasn't necessarily the case. Had I known the truth, circumstances might have been different. You should have—" She reached across to touch her mother's arm, and Clara released her mug to join hands. "I mean, I wish I would have known Dad had a mental illness—that he struggled to live his own life, let alone take responsibility for mine. And he didn't abandon us but, perhaps, spared us of his worsening condition to seek outside help."

"Who told you about that? How did you find out?" Clara's leg shook under the table, making the coffee shift back and forth in their mugs.

"The 'whos' and 'hows' are irrelevant now. I deserved to know about my father. He had a disease, Mom. There is no shame in that part of him."

Clara drew a deep breath and released it slowly. Air seeped out of her mouth like it had escaped a pinprick in a balloon. "How I adored him. Victor was thrilled to be a dad, and a natural at fatherhood. He had a knack for rocking you to sleep when none of my tricks worked. And he blew a raspberry on your cheek each morning, which made you giggle and squeal in your crib."

They both smiled through Clara's haze of nostalgia.

"He bought you a paint set and taught you how to blend primary colors. You two Picassos always had a paintbrush in your hands. And he kept a pencil behind his ear, ready to sketch a caricature of us whenever we weren't looking."

"I vaguely remember those silly pictures."

"Of course, I gave him grief, but I laughed behind closed doors." Clara chuckled. "He mastered the art of impersonation and kept comedy at the forefront of our lives. I loved every minute of his corny humor."

Two decades of waiting yielded words Miranda yearned to hear. She eased into the kitchen chair and took a sip of her lukewarm coffee.

"Above all, Victor believed in the life we would continue to build together. We had something out of a storybook until I noticed subtle changes in his behavior." Her tone shifted from pink shades on a palette to somber rusts and browns.

"Then what?"

"We struggled day after day, week after week," Clara explained. "Dad fought the good fight, and I told him to hold on and not give up. There were different forms of therapy he could try. But the sickness took over, changing him into a man I no longer recognized. As he slipped further away, I grew more desperate. His illness took him from me, from us." Her words mimicked Jake's from that night on the beach—pained and deep-rooted. "He didn't want to be a burden, so he left. There was no goodbye, and I never heard from him again."

"I ache for his suffering," Miranda said, her expression etched with grief. "He must have been so scared."

"And I was petrified for him. I spent endless nights waiting and wondering and fearing his whereabouts. I cringed each time the phone rang. I was heartbroken for you and felt betrayed by Trudy, who encouraged him to leave. There was enough stress without her intervention."

"It was a devastating time for her too, Mom. That was her only son drifting away from a debilitating disease."

"He was my husband and your father. She should have supported my efforts to keep him here."

"Did you ever consider it more courageous for Dad to leave and seek outside help than stay? Weren't you worried for our safety?"

"Your grandmother entertained those thoughts and fears," Clara replied. Her hands gripped the coffee mug, her knuckles turning white. "In my mind, your father was the gentle, caring man I fell in love with who would never hurt anyone. It may have been selfish to want to keep him home, but I never meant to put our safety at risk. I'm thankful it never got to that point."

"But it might have," Miranda said, "had he not walked out that door to get help. The way I see it, this wasn't about him abandoning us or falling out of love with us—it was about getting better elsewhere. In some respects, I think my grandmother and father were brave. Like you, they demonstrated the depths of their love by wanting to protect our family."

"I couldn't see it that way. Had Trudy not meddled in our lives, this might have had a different ending. Maybe Dad wouldn't have gone into cardiac arrest."

"Cardiac arrest?" Miranda inched in closer.

"Yes, his heart gave out. Those damn experimental drugs that were supposed to improve his life took it, so I later found out."

"So Dad didn't, um, you know—"

"No, he didn't take his life."

Miranda closed her eyes and exhaled her relief.

"But," Clara said, "he never did seek outside help once he left home. Instead, he lived on the streets."

"Oh, I assumed he admitted himself into an institution to receive the necessary care."

"That's what Trudy expected him to do once he left. I knew better."

Miranda lowered her head into her hands and massaged her temples. "At least now I know his side of the story. Trudy's too."

"And please don't forget my side," her mother replied. "Living a single day without him was painful. I was a young mom losing my best friend and trying to make sense of challenging circumstances." A defeated Clara tossed her tear-soaked napkins into the garbage along with the unappetizing eggs and burnt toast. The overhead light flickered and buzzed, and the bothersome fly circled the garbage pail. She stood by the sink, scrubbing, soaping, rinsing, and repeating. Her endless stream of tears competed with the running faucet. "If you need me to accept responsibility for how I handled things, I will take the blame."

"I've learned life isn't always black or white, Mom. There are gray areas, too, that are best left unjudged. This is about expressing our feelings and allowing the truth to heal. Don't we owe it to our future selves?" Miranda stole another affirmation from Jake.

"Even after twenty years, I find it difficult to understand what happened," Clara said. "It's been easier to harbor a grudge than to find forgiveness. Forgiving meant moving on. I never thought I was strong enough to take the next step by myself, for the both of us."

Miranda approached her mother. "You don't need to protect me anymore. And while we can't change the past, it's never too late for a fresh start. First, we need to cherish the beautiful memories of Dad, purge the bitter ones, and then forgive him so he can, finally, rest in peace." She placed a hand on her mother's shoulder and gave it a light rub. "And we need to forgive Trudy, who was also a victim, not an enemy. No more walls between us or others."

Tears rolled down Clara's cheeks. "I'm sorry it took me this long to realize how selfishly I handled things. I never claimed to be the perfect mother or wife, honey." She sobbed in her daughter's arms.

The bond her parents once shared—a love torn apart and fragments washed away like jagged sea glass—mirrored Miranda's relationship with her father. And grandmother. And Jake. And the story line in his novel. And the demise of Trudy and Randy's relationship. Their loose threads were now sewn together in an imaginary patchwork quilt through the commonality of loss.

"Everything we've endured has shaped us into today's resilient women," Miranda said. "I have a feeling this U-turn will lead to wonderful places. We have plenty of lost time to make up for, don't you agree?"

Clara pulled back from their embrace and held her daughter at arm's distance, her eyes smiling. "I'd say you are wise beyond your years."

"This summer offered me a new perspective, is all. The ball bounces up, Mom."

"Oh, is that so?" Clara cocked her head. "There's more to this enlightenment than you let on. Care to tell me about him?"

Chapter 36

Seated across from the attorney, separated by his file-laden desk, Miranda studied the rise and fall of Mr. Baxter's brows. His eyes scanned the legal document from top to bottom, resembling a fired-up typewriter from long ago.

"As the executor of Gertrude Blair's estate, I took the necessary steps to probate her will." He cleared the phlegm from his throat. "To recap what we disclosed at our meeting last spring, your paternal grandmother proposed a hundred-day arrangement as a condition for acquiring her property and assets."

With crunched toes and clenched teeth, Miranda offered a blank stare.

"Your consented departure date, as we documented here, was June twenty-first, which means the agreement would have been satisfied as of . . ." Mr. Baxter flipped through his notes. "September twenty-ninth. It is my understanding, Ms. Blair, that you have fulfilled Gertrude's final requests, as indicated herein, granting you her estate. Let's proceed."

"Well, sir," Miranda began, swallowing hard, "I only satisfied eighty-six of those hundred days. So is this where I'm reprimanded for failing her assignment, and the runners-up inherit the estate? I can provide their names if you'd like."

The attorney peered over his glasses at Miranda with dark,

beady eyes. It wasn't her intention to be disrespectful, even if she came across as brash. And she hadn't left Cobblers Hill early to be vindictive. Her emotional roller coaster didn't reserve energy for mind games.

Sabotaging her pride and self-worth by staying in Jake's hometown had not been an option. Instead, by forfeiting control and relinquishing her position as the decision maker, the property's fate would be determined by someone else. Perhaps it was another one of Miranda Blair's cop-outs—or another leap of faith.

The attorney peered back down at the will through thick-rimmed bifocals and mumbled unintelligibly as he read.

"According to this addendum, which Gertrude Blair asked me to share at this subsequent meeting, you were to inherit her estate regardless of whether or not you satisfied her arrangement."

"But there were guidelines to follow," Miranda said, rising to her feet. "You clearly stated them yourself. A hundred days. An extended season. What you're telling me now doesn't make sense."

"True, but guidelines are merely suggestions or recommendations, as it were, for you to navigate freely. Please take a seat, Ms. Blair. Your grandmother hoped you would willingly accept her proposed time frame with an open mind and willing heart. It appears you have satisfied the arrangement after all. You have inherited what remains of Gertrude Blair's history."

He removed his glasses and rubbed his squeaky eyes in a circular motion with his palms. Miranda's breakfast revisited the back of her throat.

"So, it hadn't mattered whether I stayed a week, a month, or a hundred days in Cobblers Hill? It was never a matter of time?"

"You are correct, Ms. Blair." The attorney smirked. "The decision was always yours."

Miranda slouched in the unsupportive leather armchair as she realized the arrangement wasn't an enemy. Trudy hadn't intended it as a personal challenge but instead presented it as a gift of opportunity.

"Now we need some signatures on these documents." With the notary summoned from an adjacent room, Mr. Baxter held out a pen and pointed with his finger. "Sign here, and here. And over here, Ms. Blair."

Reviewing documents and acquiring signatures was typical of Mr. Baxter's profession. But there was nothing ordinary about the day. Rather than relinquishing liability before flying on the circus trapeze, Miranda would be accepting responsibility for someone else's legacy. Her signature on the dotted line, alongside Trudy's, would affect the rest of her life. But how?

Blood whooshed in her ears as she held the dampened will in place with a perspiring hand and took the attorney's pen. The crisp, black ink dragged across the document, giving proper attention to every letter in her name. Like trains that never intersected or the characters in Jake's novel who failed to cross paths, Miranda and Trudy's lives had always been parallel.

Now they converged.

"Onward we go," Mr. Baxter said. "If you'll look here, we can review the assets of your inheritance together." He unveiled a thick folder and removed the first two typed pages of letterhead showing columns and dollar signs, some with multiple commas.

Miranda gasped. She inched forward in her chair, planting both feet firmly on the ground, and gripped the armrests. There were not enough complimentary water bottles to quench her dry mouth.

"You are one wealthy young lady, Ms. Blair," he pronounced with a snort.

Not only had she questioned her vision but her hearing too.

He walked Miranda through the different accounts and advised her on the necessary steps to claim funds from various banks. She would need a financial adviser, or a team of them, to help navigate the unfamiliar territory of proper investing and asset allocation. The sheer magnitude of the estate would secure her financial future and the generation that followed. There was no longer a need for coupon cutting, college loans, bargain outlets, or two-for-one specials. She could pursue any dream and travel the globe like Jake. Miranda Blair's life no longer needed to be a single scoop of vanilla.

Mr. Baxter's foot tapping grabbed her attention from the page. Unlike her nail biting and cuticle chewing, his tics seemed to stem from impatience rather than anxiety.

"At our initial meeting, you had expressed an interest in selling Gertrude's home on Primrose Lane. You've probably considered the harsh winters up north, and you'll have to contend with freezing pipes and diminishing value. The estate will pay taxes whether or not you occupy the house."

Miranda's heart raced at the reference to the New England property. If only Jake had been the man she thought he was, he might have been seated by her side, determining the next steps together.

"As your grandmother was up in the years, I imagine her home reflected her age. You'll need to consider the time and energy required for renovations, Ms. Blair."

The once decrepit bungalow had become a peaceful retreat that encouraged hopes and dreams and fostered unlikely relationships. Even if those sentiments had soured, it was irreverent to discuss Trudy's home in a negative light, like talking about a former friend behind her back.

"There are no liens on the property, and Gertrude made the last mortgage payment long ago," Mr. Baxter said. "Property in that coastal community is in high demand and comes with an attractive price tag. Our affiliated realtor team can have that house off your hands in no time. The rewards will be generous, I can assure you."

The plump attorney raised his bushy brows at Miranda. His eyes reflected dollar signs, and excess saliva pooled in the corners of his mouth, creating a white paste. Her own eyebrows didn't mimic his excitement, nor did she salivate.

The cottage's fate was now in her hands. Even without Mr. Baxter's valid points, Miranda knew it would be difficult to return to New England and confront memories from the most fulfilling time in her life. Owning the hilltop property would keep an expired dream alive.

Yet if she closed the door on Primrose Lane, she might not find happiness elsewhere, anywhere, and with someone other than Jake Colby.

Miranda's stomach churned. She adjusted her posture and wiped her palms on her dress pants.

"We handle estate sales in a seamless transaction for those without an emotional attachment to a piece of property," the attorney explained. "Assuming that's the case here, you wouldn't need to be present at the closing. To satisfy your curiosity, I could have one of our distinguished realtors appraise the house within forty-eight hours and provide its current market value. Let me be frank. If we price the property right, we'll have a quick sale on our hands and put this to rest. Imagine having those funds in your pocket before the next season."

But Miranda wasn't curious. She couldn't imagine, and she wasn't ready for the next season. The attorney's reference to more large figures didn't make her do a happy dance. The door of opportunity Grandma Trudy had opened in the quaint New England town couldn't be purchased or replaced, no matter how plentiful Miranda's finances became. Selling the cottage would permanently nail its door shut and extinguish the burning within Miranda—flames that flickered in pursuit of happiness, passion for art, and desire for Jake Colby.

There was a thick financial cushion from Trudy's bank accounts and stocks without adding real estate to the portfolio. The cottage could sit vacant, as it had while her grandmother resided at the nursing home. A hired landscaper could prevent the property from becoming the neighborhood's eyesore and buy Miranda time to finalize her decision. Still, 21 Primrose Lane would remain a ball and chain shackled to her recent past.

"You've given me much to consider, Mr. Baxter." Rising to her feet, she shouldered her handbag. "But I need to weigh my options before involving the realtors."

"As you wish." He gathered the paperwork, tapped it twice, aligned the corners, and returned it to the file. "I have a feeling I'll be hearing from you soon—real soon. Until then, you'll find everything you need in here."

He handed the weighty folder to Miranda. "My assistant included the business card for LaMano's Realty and notified them of our client relationship. They are aware of your possible interest in a quick sale." Mr. Baxter placed his pen on the desk and swept dust to the side. "There is an envelope in there too, Ms. Blair, and some recommendations for financial advisers. You'll likely need guidance to handle an estate of this size."

It would have been easier to take the necessary steps to sell Trudy's property—to lay Jake's memory to rest alongside that of Miranda's grandmother and father. But she wouldn't acquiesce to pacify an impatient, dollar-seeking attorney. Even if the inheritance were a gain, he would benefit from her loss.

Miranda needed breathing space. Another few days or weeks to finalize her decision wouldn't make a difference. Then again, time could change everything.

Chapter 37

Miranda tapped the computer keys with her nails but didn't press them. While it was unlike her to procrastinate on assignments, nothing at the historical society or elsewhere in Barron Park held its former significance.

The desk chair screeched and teetered as she leaned back. Several warped ceiling tiles had brown stains, and the broken ones revealed rusty pipes. The office needed a makeover as desperately as Gertrude Blair's cottage had last summer.

The cursor flashed on the screen. It was Miranda's move, yet what would it be?

Acquaintances were making wish lists and dreaming of a white Christmas. But Miranda was stuck in another season, having missed fall's magical transformation with Jake Colby.

The dark-paneled walls of her workplace provided subtle reminders of the cozy New England cottage. There had been a palette of warm colors throughout Cobblers Hill and a blanket of leaves along the wooded path that led to Edens Cove. Harvest festivals, haunted hayrides, the town's annual pie contest, and window painting on Main Street took place. Life moved on without Miranda Blair, but time had not healed her wounds.

The front door to the office flung open, prompting a jingle of overhead bells.

"What's with the eerie silence? It's like a library in here. Did I miss the memo, and we're lending books now? No holiday music?"

Bonnie, the retiree who volunteered on Wednesdays and alternating Fridays, warmed her gloveless hands in front of the wood-burning stove.

"Where are the 'holly jollies' and the 'ho ho hos'? I don't hear any 'fa la las' either," she added with a snicker. "I'd even settle for some 'hickory, dickory, docks.'"

"I hadn't noticed. I'm too absorbed with these Holiday Show-case brochures—overdue brochures, that is."

Miranda ruffled through papers to disguise the truth. She couldn't listen to songs about being home for the holidays or gathering with loved ones by an open fire when she wasn't sure where home was anymore.

Bonnie placed her hands on her broad, curvy hips. "It just so happens I peeked in the bay window earlier. You were sulking there like you lost your BFF. Need me to spread some holiday cheer, do ya? Do ya?"

She snapped her fingers and did a little jig that swayed her candy cane earrings. Miranda pretended not to notice.

"Uh-oh. It's worse than I thought." Bonnie straddled a chair. "What's got you in a twist? Your Thanksgiving turkey wasn't moist? Were the cranberries too bitter? Not enough yeast in the bread? Was the cider too tart?" She made a sour-lemon face and stuck out her tongue.

"Funny, Bonnie." Miranda forced a grin. "I can't believe my desk calendar has only thirty-four pages left. Where did the days go?"

"Knowing you, you're keeping a close eye on those ticking hours, minutes, and seconds."

Miranda smirked. "It's just that I've never been good with endings."

"You and everyone else, my dear. And doesn't it feel like it was just summertime? I miss those long days and steamy nights, if you know what I mean." Bonnie fanned herself. "Wait, you weren't here last summer. Weren't you visiting family or something?"

Aside from the occasional chat with her mother, Miranda missed having conversations with someone who had weathered life's storms. While Bonnie added humor and a touch of sarcasm to the workday, the well-intentioned but outspoken fifty-something-year-old had never been a confidant.

"I miss those friends from last summer. I doubt I'll ever see them again." Miranda winced, the pangs of homesickness aching in every muscle. "The situation is complicated."

"Well, I'm no expert on curing the friendship blues, but if your desk weren't such a mess, you'd have room for photos of these so-called friends."

Bonnie began stacking empty Chinese food containers. She tossed slivers of bok choy and a lo mein noodle into the garbage with a *tsk, tsk*. "This reminds me of my teen daughter's bedroom. I swear, one of these days, I'm gonna see an opossum run outta there eating a week-old sammie and wearing a soiled sock as a scarf."

Had her circumstances been kind, Miranda would have displayed the photo of Jake kissing her cheek in the gondola. Everything about that moment made her insides sing, including the OVERJOYED balloon that provided the perfect backdrop. It wasn't possible to find a more appropriate word to express how she felt all summer long in his company.

"I know you've lived here your entire life, Bonnie, but there's an exciting world beyond Barron Park. Did you ever consider you might be missing out on something more?"

"You mean bust outta here for good? Nah. When I get the itch to get away, I travel. That's what vacations are for—to scratch the itch." She ran her polished fingernails up and down her forearm and reached for her back. "You visit, enjoy, and go home broke until the itch returns."

"I guess, but a visit is limiting, don't you think? It's temporary, only temporary."

"That's one way of looking at it. So, let me ask you something. If you could go anywhere in the world and the bucks weren't an issue, where would it be?"

Jake had posed the same question at the old-fashioned ice cream parlor while nostalgic music entertained them through juke-box speakers. Rather than Paris's bright lights and awe-inspiring artwork, Miranda now craved the simplicity and charm of his hometown—the untainted fairy-tale version of Cobblers Hill.

"Someplace in New England," Miranda replied without removing her eyes from the frozen computer screen. If she wasn't careful, brazen Bonnie would extract details she wasn't ready to share.

"New England, huh?" Bonnie jolted her head back. "How about checking out the painted ceiling of that cathedral in Rome? Or taking an Instagram-worthy selfie with the Hollywood sign in LA? Or eating a slice of pepperoni pizza in Pisa? Shall I continue?"

Miranda shook her head. "No, up north."

She spent days entertaining thoughts of what Thanksgiving had been like at the Colby home—Addie's cherished recipes, the warm family tradition of saying grace, children's giggles, fireside stories, and abundant love.

Jake might have worn dress pants and a knit sweater that hugged his biceps. Or it was likely he spent the day in relaxed jeans and the frayed college sweatshirt Miranda had borrowed, tossing a football in the yard with his nephews. She imagined the aroma of warm fruit pies from the Apple Dumpling Bakery and equally enticing smells trailing from Addie's southern kitchen.

Had the arrangement ended favorably, Miranda would have worn a new sweater dress, hemmed above the knee, and a stylish pair of tall leather boots for the neighbors' celebration. Welcomed through the open garden gate, she would have arrived early to tend to the litany of tasks Addie had assigned.

And when Miranda and Jake had a moment alone in the kitchen, he would have stared at her with his emerald eyes and gently touched her shoulder or placed his hand on her side, sending messages that didn't need words to convey. How she missed their chemistry!

"Girl, you need bigger dreams!" Bonnie waved her hand in the air like she was swatting a fly. "What in the world is up north?"

"I picture farm stands on every corner with overflowing wicker baskets of freshly picked vegetables and bright orange pumpkins in various shapes and sizes. Corn stalks, eucalyptus swags, and wagons filled with gourds decorate the Victorian porches." Miranda closed her eyes and drew a deep breath. "And the autumn air holds hints of sugar maple and hickory."

"Whew. It sounds like you took a lot of time dreaming up that schmaltziness. But farm stands? You wanna go up north for farm stands? You know, the local grocery store has a produce aisle. If farm stands and foliage are what you're craving, you should've taken that trip weeks ago. Life's moved on to another season. It's time to deck the halls and jingle those bells." Bonnie laughed until she snorted, then laughed some more. She swept pieces of yesterday's fried rice from the desk's surface into her palm.

"You're right. It's all in the past."

Miranda's cell phone rang several times.

"Aren't you gonna get that?"

"My voicemail will."

"Okay, where were we?" Bonnie plucked at a stray hair protruding from her chin. "Ah, yes, leaving town. If you think about it—"

A series of three consecutive wind chimes sounded from Miranda's phone.

"First a call, then texts. That's one persistent person. What's next? Skywriting? A carrier pigeon? If you don't pick up that phone and give it some love, I'm gonna dive into your handbag and do it for you," Bonnie said with a cheeky grin. "Take care of business while I go make us some joe."

Miranda huffed as she retrieved several weeks of neglected messages.

There were out-of-area missed calls and two enthusiastic messages from Joanie, who shared news of a library grant for more art-related community events. Had Miranda still lived in Cobblers Hill, she would've been delighted. The attorney's office inquired about the New England property. And then there were Jake's calls and texts leading up to Thanksgiving.

While Bonnie dumped coffee grinds and prepared a fresh pot, humming "Have a Holly, Jolly Christmas," Miranda listened to Jake's long-winded messages. As if regrets and resentment weren't heavy enough burdens to carry, hearing his defeated tone acknowledging, "I'm sorry," and pleading, "We need to talk," and requesting, "Call me," added guilt to her load.

Jake's string of texts offered many of the same gut-wrenching pleas. Miranda missed him tremendously, but she wasn't willing to subject herself to more hurt and disappointment. She wouldn't confuse empathy for the Colby family's tragedy with forgiveness.

Bonnie returned with snowflake-patterned coffee cups and handed Miranda one. "Girl, you look like you've seen a ghost. Are you stuck on Halloween? I mean Thanksgiving. Right. We were talking about squash and farm stands."

"That's okay. I should be digging back in with work before I fall further behind. But, um, let's see . . . Here, you can deliver these thank-you letters to the supporters of our Harvest Fundraiser. Everyone was so generous this year."

"I'm on it." Bonnie grabbed the pile with her free hand while blowing on the steam from her coffee. "Text me if you think of anything else. And rev up some holiday spirit while I'm gone, for goodness' sake. I'm getting depressed just standing here."

Overhead bells jingled, and a gust of air blew through the office, twirling Miranda's papers everywhere.

"Oh, and one more thing." Bonnie arched her head back through the entrance. "The winter must be beautiful in New England too. It's something you ought to think about." She winked and flew out the door as quickly as she bustled in.

Chapter 38

Miranda eyed the Roman numeral wall clock and sunk lower in her teetering chair. Her afternoon at the historical society was as unproductive as the morning, but it didn't matter—nothing did. Every muscle ached in her slender frame, taunted by last summer's overlooked red flags.

It made sense why Jake was a grown man living with his grand-mother. Miranda wasn't the only one stuck in the past. And she had been foolish to think there wasn't history between the longtime neighbors.

Jake was familiar with the cottage's quirks and the property's shortcomings. He knew how to light the gas tank by hand and anticipated stubborn windows on humid days. He even had a rela-tionship with the front door keyhole, oiling the rusty lock every three weeks with a can of WD-40 from the potting shed.

Miranda rested her elbows on the desk and lowered her head into her hands.

Of course, Jake didn't have a girlfriend last summer. He wouldn't have risked the relationship by spending time with Miranda. There weren't identifiable calls from Europe, only Miranda's assumptions about an occasional text. And while she had been transparent about her hundred-day countdown, Jake never had one for Kasey's return.

No worthy woman would leave a guy like Jake Colby behind for the entire summer anyway.

Miranda sighed loud enough for the next-door office to hear. She shifted her weight in her chair, making the seat screech.

Trudy's desk drawer brochures were likely Jake's souvenirs from his purpose-driven travels. What guy in his early twenties had the flexibility and funds to see the world but refrained from discussing his experiences with others?

Nothing made sense until everything made sense. Jake Colby had been flawless in Miranda's eyes and worthy of her trust. She'd believed what she wanted rather than accept the potential truth about her neighbor. But Miranda was wrong to seek perfection in someone else.

Now she paid the price for her naivety. The damage was done, but she wouldn't allow herself to be vulnerable again.

Tears began their slow descent down her cheeks. Sniffling, Miranda rummaged through the compartments of her handbag. She pushed aside mint lip balm and a pack of sugarless chewing gum. There wasn't a stack of Jake's badly crumpled and coffee-stained napkins when she needed them. Sadly, Jake Colby was no longer a consolation.

Grandma Trudy's love letter reappeared in the pocket of her handbag. The piece of history had been tucked there nearly three months earlier during the mad dash from Cobblers Hill. With lingering bitterness from the neighborly alliance, Miranda removed the brittle stationery and reread the words Trudy had penned to the man she left behind.

I think of you often as if you were here with me, walking beside me, hand in hand along the beach, basking in the simple joys we once shared before things became complicated. I wonder if you ever reflect on those special times. Maybe they were replaced or forgotten, or they were never cherished memories.

The historical society's Christmas tree stood naked and alone in the drafty corner. A single string of lights or a few shiny ornaments would have erased its stigma of being overlooked. Maybe Miranda failed her decorating assignment so that she wasn't the only one betrayed by a single season. But her grandmother had understood loss and emptiness too, and her written sentiments reflected a familiar pain.

As I look back on my days, I long for the history we could have made. Sadly, I am left with what remains. Life had a different plan for us, and the world missed our legacy . . . yours and mine . . . ours together.

If given another chance, I would have embraced the opportunity to change what was.

Miranda nodded her lowered head as she read.

For this, my regrets have been heavy. Rather than easing over time, they have become more cumbersome with each passing year. I have carried mine through sweat and tears. Hopefully yours, if any, were lifted and set free.

Miranda couldn't bear to live with more regret. And she didn't want to end up like Trudy and Randy or the characters in Jake's unfinished novel, tortured by what might have been. She endured enough of those from her childhood.

Maybe there was truth to Jake's claims that final evening surrounded by empty beer bottles on the wind-stricken beach. Trapeze hanging, blue-sky soaring, and Fourth of July stargazing would have failed to exist had she constructed walls from Jake and Trudy's relationship. She would have never confronted the ghosts from her past or tested her inner strength. And while Miranda wasn't ready to forgive Jake for misleading her, she was grateful for each wing-developing experience last summer.

The computer's inactivity triggered the power-save mode to kick in, turning the screen black and quieting the dull hum.

And had there been a superficial romantic involvement between Miranda and Jake early in the arrangement, it might have been short-lived. Instead, with Kasey's invisible presence, they had established a more meaningful foundation of friendship.

Time waits for no one. Relationships must be handled carefully and regarded sacredly. Actions cannot be undone, just as words cannot be retracted once spoken. The bitterness left behind can sting indefinitely. For this, I am sorry.

Miranda outlined the letter's creases with her finger, strengthening the unlikely connection with the woman she had looked at as a coward. Having shared her innermost thoughts about the man she loved on paper, Gertrude Blair proved to be more courageous with her emotions than her granddaughter. The day might come—a week, a month, or a lifetime later—when Miranda would write Jake a similar letter. If so, she hoped it wouldn't wait in vain to be discovered.

Miranda tossed her phone back into her handbag. With the New Year approaching, she was ready for resolutions and clean slates. But where? In Barron Park? Or Cobblers Hill? And should she heed Grandma Trudy's advice by seeking second chances? Or would it be too late to turn the Colby nightmare back into a fairy tale? Her life wasn't going to change unless she, herself, changed.

Activating her computer from sleep mode, Miranda clicked the print icon. The machine whirred and whooshed, spewing the final drafts of the event brochures. Her completed assignment had room for improvement, but she would no longer seek perfection.

Having jotted down instructions for Bonnie and scribbled a personal note to the director, Miranda shouldered her handbag and left the office. This time she would not look back.

Chapter 39

The season's first snowstorm blanketed Barron Park with more than a foot of snow in the days leading up to Christmas Eve. With poor road conditions and homes losing power, life came to a halt. For many, the white slippery stuff jeopardized holiday travel and gatherings with loved ones. Miranda didn't have plans for either.

Her cabin fever–inspired frenzy—organizing drawers, shredding to-do lists, cleaning closets, gathering donatable items—kept restlessness at bay. Her current finances didn't warrant the need for books referencing cut corners and money-saving tips. Garbage bags and cardboard boxes overflowed as endings yielded beginnings, making room for whatever the New Year had in store.

"Miranda, are you ever going to come down?" Clara yelled to her daughter from the bottom of the stairs.

"Soon. I just need to sort through these last two stacks of papers."

"You said that an hour ago. It's almost five o'clock, and I'd like to decorate our tree."

"Ten more minutes," Miranda pleaded.

"I'm not sure how much more you can clean. We're running low on paper towels."

A half hour later, Miranda entered the den, dragging the final bag of childhood remnants and holding an envelope in her free hand.

"I'm glad you came to your senses and decided to join me." Clara lifted glazed eyes from her checkbook. Bills covered the coffee table, and a few invoices had slipped onto the floor. A strip of paper with printed digits flowed from a calculator.

Miranda plopped down on the couch and kicked up her soiled, socked feet. Sticky cobwebs and traces of dust covered her sweatshirt. Strands of hair escaped her sagging ponytail.

"I can't believe how much unnecessary clutter I allowed to accumulate in my life."

"All that so-called clutter never bothered you before," Clara said. "At one time, you needed those items to make you feel secure, but that's no longer the case."

"I guess not." Miranda reached into the bowl of popcorn and tossed a handful in her mouth. The chewy flakes had waited in the open air too long.

"Tell me about this bucket list you've been creating." Her mother placed a pen alongside the calculator and rubbed the palms of her hands together. "I imagine you've planned some pretty exciting adventures, huh?"

"It's not what you think. Not yet, at least. I'll make one of those fun lists eventually, but I have unfinished business to settle first."

"I see." Clara gathered a pile of receipts and stapled them together. "So, I'm assuming your resignation from the historical society was on that list?"

"Yep, the first item. I'll volunteer as much as possible, but we both know it's time for me to move. To move onto new horizons, that is."

"Agreed. Don't keep me hanging here. What's the second item on your list?"

"We already accomplished that too." Miranda made a check mark in the air with her finger, borrowing Jake Colby's use of "we" instead of "I."

"Here," she said, handing over the envelope, "take a look."

Clara unfolded both pages, placing them side by side on the coffee table. She peered down through her reading glasses and gasped. "You did not!"

"Yep, we sure did. It's incredible, isn't it, Mom?"

"That's one way to put it." Clara did a little jig while holding up the papers. "I never thought I'd see a zero balance on either of these statements. If I'm this ecstatic, you must feel like you're soaring without college debt holding you back."

Miranda grinned. Having left her stained-glass wings behind in Cobblers Hill, she was slowly developing new ones through the abundant fruits of her grandparents' labor. Yet without being privy to their hard work and sacrifice, there was an overwhelming responsibility to use their gifts wisely.

"While I was at it, I wrote a one-lump check to pay off the remainder of the mortgage. I assumed you wouldn't mind. And you're overdue for a shopping spree and some pampering, so consider that on my bucket list too. No longer will we lounge on couches with pancaked cushions and worn fabric."

Fanning herself, Clara said, "It's either warm in here, or I'm going through my changes."

"I think you're slightly overwhelmed." Miranda smiled. "Hold on, though. I have some other news to share."

"Wow, bucket list accomplishment number three?"

"Number three! I've always known it was silly to take random grad classes without a goal. It was how I convinced myself I was moving in a direction without taking responsibility for finding one."

Miranda reached for more popcorn but grabbed a lukewarm water bottle instead and removed its cap. "I've been working online with a career counselor. First, he gave me homework assignments that took a personal inventory of my strengths. We discussed my graduate credits and course completions. And then he offered suggestions on careers that matched my interests."

"And . . ." Clara inched toward the edge of the couch.

"I am an artist, Mom."

"You had that epiphany from the career counselor? I could have told you that two decades ago."

"No, I've always known I'm an artist. It's in my genes, and creativity runs through my blood. But I denied that part of me beyond a hobby and never believed in myself. Before now, that is. I will no longer shortchange myself or others of the gifts I can offer, including my past experiences. Those trials are responsible for who I am today. And I have a wealth of knowledge to share. How would you feel about having an art therapist in the family?"

Her mother's eyes widened.

"I envision a little storefront where I'll offer group art classes and individual painting lessons for children." Miranda stood and paced the room while communicating with her hands. "My focus will be on healing and renewal through self-expression and imagination. Of course, music will guide the meditations. And we can donate completed artwork to the local children's hospital to decorate the uninspiring walls and hallways—picture colorful ceiling tiles above examining room tables and murals stretched across intimidating waiting areas. We'll uplift others through our brushstrokes while restoring ourselves. I also foresee paint parties and summer camp, wine-down Wednesday evenings for the adults, and volunteer events to benefit the community. The possibilities are limitless."

"Sounds fantastic, honey! You certainly have taken enough psychology classes, and art has always been your passion." Clara beamed. "My daughter—a therapist. I like it!"

"It was once unthinkable that someone like me could help others," Miranda said. "Now I know I'm qualified for the job. The career counselor determined many of my credits will carry over, and we outlined the remaining courses I'll need to complete the program. There's a grueling thesis I'll need to write, but still, I can't believe how close I am to receiving my master's degree."

"That's amazing! Put another check mark next to registering for the spring semester here."

"Um, not yet." Miranda drank a few sips of water and took her time twisting back the cap. "The one thing I forgot to mention was that my talks with the career counselor began late last summer while I was still in Cobblers Hill. A representative from the local university suggested I apply to their renowned art therapy program. I knew it was a long shot I'd get accepted, let alone afford out-of-state tuition, but I allowed myself to drift from reality. I applied on a whim." Miranda stared down at her mismatched socks and picked lint off her sweats. "They accepted my application. They want me!"

"Oh, I see." Clara sunk into the couch. "That's fantastic news, but, um, I can't believe you'd consider leaving town again."

"I wanted to have options, you know? Both programs, the one here and the other in New England, are highly regarded. But since plans didn't work out as I hoped, it looks like I'll be finishing my studies nearby."

"I'm overjoyed by the check marks on your bucket list." Clara gave an exaggerated sigh. "And I'll credit your grandmother for making this possible for you, for us."

Her mother's word choice of "overjoyed" triggered warm summer memories of hot-air ballooning, distant on a dismal winter's night.

"Thanks, Mom. I never found my purpose in life, but that's changing. Finally, I have a destination for my studies and goals for the future. No more missed opportunities—I'm excited about a new beginning. And rather than avoid relationships, I welcome them."

"Speaking of new beginnings, I kind of made some strides myself while you were away."

Clara stood, stretched, and walked over to the artificial tree they had intended to decorate days ago. Dust lifted into the air as she rummaged through boxes. "Change was never my strong suit, but your arrangement pushed me beyond my comfort zone last summer." She emerged with a glass ornament dangling from each hand, luring Miranda from the couch.

"Oh? In what way?"

"Well, this house had a chill without you, so I looked for social outlets and jumped on every opportunity not to be alone." Clara's eyes darted back and forth across the branches. "Remember when we would see Mrs. Stewart leaving her house in an evening gown and a flowing strand of pearls?"

"Yep, and we would make up stories about where she was heading—a Great Gatsby gala, a castle ball."

"A costume party, a senior citizen's prom." Clara chuckled. "Little did we know we have celebrities living on our block. Mrs. Stewart—Jennie—is a concert pianist who has performed at Lincoln Center, the Metropolitan Opera House, and Albert Hall, to name a few prestigious venues. She craves an audience, so I spent my Sunday mornings getting acquainted with pieces from Chopin and Debussy from her living room sofa. I don't want to hear, 'I told you so,' but I enjoy classical music now."

Miranda pretended to zip her lips.

"And Harris Stewart sings baritone in a barbershop quartet. What a powerful voice! I'm telling you, that old couple is nothing like we thought from our quick exchanges over the years. They are quite the dynamic duo!"

"It's a shame we never bothered to know our neighbors," Miranda replied. "Maybe it's time we built a front porch instead of a wall."

"You might be onto something. I also participated in a book club. I never understood the appeal of gathering with others to discuss plot and prose, but I finally got it. Who would have thought a single story could prompt so many conflicting reactions in readers? I was intrigued by the various perspectives on the authors' intent and purpose. Look at me sounding all intellectual," Clara said with a giggle. "Anyway, I have suggestions for your winter reading, honey."

Clara straightened a crooked branch and spread apart others, filling in the gaps. "These mom legs completed a 5K charity walk, not once but twice. And I learned to Zumba even though I have no rhythm whatsoever. But the best part—the best part was—"

"Was what? Don't leave me in suspense here."

The den fell silent. Even the walls yearned to hear what Clara Blair had to say.

"I went on a date with someone I met through a ballroom dance class." Blushing like a schoolgirl, Clara turned away from her daughter. "Okay, so it was a handful of dates. And there are more to come. Hopefully, a lot more."

"You're kidding me? That's fantastic, Mom." Miranda reached over to hug her mother with a triumphant smile, brushing up against the weak branches and making the ornaments sway. "Why did you wait so long to share this with me? I would've been as happy about the news a few weeks ago as I am now."

"Because I wasn't sure how to handle recent developments in the romance department. It's kind of new territory for me again." Clara placed hooks on the remaining ornaments with distracted hands. "Besides, I was afraid of your reaction to change, and I didn't want to make the situation awkward between us or with Anderson. I'm sorry I hesitated. I should have known better than to sneak around."

Miranda hung a shiny red star on a low-hanging branch and an iridescent one above it. She stood back, swapped the two ornaments, and nodded her approval.

"I figured I would wait until it was newsworthy to tell," her mother explained timidly.

"Well, then, Anderson must be worth reporting. You deserve to find happiness again."

The corner streetlamp's glow shone through the front bay window. The colorful lights of the pre-lit Christmas tree twinkled like a spinning disco ball within the modest room.

"So much for me being open and honest, huh?" Clara didn't meet Miranda's stare. "It'll take time to unlearn old habits, but I'm working on it."

The tune others sang—wanting to protect Miranda and being afraid to share information—was becoming annoyingly familiar. But Miranda had been equally guilty of withholding details during and after the hundred days. And if she could justify her reasoning, then her mother, and possibly Jake, deserved forgiveness too.

"We are a work in progress. I'm over-the-moon thrilled for you." Miranda reached for a box of tinsel. The tangled Mylar strands, recycled from previous holiday seasons, clung to everything but the branches.

"I'm so relieved, honey, and I can't wait for you to meet him."

"That makes two of us. And for the record, your face is brighter than this tree."

"Um, there's something else." Clara removed a silvery strand from her ugly Christmas sweater and placed it on the tree. "He asked me to go away with him over New Year's weekend, and . . . I said yes. Before your mind wanders with assumptions, please consider joining us. Anderson was genuine when he extended the invitation."

"Wow, I didn't see that coming, but I think it's fabulous you two want to celebrate together. As much as I appreciate the offer, I will pass." She busied her hands, fixing and shifting ornaments and fighting with tinsel. "Another time, I hope."

If things had been different, Miranda would have headed to the winter wonderland in Cobblers Hill for delicate snowfall and crackling fireplaces, frosted windowpanes, and handsome Jake Colby. If only.

The quintessential New England town likely resembled the Dickens Village with velvety red bows, fresh garland, and wreaths adorning every lamppost. The gazebo in the square welcomed tired shoppers to rest on its benches. A fragrant balsam fir took center stage within its octagonal posts. Carolers of all ages sang songs of reverence around St. Therese's nativity scene on the snow-covered lawn.

"Are you sure?" Clara chewed her lower lip. "Because I can cancel my plans. The three of us can stay here and binge on old movies and order takeout." She began stacking empty boxes, placing some inside others. "What am I doing? It's foolish of me to think I have a second chance at something unforgettable."

"Absolutely not! Take that trip. Mark Twain once said you must be willing to go out on a limb if you want to discover life's fruit."

"Thanks for sharing, honey." Clara picked up loose strands of tinsel from the rug. "I've never been one to venture anywhere in life, but Anderson brings out a bolder, more confident side of me. He restores hope that I haven't had in a long time."

"He sounds wonderful. Until we meet, how about sneaking me a few details?"

"Well, he's a few years older, making him wiser."

"Divorced?" Miranda raised a brow.

"Nope, a widower with two married daughters, Mary and Gianna, and three adorable grandsons. Is it Bradley, Brice, and Bryan? Or Brandon, Brett, and Byron? Oh, I forget their names all the time."

"At least you remember they start with the letter 'B,' right?"

"You have a point," Clara said. "Unlike us homebodies, Anderson has this wild, adventurous side that makes my adrenaline surge. He's been begging me to skydive."

Miranda cupped her mouth.

"I know, I know. It's a ridiculous thought—your mom, jumping out of a plane. But Anderson's easygoing temperament has a soothing influence over me. With him, anything is possible because I feel safe. We're opposites, but maybe that's what fosters a good team. I'm just lucky to have him on the other end of my seesaw."

"Sounds like he is a keeper, and you, Mom, are starstruck."

"Let's not go ringing wedding bells or anything." Clara giggled, and joy covered her face. "You can't possibly know a person's true self in a few short months. Only time will tell."

She draped her arm around Miranda, and they gazed at their decorated tree. Many glass balls had shattered over the years, and the ornaments became scarce on the four-foot Fraser fir. Although modest, standing a little crooked with several misshaped branches, the tree had celebrated with them since the first Christmas after Victor Blair's disappearance.

Neither Miranda nor her mother exchanged thoughts, but it was time for new traditions. Change had crept in. Nothing would be the same next year or ever again.

"I think I'll make some hot cocoa," Clara said. "Care for a cup? I bought those tiny marshmallows you like."

"I'll hold off. I haven't exercised much with this weather, and I'm feeling it around my waistline."

"If you say so." Her mother waltzed toward the kitchen, twirling through the doorway, losing balance, laughing, and fading from sight.

Outside, a sheet of white blanketed her neighborhood and hushed it to sleep. But in Miranda's imaginary Cobblers Hill snow globe, sleigh bells rang on each street corner. The winter chill invited couples to snuggle a little closer.

Jake bundled up in a burgundy plaid scarf with his eyes matching the evergreens of the season. And festive mistletoe suspended from doorways, beckoning romance for lovers and those looking to become them. There was likely no place more enchanting than Jake's hometown at Christmastime.

Having someone special made each sunrise hopeful, each sunset magical, and the moments in between memorable. How Miranda missed that someone. Even if Jake had been the wrong tree to venture out on a limb, the forest was full of others.

In heeding his advice, Miranda would allow herself to believe something crazy good was in store. She owed it to her future self to be open to the possibilities.

It was time to give someone other than Jake Colby a chance at being *the one*. Like Clara, maybe Miranda could find love again after all.

Chapter 40

"Are you sure you don't want to join us for the holiday weekend?"

Clara stood in her daughter's bedroom doorway, clutching a suitcase handle and shifting her weight on alternating hips.

"You could use a change of scenery for a few days, and, who knows, the mountains might inspire your next masterpiece. Anderson promised the views would be breathtaking."

"I appreciate the offer," Miranda said, "but I should stick to my original plans. I'm due for another check off the bucket list."

"You're referring to Primrose Lane, aren't you?"

Miranda nodded. "I'll review the realtor's paperwork and start the process. I won't allow Grandma Trudy's property to hold me back in the New Year."

"I see." Clara's raised forehead revealed a series of horizontal lines. "It's your cottage now, no longer Trudy's, but if selling it will bring you happiness, then that's what you need to do. Just don't forget to eat. You've already missed two meals today. I know how you get lost in the hours."

"I'll order Chinese takeout and watch *It's a Wonderful Life*." Miranda stifled an unbrushed-teeth smile. "For someone who has never been a New Year's fan, I'm looking forward to the ball dropping tonight. The time can't pass quickly enough for a fresh start."

"Chin up. I know exciting things are in store for you—for both of us." Clara approached Miranda's bed, her motherly hands smoothing the covers. "Are you sure you don't mind being alone?"

"Go have fun." Miranda shooed her mother. "You've waited a long time to be this happy. Enjoy every moment together, and don't look back."

"I'd better be on my way then." Clara pressed a kiss against her daughter's forehead and scurried off with teenage excitement.

Once the front door locked, Miranda sat up in bed and smeared tears across her face. On the year's last evening, there wouldn't be streamers or celebratory noisemakers—only water rushing through rusty pipes and restless wind banging against vulnerable shutters. The attorney's folder, outlined by dust and visible from every bedroom angle, had taken up a residence on her nightstand. She located the realtor's business card, held it between her fingers, tapped it against her palm, and analyzed the calibri font. The attorney had assured her relinquishing the cottage would be a seamless process requiring minimal involvement.

Miranda reached for her cell phone with a trembling hand, tapped the eleven digits on the keypad, and pressed the call button. Each ring on the other end constricted her throat. Not only was it difficult to swallow, but she might choke on her words.

"Good afternoon, LaMano's Realty. How may I assist you?"

"Yes, hi, um, hello. This is Miranda Blair. I'd like to speak with a realtor, please."

"I'm sorry, but you have reached the answering service. In light of the holiday, the office has closed early. I'll gladly take your message and have someone return your call."

Miranda was pleasantly surprised by the woman's British accent. She had anticipated—even deserved—a gruff greeting, having ignored the office's weekly calls.

"Hello? Are you still there?"

"Yes, then I'd like to leave a message, please," she said with a groggy voice. Having slept half the day, she was still tired—tired of wallowing in sweats, tired of feeling uninspired, tired of being home-sick while at home. "I'm ready to sell my property at 21 Primrose Lane in Cobblers Hill—"

Despite a few rehearsals, saying, "Primrose Lane, Cobblers Hill" and "sell" in the same sentence, followed by her contact information, made it frighteningly real. Miranda was officially closing the door on what might have been—a finality that made her mouth water from nausea.

"I'll pass along this message," the woman assured her. "Is there anything else I can assist you with?"

Please sever ties to Jake Colby as quickly as possible, so there's no other choice than to learn to live without him.

"Um, you can mention I'm Felix Baxter's client, and I'm eager to get this sale underway." Miranda's eyes wandered back and forth from one corner of the uninspiring bedroom to the other.

"Very well, then. I'll take care of this for you. Happy New Year, Ms. Blair. Goodbye."

Perhaps Miranda would hear from an agent in a few minutes or hours. She might even have to wait until the long holiday weekend drew to a close. She sorted paperwork into neat piles between frequent glances at her phone, willing it to vibrate, ring, or send out smoke signals.

As someone who struggled to balance a checkbook and add without a calculator, how was Miranda supposed to interpret mutual funds and stocks? She scribbled notes and yawned, then highlighted bank names and stretched. As her to-do list lengthened, the attorney's folder emptied. Only a cream-colored envelope remained.

Miranda's pillow conveniently kept an imprint from her recent naps. It would be easy to pull the covers up to her chin and ignore the thickly laid responsibilities across her comforter. New Year's resolutions wouldn't allow for procrastination, but the ball hadn't yet dropped. The folder's final item could wait until after the holiday weekend, along with the other incomplete tasks she never asked to inherit.

The nightstand clock ticked more emphatically with every passing minute. While the freebie T-shirt Miranda threw at it may have blocked the ever-changing digits, loose ends still hovered over her conscience like a past-due term paper at the semester's end.

With positive affirmations still cheerleading from her trapeze adventure, Miranda tossed her final tissue in the pail and slid a finger under the envelope's sealed flap.

My dearest Miranda,

By the time you read this letter, I will have left this life behind for another purpose. Not knowing how the years will unfold has challenged my words as I sit in my sunroom with a hesitant pen. Thoughts are running circles in my head, and there's an ache for forgiveness in my heart. However, my view of golden fields and amber treetops fills me with warmth and nudges me to press on.

I wasn't the grandmother I hoped to be during my time here. I am genuinely sorry for the disappointments my words and actions, or lack thereof, may have caused.

Please know I have paid my dues for these mistakes. I'm afraid that regret is a heavy burden to carry on a lonesome journey.

But the past should not dictate the future, my dear granddaughter. And so, it became the purpose of my remaining years to help secure your happiness after my passing. I created the arrangement summoning you to Cobblers Hill with the purest of intentions.

I have witnessed the cottage's inspiration, the magnificent coastline's healing power, the community's affection, and the town's encouragement. I have faith in new beginnings, and I believe in your bright future here, Miranda.

As one can't predict their final hour, I had no idea of your life stage during the arrangement. You might have been a young adult on a quest for freedom and independence in New England. Or perhaps an experienced mom with a growing family in need of a gathering place for summertime fun. Or maybe a single woman looking to mend a broken heart and piece together her soul during a cozy New England winter.

Regardless, you would never be alone in Cobblers Hill with such wonderful neighbors. To know the Colby family is to love them, especially that charming Jake. I often thought he would be favorable in your life if you weren't spoken for at the time of your visit. But even with my lack of experience as a grandmother, I knew better than to overstep and play matchmaker.

If you fulfilled my arrangement or even satisfied a few of those hundred days, you witnessed some of the things I referenced firsthand. What you choose to do with the property after I am gone is ultimately your decision. I will rest in peace.

Dearest granddaughter Randy, I trust you have read my other letter, too, by now. You were barely a teenager when I wrote it, and I was a younger version of an old lady. I held on to that piece of paper throughout the years and reread my words whenever I sought comfort. Somehow, it eased my pain.

I hoped my heartfelt sentiments would heal any grudges toward me. I prayed you would realize that I loved you from afar despite our lack of history. Eventually, I turned the envelope over to Jake and made him promise to leave it for you at the appropriate time.

These are just a few more thoughts of grandmotherly wisdom. Love comes in various forms, under unique circumstances, and during special seasons of our lives known only to a higher power. It is the greatest gift of all but a fragile one.

When you are lucky enough to find love, embrace it with endless gratitude. Resist turning your back on what could be, Randy, and don't give in to fear or crumble with challenges. Complacency and pride should never settle where they don't belong. Nothing in life is perfect, nor will it ever be.

Please travel mindfully wherever your journey may lead; not every road winds back around for a second chance.

And so, I must leave you now, but this time with love, laughter, and sunshine.

Grandmother Trudy

Miranda folded the letter and tucked it into the cream-colored envelope. Then, with a surge of energy, she tore the realtor's business card into pieces and leaped from her bed.

Chapter 41

The year's countdown dwindled on the dashboard clock. Miranda gripped the steering wheel in the nine and three positions. Like spinning tires on the highway pavement, her thoughts raced in different directions from Jake Colby and Cobblers Hill to Grandma Trudy and Addie, then to the hundred-day arrangement and back to Jake.

With a heavy foot on the gas pedal, she ignored the ever-changing speed limit and the disappearing cars in her rearview mirror. The headlights' cast illuminated the darkness and brought clarity.

I am Randy! Miranda—Randy.

Jagged pieces of a confusing puzzle had smoothed, and previously missing ones were finally falling into place. Either Miranda was too young to remember the name coined by her grandmother, or Clara never acknowledged it. Jake's little niece had been right; everyone in Cobblers Hill had a short name—Addie, Bree, Linz, PG, the nephews, Jake, and even Trudy.

After twenty-five years of answering only to Miranda and the more recent kiddo or darlin', she now had a nickname. It was another validation she belonged in the coastal New England town with the others.

The original pink envelope lay in the passenger seat, accompanied by the newly discovered cream-colored one. Both letters provided grandmotherly wisdom Miranda yearned to hear. Through Grandma Trudy's written profession of love and remorse, she had been addressing Miranda, not some old flame. And throughout the hundred-day journey, her affection had been present in sunrises and sunsets, within the cottage's serenity and excitement of Miranda's budding relationship with Jake. It was present now, too, offering encouragement for the evening and the promise of tomorrow.

The passage of green highway signs brought Miranda closer to where she hoped to reclaim her happiness. While Barron Park would always be special, she was heading *home* now. There was no word more meaningful nor place she desired to be on the last evening of the year. All she needed and wanted was wrapped up in the simplicity of life in Cobblers Hill with the unmistakable presence of Jake Colby.

Miranda pressed the gas pedal, nudged by thoughts that Jake wasn't spending the holiday alone. Or maybe the neighbors were out celebrating. She would have contacted Jake and Addie before leaving Barron Park if there had been minutes to spare. But every second of separation, consumed by misunderstandings and regret, tugged at her heartstrings. The "whys" and "how comes" waited impatiently to be satisfied. Miranda would not miss her opportunity to seek the truth, nor would she fear the answers. Her mistakes and those made by others were learning experiences from which to grow. Not every road winds back around for a second chance.

At last, her Toyota exited the highway and headed toward the quaint New England town. Along neighboring streets, gingerbread-trimmed Victorians nestled in what looked like a Currier and Ives scene. Miranda had disregarded their grandeur during her initial shortsighted drive. Although the road led to the same destination, she, the traveler, had changed.

Through picture windows, families gathered in joy and laughter, building anticipation for the life Miranda would create in Cobblers

Hill. Jake had opened her eyes to the beauty of his hometown and her heart to the possibilities that existed there. And Grandma Trudy had validated Miranda's place in the story.

Around the bend of Primrose Lane, the partially boarded-up cottage stood amongst a backdrop of bare trees. Snow blanketed the once-green property, but it was familiar and welcoming, like seeing an old friend after a long absence. Resisting the urge to wave, Miranda smiled at her home instead. Someone had shoveled her driveway, although there had been at least a day's dusting of fresh snowfall. Jake was likely that someone.

The crocuses would peek their hellos in time, and the garden would bloom in a menagerie of colors. Ripened fruit would drape from backyard branches and perfume the crisp air. The curtainless cottage windows would reflect glorious sunshine and offer a magnificent hillside view.

Clara would grow to love it there. Anderson and his family might too. Love didn't divide; it multiplied. Miranda would sow seeds of happiness that embraced everyone, and her home would foster lifelong memories.

Snow crunched under her boots as she trudged through the open gate and down the path to the Colbys' back door. Except for the temporary beam from motion detectors, the neighbors' home was sleepy. Fog came from Miranda's quickened breath, and her teeth chattered with anticipation. She knocked lightly at first, followed by knocks of more intent until the inside light turned on, and a weary Addie opened the door.

"Heavens to Betsy, will ya lookie here! What in the world? Come in, come in, ya gotta be freezin' out there."

"Hi, Gram." Miranda choked on emotion. "It's wonderful to see you." She reached forward to meet the cherished old woman's extended arms. "I know it's late. Am I interrupting anything?"

"Not at all, darlin'." Addie's wrinkled pajamas and messy hair answered otherwise. Disguising a yawn, she reached for Miranda's coat and escorted her into the den.

"Why, ain't that a pleasant surprise? I was sittin' here watchin' 'em New Year's Eve programs. They get crazier each year, I tell ya. Would ya look at 'em outfits 'em gals are wearin'. Sinful, I say."

A dim light came from the dated television, and a winter chill penetrated the air. The Colby home lacked the summertime warmth and old-world charm that Miranda fondly remembered.

"Let me grab my robe, darlin'." Gram rubbed her arms. "Be right back. Get comfy."

Not only had Miranda disturbed the old woman late in the evening, but there was no sign of Jake. Just because she was still entangled in their web of summer memories, it didn't mean he hadn't moved on to make new ones in another season.

A bundled-up Gram returned, sporting furry slippers and a hot-pink fleece robe.

"Let me put this here lamp on so we can see each other." Jake's grandmother rotated the switch. The lighting remained dim; perhaps the lamp needed a new bulb or higher wattage or a modern replacement. "Ah, look at ya there all gussied up. You're as pretty as a peach."

Miranda glanced down at her tight black dress. She scratched an imaginary itch on her blushed cheek.

"I'm sorry, darlin', but ya missed Jake."

Miranda bit her lower lip and stifled a gasp. The sweet old woman mirrored her disappointment.

"He went out hours ago. Said he wouldn't be back till Sunday." Gram shrugged. "Wish I knew more, darlin'. You can send him one of 'em texts, though."

Assumptions about where Jake went and who he was with and what they were doing beckoned Miranda to cruise anywhere self-imposed blame wouldn't follow. But assumptions, she knew, could be misleading. She wouldn't surrender to fear this time or crumble from a setback.

"What can I get ya? A nice glass of wine or a hot cup of tea?" Gram had a renewed sparkle in her eye. "How about some creamy eggnog with a sprinkle of cinnamon?"

"That's okay. I'm fine," Miranda said, although there was no escaping southern hospitality.

"Ah, I know, a little piece of pie with a dollop of my homemade whipped cream. Be right back." The old woman disappeared into the kitchen and called out, "Ya mind clickin' on that there tree?"

Miranda fidgeted with the switch until the balsam fir's branches illuminated a wondrous glow. The vibrant-colored ornaments came to life and spread holiday cheer across the once drowsy room. Still, nothing was the same. The prized sea glass collection had relocated from the fireplace mantel to a more visible end table. The hand-tufted area rug lay horizontal rather than vertical, allowing more walking space. And the couch had moved to the other side of the room, where it no longer blocked the radiator. Even the formerly bare walls now had something to celebrate.

The grandfather clock had ticked steadily, and life continued during Miranda's three-month absence. Change was inevitable, but now she hoped to be part of it. Wending her way around the room's perimeter, Miranda inched in at the newly decorated walls and gasped.

The Colbys' den had become an exhibit featuring original works from the town's newest artist, Miranda Blair. With her mouth gaped open, she rekindled each warm summer memory from her hundred-day journey, lost and found, preserved in thick acrylic brushstrokes on framed canvas.

"Beautiful, huh?"

Jake's voice resonated from behind.

Chapter 42

"I hope you don't mind," Jake said, "but those paintings deserved to be put on display rather than occupy some landfill. Luckily, I retrieved them before the sanitation truck did."

With her Jake-radar faulting, Miranda hadn't heard the rumble of his Jeep or the jingle of his keys as he hung them on the hook.

Earlier that day, it seemed likely they would never see each other again. Yet there he stood in the doorway with his coat in his hand and a buffalo plaid scarf draped around his neck. The sight of him, like a mirage, made Miranda catch her breath. They stared at each other from across the room, breathing in the same scent of Christmas pine.

"Hey, you."

"What are you doing here, Miranda?"

"I could ask the same question. Gram said you were gone for a few days."

"I had a change of plans."

"Um, same here," she said. "I hope you don't mind me dropping by uninvited and empty-handed. I should have stopped at the liquor store but assumed there would be long lines. The bakery closed early."

She placed her palms on her hips, entwined her fingers, shifted her weight back and forth, and ultimately let her arms dangle at her sides. Gram entered the room with the piece of pie but quickly retraced her steps and trudged down the hallway in her noisy slippers.

"We've always welcomed you here, you know that." Jake's reply came barely louder than a whisper. He tossed his coat onto the chair and fussed with his cuffs. "Just curious, though, why did you return tonight after all these weeks? What's changed?"

"Nothing and everything. I was hoping for a few minutes of your time to explain."

Jake knelt before the stone fireplace. From behind, she noticed his hair was shorter, and he wore thicker layers of unfamiliar winter attire. Although the seasons had changed, the way she felt about him hadn't. He maneuvered a few logs and kindling like a seasoned player on the reality show *Survivor*. The room reflected an orange glow with a single stroke of a match. Wafts of warm air thawed the tips of Miranda's toes, but an anticipated chill still lingered.

He took a front-row seat by the fire and patted the spot beside him. Miranda smoothed her dress and settled cross-legged on the area rug.

"I should have never abandoned you that night at the beach, Jake," she said ruefully. "I admit it was selfish and hypocritical to run from Cobblers Hill as I had accused my father of doing all those years ago. And it was inconsiderate to ignore your calls and texts these past few months. I was confused and afraid of my feelings, so I looked for excuses to leave instead of finding solutions to stay." Miranda's lips quivered, and she steadied her jaw. "I've learned from my mistakes, though. You deserved better, and I'm deeply sorry."

She reached out and placed her hand on Jake's; his fingers did not budge.

"I'm a slow learner." Miranda rescinded her hand. "But you always had my back even when it didn't appear that way. Gram did too. I should have never doubted you—it was my insecurity. And I know my grandmother loved me from afar. So did my dad. Realizing this, and understanding the reasons behind his disappearance, have made a world of difference in my life."

"You sound at peace with your past. I knew, in time, you'd find closure," Jake replied dryly, his attention directed at the dancing flames. "So, you're here to clear your conscience before moving on, then?"

"That's not it at all. Well, um, it's partially true, but there's so much more. You're such a blessing to me, Jake, and I'm grateful the arrangement brought us together." Miranda's voice cracked, but she was too absorbed at the moment to care. "These past few months in Barron Park were challenging but necessary. Beyond delving into my history and taking responsibility, I had no choice but to gather my broken parts and develop a new set of wings—this time, stronger, more resilient ones."

Any reaction from Jake was justified—a heavy sigh or low groan, a loud huff or snickering laugh. He could whisper or shout, grit his teeth or roll his eyes. Instead, Jake kept a poker face and the fire poker in his hand.

Miranda picked up a lonesome strand of tinsel and twined it through and around each finger until it left dark marks on her skin. Eventually, it snapped in half, and she surveyed the room for another distraction from his lackluster replies.

"The pieces seem to be coming together in my life," she explained. "All except for one."

"What does that mean?"

"I needed these months without you to discover where I belong. Since that revelation, I have closed the doors back in Barron Park. I resigned from my position at the historical society, paid off my student loans, and donated items that once defined me."

Miranda sat up a little taller. She kept her manicured hands clasped in her lap rather than hide them, bite her fingernails, or chew her cuticles.

"Mom and I found forgiveness—no more wallowing in lost decades or moseying without a direction. There won't be any grudges or half-empty glasses for the Blair women. And lately, I've stripped my self-imposed blinders too."

"All good stuff. Sounds like you've made huge strides since leaving Cobblers Hill."

"I wouldn't say huge, but I am a work in progress committed to change. And get this . . . Mom has a new boyfriend now. She's smitten."

"I'm happy for her—for you both. I know you never wanted to move on without your mother."

"Wait, there's more." Miranda's grin spanned her face. "I'll be receiving my master's degree in art therapy as early as next summer. After that, I have plans to open a studio and offer classes and workshops."

"I had no idea you were close to another graduation," Jake said.

"Me either, but it's true. You and Gram helped me realize being surrounded by the right people can make all the difference in overcoming life's roadblocks. I want to be that person for others."

"With such a loving and compassionate heart, you're destined to touch many lives," Jake replied, feeding the fire with his back to Miranda. "I admire your grit, and I've always said you're a talented artist."

"Thank you. That means everything to me."

"Was there anything else you came here to say, Miranda?"

She took a deep breath. "There is. I hope it's not too late for us to continue learning about one another. I'd love to pick up where we left off last summer, if you'll give me another chance. I never had a more fulfilling relationship before. We made a terrific team."

Aside from the crackling fire, Miranda's sentiments met deafening silence. Still, she pressed on. "The days we spent together were the happiest times. To be honest, I pictured us together whenever I thought about tomorrow."

"That's what you want? You and I to be 'we'?" Jake narrowed the distance between them. There was a slight curve in the corners of his mouth—a glimpse of his old self.

"Oh, more than anything. I may have a funny way of showing it, but you mean more to me than I thought anyone ever could. I don't want to paint the future without you in it, Jake."

Free-falling, Miranda hoped to land safely in Jake's muscular arms. Instead, she lowered her head into her hands and massaged her temples. "Wow, this is more difficult than I thought. I'm so overwhelmed being here right now."

"What does that mean, 'right now'?"

"At this moment, here with you. A hundred days together wasn't long enough. I'm not sure a lifetime would be either. And since the local university accepted my application for their art therapy program and transferred my grad credits, I plan on registering for the spring semester as soon as the registrar opens Monday morning."

"You'll be staying at Trudy's!"

"Well, not exactly. I'll be living at home."

"That doesn't make any sense." His shoulders slumped. "I'm afraid I'm lost here."

"I was the lost one, Jake, but I recently discovered who I am and where I'm heading in life. With no minutes to waste, I plan to appreciate every hour of the journey. You're looking at your new permanent neighbor. This is home now."

"Are you serious?"

Jake gazed at her with his brilliant emerald eyes, fostering a connection for the first time that evening. The once chilly den had become a comfortable room temperature. "That's fantastic news!

I'm not sure if I can top that, but I'd like the chance to say a few words."

Miranda placed her hand on his bare forearm. Warmth radiated from his skin.

"Okay," she replied with an endearing smile. "I'm all yours."

Chapter 43

"For starters, I want you to know how much I enjoyed accompanying you on your hundred-day journey," Jake said without removing his gaze from the dancing flames. "Before we met, I was stuck in the past, lonely and uninspired, without knowing how to break free. Time was passing, and yet I had nothing to show for it. But my luck shifted that afternoon in Gram's kitchen."

The memory of a half-dressed, facial-haired Jake rescuing his grandmother's teakettle delighted Miranda.

"Your receptiveness to change last summer inspired me to take inventory of my shortcomings and believe I, too, was capable of more," he continued. "I was intrigued by our differences and comforted by our similarities. I found myself drawn to your natural beauty, humility, and innocence. I wanted to fill my bucket list with rewarding experiences because *you* would be the one to share them with me. I could go on and on."

"Don't let me stop you." Miranda chuckled.

"The point is, my days had new meaning again—to help you find happiness in Cobblers Hill so you would extend your stay. By the summer's end, you were the one who healed me. You made my life whole in ways no one else had before."

"I'm grateful we helped each other. And to think Trudy had a heavy hand in it as well. I'd love to know more about my grandma, Jake."

"Well," he said, running his fingers through his hair, "she was a strong-willed woman, which probably doesn't surprise. Gram would say Trudy was as tough as shoe leather–a side of her that kept us on our toes. But like you, she had a compassionate heart and gentle spirit."

"She did, didn't she?"

"Yep. Trudy led a simple life alone here in Cobblers Hill. When she wasn't wearing her gardening gloves, she had a piece of sketching charcoal in her hand or an open Bible across her lap."

"I knew my grandma was modest and spiritual and artistic! All the signs were there."

"And don't forget talented with those crochet hooks. Every Veteran's Day, she would donate handmade blankets to the local VA hospital. Trudy never expected anything from anyone. There was also a fragile side under that tough exterior of an independent and capable old lady. Gram and I learned to handle it with care. That revelation came after Trudy shared her lifelong regrets and intentions for your visit. She wanted to inspire happiness, so you would experience the joy she had never provided–the joy she denied herself. Would you like to see pictures of her?"

"I'd love to," Miranda replied, the unfamiliar memories no longer a threat.

Jake removed a worn, leather-bound album from the bookshelf. Then, resuming his spot beside Miranda, he placed it across their laps.

"Before Trudy went into the nursing home, she gave us this album for safekeeping. It's yours now." He pointed to a creased photo on the first page. "There's your grandmother."

Miranda beamed. This time, the words "your grandmother" instilled feelings of pride and gratitude. Gertrude Blair was a piece of Miranda—a forever branch of her family tree and a link to what her future might hold.

Seeing old photographs of Trudy in her garden, smiling against a backdrop of wisteria, and others with a younger Jake and Addie in front of the cottage provided an overwhelming sense of family.

"It would have been easier to spend those hundred days convincing you that Trudy was a good-natured, well-intentioned woman. That was not her plan. Your grandmother needed you to come to that realization on your own during your time in Cobblers Hill. She made it clear Gram and I weren't to interpret the past."

"I know that was a tough request to honor."

"It would have been, but since you never questioned or dug for answers, we could respect Trudy's wishes. She asked that I pass along a piece of history to you at the appropriate time. Delivering that pink envelope, Miranda, was the extent of my arrangement with your grandmother. That and steering clear of your past, of course. Everything else I said and did this summer was genuine, from deep within my heart, out of want and desire, not as an obligation. Anyway, I kept my promise to Trudy by slipping the envelope into your picnic basket that day at Edens Cove."

He turned another page and pointed to a photograph of a younger woman holding a bright-eyed, pig-tailed little girl on her lap. "Randy—that was how she referred to you."

Miranda's heart leaped, hearing Jake address her by her nickname and seeing the joy on her grandmother's face.

"How I spent the arrangement making assumptions about that letter," Miranda said sheepishly. "I wasn't aware I was Randy until earlier this afternoon."

"Really?" Jake cocked his head to the side. "You're kidding? Oh, I just figured—"

"Honestly, I thought Randy was an old boyfriend. Why didn't you or Gram ever call me by that name?"

"You introduced yourself as Miranda Blair. And you deserved the chance to establish your own identity here. At least that's how we felt."

Jake poked at the fire while narrating tidbits of Miranda's history. Embers glowed and crackled, and the logs shifted and burned. Gingerly, Miranda turned each unchronological page featuring youthful photos of her father and grandmother.

With deep, self-assured breaths, she exhaled doubt and insecurity. There was no longer the urge to bite her cuticles, crack her knuckles, or consider what-ifs. The past was the stepping-stone upon which she would lunge into her bright future.

"As the summer moved on," Jake continued, "you and I grew closer. Still, details withheld to respect your grandmother's wishes formed a wedge between us. I couldn't be the man I wanted to be while keeping the two worlds—yours and Trudy's, and ours—separate, if that makes sense."

"Perfect sense," Miranda said. "I'm sorry you were stuck in that position, and I'm humbled by everyone wanting to protect me and be a part of my life." She placed the album by her side and smoothed her hand lovingly over its cover.

"I reminded myself the summer was never supposed to be about you and me becoming 'us.' Instead of compromising Trudy's arrangement," Jake said, "I enjoyed your friendship and hoped something more meaningful would develop beyond those hundred days. It was difficult being around you, not knowing if I could be with you."

Miranda's pulse raced as her stomach danced to the words she longed to hear.

"Even though I had good intentions, I should have never misled you with Kasey." Jake's face was apple red.

"I understand now. The facade of your girlfriend helped our relationship develop. There was never any awkwardness or expectation to complicate things. I'm grateful to Kasey for that. Honestly, I am."

"Anyway, I blamed myself for how Trudy's plan had ended. I had let you both down, and my hesitancy ruined what I hoped for deep inside." His eyes met Miranda's gaze, conjuring flattery and sadness, relief and anticipation. "I tried to get through to you, to apologize and tell you how much you mean to me. I found myself hibernating on the couch and wasting the days away when you wouldn't reply. Then Gram got on my case and began hollering at me. Her words were, 'Sittin' there lookin' like a grizzly bear, feelin' sorry for yourself, ain't gonna bring that gal back.' She threw me out of the house."

"She did not!" Miranda cupped her mouth.

"Yep. Tough love, as they say. The point is, spending all that time with you last summer made me realize who I wanted to be, and that meant no longer living someone else's dream or running from the disappointments in my past. Like you, I found those months apart to be humbling and lonely, but they also pushed me in the direction I'm headed today."

The grandfather clock chimed, alerting them of the final hour, but Miranda barely blinked during Jake's fireside story.

"Gram reminded me as long as I didn't see a 'For Sale' sign on your lawn, the cottage was still yours, and you'd be back someday. I remember her words. 'Ya two gotta make history together, and that's that.'"

"How I missed her!" Miranda smiled as if the joyful expression would somehow conceal how close she had come to permanently severing ties with her neighbors.

"It was the glimmer of hope I needed to get off the couch, shower, shave, rescue Gram's whistling teakettle, and then dig back in with life. I thought it best to give you space—no more calls or texts—and I would take time to regroup." Jake pushed Miranda's hair back and stroked her cheek. "I committed to becoming a better version of myself for you."

"For me?"

"Yeah, you. I threw myself into my novel, where I expressed the feelings I withheld all summer. I wrote before the sun rose and late into the evening hours. I poured my heart and soul into each sentence, and those sentences yielded paragraphs and pages."

Jake's eyes surveyed the room but returned to meet Miranda's gaze. "It was liberating to escape into my story line. Unlike reality, I could determine the appropriate ending."

"What about the store?"

"Colby's Hardware changed, everything changed," Jake said. "After you left town, my assistant Jeffrey stepped up to cover during my absence. Jeff's quite the lucrative replacement, offering workshops and product tutorials on weekends, which he enjoys and the customers love. Business has been through the roof since he expanded product lines and negotiated deals with our suppliers."

Miranda's eyes widened. "That's fantastic! I'm sure it wasn't easy relinquishing control, but it sounds like Colby's Hardware is in good hands."

"Better hands than mine, that's for sure. I'm not removing myself entirely from the store, but I am focusing on my happiness now, which means pursuing the dreams I put on hold and allowing Jeff to follow his vision as the manager. I know Pop would want that for Colby's Hardware, for me—for all of us."

Not only had Miranda spent the summer taking his meaningful advice, but Jake heeded her affirmations as well. Like the promise of Christmas, continuing to spread joy throughout the room with flickering lights and animated ornaments, hope abounded.

"Being apart for so long, you'd think things wouldn't matter as much, and feelings would fade. Today proved that's not the case." Jake reached for Miranda's hand. "Friends had plans with their significant others or traveled over the break. I didn't want to be alone on the year's final evening, so I gave into temptation."

Jake avoided eye contact with Miranda. "After weeks of being pursued by this woman from the gym, I, um, accepted an invitation to her Berkshires ski house for the holiday weekend, and—"

"And what, Jake?" Miranda squeezed his hand. The blood whirred its familiar tune in her ears. "What?"

"I was halfway there to meet her, knowing she was willing and eager to take things to the next level, but I made a U-turn and came home. I couldn't go through with it."

"Why didn't you, you know—"

"She wasn't you, Miranda," Jake pledged, entwining his fingers with hers. "It would have been meaningless to move forward and mislead her when all I wanted was to be with you. I wasn't ready to give up on us."

Like the fire log that had shifted into place, embers burned, and sparks flew. Miranda patiently awaited where their chemistry would lead them.

Chapter 44

"I have a little something for you." Jake reached under the tree for the one remaining gift and placed it in Miranda's hands. "I've waited a long time for this opportunity."

There were several creases and a tear in the foil wrapping. Strips of tape stuck to the paper without purpose. Jake was right. Gift wrapping wasn't one of his talents. But Miranda no longer sought perfection in him, herself, or anyone else. Everything he represented and aspired to become was more than enough.

Off to the side, Miranda's handbag sat idly on Gram's sofa table without the accompaniment of a wine bottle or poinsettia. Even a generic card wishing "Greetings of the Season" would have sufficed.

"Pulling up and seeing your car in the driveway tonight . . ." Jake stroked her cheek with the back of his hand. "I mean, being here, together, is the best gift of all."

Sliding her finger under the wrinkled foil paper, Miranda lifted the trinket box lid and gasped.

"You found it!"

"I always felt you deserved something special, reflective of what you mean to me."

"It's more beautiful than I could have ever imagined!"

She held her hair to the side while Jake removed the red sea glass pendant from the velvet lining and placed it around her neck.

Leaning back, he said, "Now I can admire both gifts—the one I gave and the other I received."

Miranda reached her hand up and caressed nature's perfectly weathered souvenir against her skin. "Thank you for sharing your treasure with me." She leaned in to hug Jake and settled there, snuggling against his chest. "But don't leave me hanging. You have some explaining to do."

"After you left town and Gram tossed me out of the house, I went to Edens Cove. Our memories still lingered there." Jake held Miranda tighter and nuzzled his cheek against her hair. "I remember how different the beach felt—it was wider than usual, and the packed sand was cold. I walked several miles that day, doing my usual skipping of stones and missing you tremendously."

Blissfully wrapped in the warmth of Jake's arms, Miranda breathed in his clean scent as she had the night she wore his frayed sweatshirt. Still, her insides ached from his pained words and shared suffering.

"I was looking for a sign—anything—that I would find you again if we were meant to be together. We had followed in the footsteps of my novel's characters, and I couldn't bear for the wrong story line to come true. I was turning back when I noticed something red in the sand. I thought for sure my eyes were deceiving me like they had done so many times before. But as I bent down for a closer look, it was the smoothest piece of bright red sea glass. I wish you could have been there, Miranda, but somehow you were."

The wonderment and joy of Christmastime reflected in his eyes. "This piece must have endured plenty of storms and waited for that precise moment. My search was finally over."

He squeezed her hand, or perhaps, Miranda had tightened her grip.

"Just as I had found this rare treasure at the right time, I had renewed hope that circumstances would lead us back to each other. I lost you once. I never want to lose you again."

"Good, because I've planted new roots, and I'm here to stay."

Despite everything she was or wasn't, this incredible man—this kind, loving, honorable man—had fallen for her.

Miranda had never been alone while waiting through the darkest years and loneliest hours. Jake's words echoed from their first date at Edens Cove: "God looks down the road and places people where they need to be." There had been a plan in place long before Jake and Miranda met. Life had strategically placed their footsteps throughout their joys and struggles, achievements, and hardships.

"And there's something else . . ." Jake released his fingers from hers and made his way over to the antique rolling desk in the room's corner. He returned with a gray cardboard box. "Here, for you. I hope you don't mind I didn't attempt to wrap it."

"It's heavy." She balanced the weight of it on her lap. "I can't imagine, Jake—"

"You don't have to imagine. Open it!"

Lifting the lid, Miranda clutched her chest. "Is this what I think it is? Tell me you finished your manuscript!" She grazed her fingers across the cover page. "*A Hundred Days Till Tomorrow.* I must say, I'm intrigued by the title."

"Those were our hundred days, Miranda—the ones we spent together. I hope you don't mind, but you inspired my revisions. You fixed my laptop and encouraged me to pursue my dream. I have you to thank for believing in me, and my characters do too."

Jake beamed like a proud schoolboy. "It took longer than I expected to finish, but like I promised that night in the town square, it would be worth the wait—and we would be worth the wait. I hope you'll agree."

Hearing the music and lyrics of Jake's soul together in perfect harmony created the most beautiful song. Miranda had become his muse after all.

"Should I stock up on tissues before I dig in?" She skimmed the first page and flipped through the chapters, reading a sentence here and a paragraph there.

"I can't guarantee there won't be a few tears, but, unlike my first draft, the proper story line comes true. You changed the course of where my characters' lives were heading. That's all I'll say, so I don't spoil the ending."

He placed the manuscript back in the box and set it to the side.

"This was another incredible surprise, Jake. I'm beyond proud of you."

"Thanks. My mind is already churning with ideas for a sequel, although I think the setting will be Paris."

Miranda drew back at the mention of the word.

"There's a catch," he said, his tone serious. "I think I may have to venture there next summer for research. You wouldn't happen to be interested in coming along to help me learn about European romance, would you? After you receive your graduate degree and before the grand opening of your art studio, that is."

"Are you kidding? Yes, of course!"

This time, there were joyful tears, and Miranda allowed them to flow freely. "I love my copy of *A Hundred Days Till Tomorrow*." She caressed her necklace. "I love my once-in-a-lifetime treasure." Then, without faltering, she ventured far out on a limb. "And I love you, Jake Colby."

The crystal ball was making its final descent on the old-fashioned television screen as the spirited crowd in Times Square counted down with anticipation:

"Three . . ."

"Two . . ."

"One!"

"Happy New Year, Jake!"

"I'd like to think of it as happily ever after," he replied.

The reassurance in Jake's emerald eyes and the confidence in her wings were all she needed to trust the journey ahead on an unfamiliar stretch of winding road.

Jake lifted her chin and cupped her face in his hands, making her tremble with his touch. Tilting his head, he leaned in closer. Miranda fell into his arms, melting into the warmth of his kiss, more than a hundred days overdue but every second worth the wait.

Fireworks exploded in the distance and noisemakers sounded from afar, commemorating the moment that seemed reserved for them. The New Year couldn't have been off to a more promising start, and it was only the beginning of tomorrow.

Acknowledgments

I believe that God looks down the road and places people where they need to be. *A Hundred Days Till Tomorrow* would not have been possible without the support from cheerleaders, who waved pom-poms and shouted words of encouragement at me. And so, with the utmost gratitude, I wish to acknowledge the following people:

My husband. Thank you for your tireless patience and influential pep talks. It is with your unconditional love and support that I embrace tomorrow. You are such a blessing to me!

My children. There has been no greater privilege in this life than to be your mom. Thank you for embracing this fourth child—my novel—into our home. Be open-minded to the possibilities for tomorrow, and never place a period where there should be a comma.

My parents. You are amazing role models and my greatest source of strength. Thank you for keeping this dream within reach and reminding me I have what it takes to soar. I will always strive to make you proud!

My grandparents, great-grandparents, and yesterday's heroes whose sacrifices make it possible to enjoy today. Future generations will proudly follow your footprints and benefit from your impact on this world. You are forever appreciated and never to be forgotten.

Laura Heubish, Karen Witty Gage, and another shout-out to my amazing mom. You've been my prayer warriors whose unwavering faith in this novel knew no bounds. Thank you for believing in me!

Dina Santorelli. Thank you for the knowledge and wisdom you so generously shared when I needed it most. As a writing coach and mentor, you helped establish my roots for this novel. I am grateful to our wonderful friend Tricia Danulevith for playing matchmaker.

Laura Engel. Thank you for being my friend throughout the publishing process and guiding me with a patient, kind heart. You are proof that God places people in our life for a reason.

Andrew Buss and Carissa Ganelli. Thank you for being so supportive and lending your time and talent.

My readers. Each page was written with you in mind. Thank you for embracing this journey with me and welcoming my characters into your heart and home. I hope Jake and Miranda's love story instills faith in the possibilities for tomorrow.

SparkPress. I appreciate your commitment to making my book-publishing dream a reality. It has been an honor to work with such a talented team of professionals.

Above all, I thank God for placing this dream in my heart. With gratitude for every roadblock, detour, and dead end that somehow led me to *A Hundred Days Till Tomorrow*. It is through His goodness that all things are possible.

My readers are at the heart of every word I write. Thank you for each review, social media comment, and email. Let's keep in touch and continue to inspire one another!

www.lscasenovelist.com
Facebook: lscasenovelist
Instagram: @lscasenovelist

About the Author

A lifelong resident of Long Island, L. S. Case is a twenty-year volunteer wish granter for the Make-A-Wish Foundation and a Phi Beta Kappa graduate of Hofstra University. Before embarking on her author journey, she spent over a decade as a proud region leader, recruiter, trainer, and multi-award sales achiever for lia sophia jewelry. With her passion for helping others, she transformed countless women's lives one necklace at a time. In 2017, she cofounded a nonprofit organization and currently serves on its board of directors. Her life's joy is the time she spends with her husband, family, and a temperamental cockatiel.

SELECTED TITLES FROM SPARKPRESS

SparkPress is an independent boutique publisher
delivering high-quality, entertaining, and engaging content that
enhances readers' lives, with a special focus
on female-driven work. www.gosparkpress.com

Charming Falls Apart: A Novel, Angela Terry, $16.95, 978-1-68463-049-3. After losing her job and fiancé the day before her thirty-fifth birthday, people-pleaser and rule-follower Allison James decides she needs someone to give her some new life rules—*and fast.* But when she embarks on a self-help mission, she realizes that her old life wasn't as perfect as she thought—and that she needs to start writing her own rules.

And Now There's You: A Novel, Susan S. Etkin. $16.95, 978-1-68463-000-4. Though five years have passed since beautiful design consultant Leila Brandt's husband passed away, she's still grieving his loss. When she meets a terribly sexy and talented—if arrogant—architect, however, sparks fly, and neither of them can deny the chemistry between them.

The Sea of Japan: A Novel, Keita Nagano. $16.95, 978-1-684630-12-7. When thirty-year-old Lindsey, an English teacher from Boston who's been assigned to a tiny Japanese fishing town, is saved from drowning by a local young fisherman, she's drawn into a battle with a neighboring town that has high stakes for everyone—especially her.

The Opposite of Never: A Novel, Kathy Mehuron. $16.95, 978-1-943006-50-2. Devastated by the loss of their spouses, Georgia and Kenny think that the best times of their lives are long over until they find each other; meanwhile Kenny's teenage stepdaughter, Zelda, and Georgia's friend's son, Spencer, fall in love at first sight—only to fall prey to and suffer opiate addiction together.

On Grace: A Novel, Susie Orman Schnall. $15, 978-1-940716-13-8. Grace is actually excited to turn forty in a few months—that is until her job, marriage, and personal life take a dizzying downhill spiral. Can she recover from the most devastating time in her life, right before it's supposed to be one of the best?

Elly in Love: A Novel, Colleen Oakes. $15, 978-1-940716-19-0. Elly is about to get everything she's ever wanted when a stranger shows up at her store with a request that changes every aspect of her life. As she struggles to stay calm, Elly will learn the true meaning of love and sacrifice.